THE STRADIVARIUS

THE STRADIVARIUS

by Rae Knowles

Edited by MJ Pankey
Proofread by and formatted by Stephanie Ellis

Cover illustration and design by David Román (Max Stark)
First Edition: May 2023

ISBN (paperback): 9781957537528
ISBN (ebook): 9781957537511
Library of Congress Control Number: 2023932795

BRIGIDS GATE PRESS
Bucyrus, Kansas
www.brigidsgatepress.com

Printed in the United States of America

For everyone who wasn't sure if it was real.

Content warnings are provided at the end of the book

PROLOGUE

Landrum, South Carolina
Spring 2008

Detective Williams gasped, though no one heard. Whether the sound was hushed by heavy curtains or gobbled up by the blood-soaked carpet, he didn't know. But the fact remained the same: at the foot of a snaking staircase, below flowery wallpaper and cherry-stained wainscoting, Richard Pruitt lay sprawled, an axe in his skull.

Beside him and still as a porcelain doll, a girl's head barely cleared the banister. Her nightgown dragged, leaving a trail of bloody streaks on the hardwood. "The bangin' woke me," she said, a voice like spun sugar. She was Mae Pruitt, according to dispatch, the victim's daughter.

Uniformed officers buzzed around the scene, their careless steps peppering dirt around her already soiled home.

"Give me the room," Detective Williams said.

Mae watched them scuttle to the front door, an oversized trail of ants. Her sandy hair drooped around her shoulders in loose curls, brushing the silky hem of her ruined nightgown, her wide eyes sitting atop deep purple recesses, unnatural on a girl her age. Williams crouched to meet them, hazel irises searching him for answers he couldn't provide.

"It's okay, sweetie."

Though, it wasn't.

He cuffed his arm around her shoulders, turning her tiny frame with a gentle nudge away from her father's body. Shards of glass glistened against wide oak floorboards, triangles large and small, a clustered mosaic dyed burgundy by specks of blood spray. He lifted Mae, sparing her vulnerable toes.

"Do I have to go to my aunt?" she asked, her voice mousy. "What if he wakes up?"

A twinge. Williams shielded her view with a curved palm and glanced back at Richard Pruitt. The axe remained upright, steadfast, posed and ready for its closeup from forensic photographers.

"It's just for a while," he said.

Glass crunched under his heavy boots as he maneuvered around the crimson spatter. He hesitated in the entry, stealing one last look at the empty display case hanging above the mantle.

A robbery gone wrong, they'd told him.

Surviving glass clung to the wooden frame in violent spikes, haphazard arrows pointing to the empty space in the middle, the small black prongs and hourglass stencil of dust tracing the void. It was a position of honor, centered over the fireplace. In the time the home was built, Williams imagined a grand portrait had hung where the shattered case did now. Oak floors groaned as he carried Mae across. Stained glass embedded in the front door bent and colored the light cast by gas lamps outside. On the wraparound porch, bloody footprints were stark against white paint, surrounded by rainbow patches of filtered light. Williams hopped from one foot to another to avoid the blood, over the vibrant patterns which dared to be beautiful despite the tragedy congealing around them. Down the steps he found a soft patch of grass and eased Mae onto her feet, hoping the blades would be kind to her exposed soles.

A wiry-haired woman waited for him beside her sedan. She wore her blazer over a sleep shirt and clutched a cup of coffee.

"You the social worker?"

The woman nodded, her face bare and eyelashes crusted with sleep. "Lydia Co—ollins," she said mid-yawn, "DSS." She flashed credentials and her eyes perked when she noticed Mae's bloodied nightgown. "Does she have anything to change into?"

"Ay! Jenkins!" Williams shouted.

A thin, uniformed cop popped out from around the corner, carrying a bag and passed it over to the social worker. "Anything to help, Williams, sir."

"We'll keep her for the night," Lydia said, tossing her empty coffee cup into her passenger seat. "Figure out next of kin in the morning." She bent over and addressed the girl with a softened tone. "And you must be Mae. Does that sound okay, honey? I have a big girl bed at a very safe place with your name on it. And tomorrow, we'll sort out what's what."

Mae nodded, but her eyes drifted across the winding gravel driveway, coming to rest on a tire swing. Suspended on the hefty bough of a mature oak, it swung that night, as if pushed by some benevolent specter, longing for joy amongst the dark.

"She mentioned an aunt," Williams said in a gravelly whisper.

Mae accepted the woman's hand and took a few steps toward the backseat before Lydia stopped her, eying the rusty ombre of Mae's nightgown. "Let's just—" She popped her trunk. It was stuffed with papers, folded beach chairs, a bottle of bug spray, and two, sun-bleached towels which she pulled out and spread across the booster seat and floor. "It'll be more comfortable for you, dear."

Williams's expression twisted into a scowl.

Lydia's face responded, *It's not your car, is it?*

Williams glanced over to see if Mae was hurt by the social worker's hesitation and found her staring over her tiny shoulder at the old Victorian. With a gentle nudge from Lydia, Mae crawled inside and settled.

"She's gonna take good care of you, sweetie." Williams shot Lydia a *you'd better* look.

With Mae buckled in and the doors shut, the sedan growled to life, its tires crunching the gravel drive as it rolled away and turned right onto Alquist Ave.

Williams caught sight of his men congregating around the newly erected caution tape barrier. "Nothing else?" he called as he approached.

"Nah." The uniformed officer examined his notebook. His outfit was pressed, his shave fresh. He pointed his pen at his writing. "Watches still there. Cash still there." Another point. "Tablet—"

"Yes, Jenkins, I get the picture."

"I don't get it, man," Ruthers chimed in, "I mean … all this shit lying around, but he only makes off with something he'd have to pawn, and for what? A hundred bucks?"

"Maybe it was worth more," Williams mused.

"I don't know about that," Ruthers said with a self-satisfied puff on his cigarette. "Seems to me, this was personal. A vendetta or something. The theft was maybe a *fuck you* after the fact, to stick it to him and throw us off."

"And the glass?"

Ruthers stopped mid-drag.

"How would the killer have smashed the glass after the fact, when the axe is still lodged in the guy's head? Did you see any shards on the body?"

"No."

William double-tapped the side of Ruthers's head with his index finger. "That's because they're under him. Glass was smashed first. The killer took it, Pruitt came downstairs and caught an axe to the head."

Ruthers sucked his teeth while the uniformed Jenkins confined his smile to his eyes. Williams motioned them away, watched Jenkins throw an elbow into Ruthers's side as they trudged up the porch steps, then took in the property. Woods bordered the 1800s Victorian on the east, west, and south sides, and a quaint, family cemetery peered down on the grounds from the north. The yard stretched far enough to accommodate a small barn and greenhouse, built by long deceased owners who likely rested in the dirt over the north property line.

Richard Pruitt restored it to historical perfection, painting the slatted siding a rosy pink. A strange choice, Williams thought, for a single father. The house's proud three stories culminated in a grand iron finial atop slate tiles at a steep pitch. A high stained-glass window towered above—a dollhouse come to life.

No doubt Richard thought he'd walk Mae down this gravel driveway in her prom dress, reluctantly turn her over to the care of her date. That he'd one day tend to the greenhouse for only himself, after she'd moved away for college. That she'd have a family of her own, maybe a young daughter to enjoy the rosy Victorian before she inherited it.

Williams's eyes trailed down to the wraparound porch, alive with plants. To the surrounding, manicured garden beds. To the rock between them, carved with Mae's name.

It was then that the full breadth of tonight's crime struck Williams.

All this ... he thought. *All this for a violin.*

CHAPTER ONE

Chipley, Florida
Late July 2018

Auntie Bel, with the frame and voice of a toad, leaned against the mildewed screen of her open window. Her chubby fingers, nicotine yellow and strangled by too-small, bejeweled rings, held her lit cigarette, smoke curling in the wind. "Hurry up!" she croaked.

Mae, arms laden with puck-sized mineral disks of mysterious composition, blew a puff of air at her wispy flyaways to dislodge them from her eyes.

"Over there," her aunt commanded, but if she gave some sense of direction, Mae hadn't seen. "Or do you want the Wi-Fi to do me in? Hah!" Auntie Bel grunted. "Wouldn' surprise me one bit!"

Mae stumbled over a stray piece of rebar and struggled to hold onto the last two speckled lumps in her arm. *First, they were for 'imposters', now they block the Wi-Fi.* She scraped the orgonite disk with her fingernail. *Look like bath bombs to me.*

"Not there! Shit, girl, toward the mailboxes."

She reversed course, phone buzzing in her pocket. Placing the supposedly mystical disk where the curb met the weedy grass, she fished out her phone. *Unknown number.* Mae slid the bar to answer. "Hello?"

"Busy, busy lady!" Auntie Bel mocked from the window.

"Hello, may I speak to Mae Pruitt?"

"This is—" Auntie Bel's window slammed shut. "She," Mae finished firmly.

"This is Robert Feinstein, I'm the trustee of your father's estate."

Estate?

"I'd like to speak with you at my office. Do you have any availability this week?"

"I, uh, you said your name was Robert?"

"You can call me Bob."

"Bob, okay." Mae walked a tight circle in the grass. "What is this regarding?" She enunciated more than she was used to, trying to sound older, more collected, thinking Bob would laugh if he saw her ill-fitting tie-dye T-Shirt, her tousled bun which flopped from one side of her head to the other at the slightest movement.

"It's regarding your inheritance."

Inheritance? The thought had crossed Mae's mind before, but when her eighteenth birthday came and went with no news of it, she'd chucked her hopes of inheritance to the wind. "I'm free tomorrow," she blurted.

"Tomorrow," he mused. A beat passed and Mae pictured him checking his schedule, better yet, calling in his prim secretary to check it for him. "Yes, tomorrow will do just fine. Three o'clock."

"Three o'clock," Mae repeated, perfect diction. "See you then." The call disconnected, Mae shook her head, exchanged her phone for the vape pen in her pocket. *Inheritance?* She took a long toke as the word bounced around in her head. Oil crackled as it vaporized and sailed into her lungs. What could he have left her? A college account? Why wait until now? She was already twenty, that money could've gotten her out of here years ago, saved her countless errands for Auntie Bel, offered her independence. Excitement distilled into acidic resentment. She squeezed the last orgonite disk in her palm.

Ten years from now I'm sure we'll hear that these things cause some new kind of cancer, she thought, digging her nail into the mineral cake. *Two years longer of exposure.* She took another sharp pull on the vape.

But hey, maybe the Bayou's Angel is right, and we'll all be murdered by the New World Order before the cancer takes hold.

She chuckled quietly, the vapor escaping her mouth in puffs.

Better late than never. Mae stole one more hit before sneaking the pen back into her pocket.

The screen door creaked shut behind her and Auntie Bel was lighting a fresh cigarette at the kitchen table. The warm hug of THC engulfed Mae's body.

Auntie Bel grumbled something Mae couldn't discern. "Who was that on the phone?" Her eyes were slits.

"Oh, nothing. Telemarketer."

Auntie Bel harrumphed and Mae realized she was still holding the last disk. She braced for the diatribe. "I know you think you're way too smart, way too *sophisticated* for all this. But I tell you what. When they do come for me, and best believe they comin' sweetie, they gone' get more than they bargained for!"

Mae nodded and smiled in agreement. She learned long ago not to argue with conspiracy logic. The microwaved beeped a sweet respite.

"Don't trouble yourself," Mae said, though she knew her aunt wouldn't have budged either way. Anything to distract from another lesson on the New World Order. She placed the disk on the counter and wrapped a paper towel around her fingers. The blazing Mac 'n cheese bubbled, its plastic bowl threatening to melt beneath her fingers.

"Well?" Auntie Bel called.

Mae held up the container. The bottom warped and sagged. "Just a minute."

She pulled a bowl from the cupboard, quickly dumping the steaming contents inside. The wafting scent of cheese nuzzled her nose. Her stomach grumbled in response. Mae eyed the pantry, the sandwich cookies seducing her from their shelf.

"WELL?"

Auntie Bel's call snapped Mae back into reality.

"Here you go." She laid the bowl on the TV table beside the worn sofa. Auntie Bel, who was already absorbed in a low budget documentary, grunted in acknowledgment.

Mae glanced at the time. *Six twenty-two.*

"Need anything else?"

Auntie Bel waved her off.

"I'm just gonna … " she trailed off when Auntie Bel didn't look up. Mae snatched the box of cookies and slid out the front door, closing it gingerly behind her. She took long strides across the narrow street, skipping over potholes as she passed a dozen trailers in various stages of decay. When she reached the white metal fence, stained brown where the sprinklers beat down, she peered around the corner in anticipation. Fingers rolling around the vape pen hidden in her pocket, arms encircled her. All went black as he pulled her face to his chest.

"Ah, babe! I came early. Just couldn't wait to see you."

Carter released her, and she beamed as she took him in. His angular jaw adorned with rugged stubble. His thin black T-Shirt drawn tight across his broad chest. Men her age never cared enough about their appearance to work out. But Carter was different.

A finger slid beneath her chin, tilting it upward. Her bottom lip brushed his top. They mingled together in a kiss that radiated throughout Mae's chest and, surely, stopped time. Birds floated lazily by. The warm air caressed all in its stillness. Children peered through their windows, envious. When she finally felt him pull away, her body ached for more.

"So? Have you made up your mind?" He stepped back to inspect her face.

Her eyes wandered as she pulled in another hit from her vape. "I don't know, I mean, I'm not sure."

"Not sure? We've been waiting for this."

Mae couldn't help but giggle. "Carter, come on. We've only been dating a couple weeks."

He put his arm around her waist, pulled her closer to him. "I know, but it's like I've known you forever."

Carter's eyes sparkled the way they had at the skating rink that night, when Mae spied him in the center of a group of ogling girls. But he didn't seem to notice their bare bellies or how their shorts rode up high. He'd watched her skate circles under the disco ball, and when she did that final loop around the rink, held out a strip of paper between two fingers for her to snatch as she glided by. On the paper he'd scrawled his number, and a day hadn't passed since without a clandestine meeting. "We could just," his hand motioned like a bird taking flight.

Mae shook her head with a wide grin. "I told you; I'll think about it."

Carter withdrew. "It isn't *her*, is it?"

"Who? Nat?"

"Yeah, the one you told me about. From last summer."

"No!" Mae pulled back, felt her cheeks turn red. "She was so … immature. She could never compare to you."

Carter squeezed her hand. "If you say so."

"People my age just don't get me." Mae settled into a pool chair, and Carter behind her, smoothing her hair and rubbing her shoulders. She popped open the box of cookies and tossed one into her mouth.

"How was your violin lesson?"

"It's tomorrow," she crunched.

"I would love to hear you play sometime. I'm sure it's amazing. You've been practicing how many years?" His thumb pushed delicious pressure into a tense spot along her vertebrae.

Mae closed her eyes to focus on the sensation. "Since I was a kid. The one thing Auntie Bel's willing to dole out money for on my account."

"I've never stuck to anything that long."

"Well, music has always been *a thing* in my family."

"You're just …" He pushed her hair to one side. His lips danced on her neck.

"Just what?"

The tickle of his breath sent a shiver down her right arm. "I could take care of you, you know. I could send you to a real school. I make plenty of money."

The offer was tempting. Since graduation, she'd felt like a caged bird. She never saw herself staying in Chipley. The tragedy of living there was almost as terrible as the one that sent her.

"You aunt wants you close because she thinks you're her ticket out."

Mae winced. Hearing this truth from another's mouth stung. "I know."

She tossed another cookie into her mouth.

Carter reached over her and grabbed one for himself. The sun dipped below the skyline as Carter taught Mae a few words in French, regaled her with stories of his travels in search of valuable antiques. Dusk left them in the company of the chirping crickets.

"I'd better get going. She'll be callin' me for dessert."

"I'll be thinking about you, Mrs. Duvall." He winked.

Once Carter was out of sight, she took high steps along the road. "Mrs. Duvall," she repeated.

It's got a nice ring to it. A ring.

She envisioned the white dress, Carter's face at the end of the aisle. As the trailer came into view, her pace slowed. She took the last heart-wrenching steps back toward Auntie Bel.

Home sweet home.

She lingered out front, anticipating the stale smell and her Auntie's demands.

Wouldn't it be nice to never walk through that door again?

"Mae!" she heard through the door. "That you?"

Mae dragged herself inside. "Yes, Auntie Bel."

"Hah, back from one of your secret walks again I see. Very sneaky," she scoffed. "You just keep him away from my home, ya hear? I don't need him or none of those clones comin' in here. Fishin' around."

"Of course, Auntie."

Mae's strings bellowed inside the disheveled mobile home, bouncing *Partita No. 2* off the tin walls. Geraldo sat, perfect posture, in the slouchy beige loveseat usually reserved for Auntie Bel. His pressed button-down and creased dress pants were out of place amongst the collector's editions Barbies in dust-covered boxes, the heaps of Christmas garland speckled with mouse droppings, the fan that circulated ammonia stench. He swatted at a fungus gnat and his face clenched, accentuating his wrinkles. "You're cheating notes."

Mae cradled the instrument, her chin nuzzled in the rest, but her eyes wandered the room as her bow sawed over the strings. Jagged chords filled the trailer with unease. The last note eked out.

Geraldo had enough. He raised his hand. "Stop!"

Mae lowered the bow.

"Tell me Mae, did I drive all the way from Tallahassee for this?" His scrunched mouth pressed his auburn mustache to the tip of his nose, and Mae felt that familiar sinking feeling.

Auntie Bel leered from the kitchen table, shaking her head in disapproval. "Mr. Engleman said it back in eighth grade, and I'll be damned if it ain't as true today. *Lots of potential, but she doesn't apply herself.*"

"I'm sorry, I know." Mae sighed. She cracked open the violin case, exposing the crushed red velvet interior and rested the instrument inside. "I've just been distracted lately."

"I see that." Geraldo stood, smoothed hairline creases from his slacks.

"Thinkin' 'bout that guy, no doubt," Auntie Bel added.

A faint smile cracked through Geraldo's cheek. "A man in your life, Mae?"

Mae flushed.

"Nothing to be ashamed of," he added.

"Speak for yourself!" Auntie Bel croaked. "Damn shame if you ask me!" She stubbed her cigarette in the ashtray. "But I know you ain't." She lit another.

"I haven't been practicing, I'm sorry." Mae fiddled with the lace trim of her navy tank.

"It's not just today, Mae. The past few months it seems, your heart isn't in it."

Mae frowned but couldn't argue, knowing it was true.

"And that's okay!" Geraldo assured. "Classical performance, at this level, it's not for everyone."

Mae breathed in deep. "It was for—"

"For your father, yes." Geraldo collected his sheet music and lifted the black metal stand. "He was truly something. And don't get me wrong, you could be too. But only if you want it. More than anything else. But most people don't. They want other things. Love, a family, a life outside the strings. And that's okay."

Mae's posture straightened; she pushed her dirty blonde locks away from her eyes.

"A waste," Auntie Bel hissed, slamming the fridge shut and sulking off to her room.

Geraldo leaned into Mae's ear, whispered so Auntie Bel couldn't hear. "He would've been proud." He glanced around the trailer from the stacks of ancient, unread magazines to the towering pile of fast-food wrappers in the trash. "You do what you gotta do. Get yourself out of here."

Mae threw her arms around his shoulders, pulled him in for a deep hug. "Thank you," she whispered back.

Sensing the lull in activity, Auntie Bel called from the kitchen. "Gerald, y'all almost through in there? It's time for Mae to make my lunch."

Geraldo pulled a long, slow breath through his nose. "Just about."

"I swear, y'all are slower than the second coming," she mumbled.

"It'll be the second coming before she gets your name right," Mae whispered.

Mae and Geraldo shared a smile.

"Coming, Auntie."

Geraldo peered around Auntie Bel's bedroom door frame and nodded goodbye. She grunted in acknowledgement. No sooner had the door clinked behind him did Auntie Bel start on with her lecture.

"What're you thinkin' with that shit?"

Mae hesitated. "About playing?"

"About not playing. Come on, now. How're you and me gonna get out of this shithole? I'm sure as shit not winnin' any beauty pageants!" she snorted.

"Auntie, I just, I'm really not that good. Honestly. I know you've been hopin' I'd get somewhere with my violin, but I'm just … I'm not—"

"You ain't your father."

Mae sighed. "Right."

Auntie Bel stamped out her cigarette. "Damn shame you ain't." She drew another from the pack. "But you ain't even tryin'. Not really. I took care of you how many years? A damn decade! My best years. All for what?" She harrumphed. "And here I got the park callin' me over some late lot fees, makin' threats; but you ain't worried about that none, prob'ly fixin to run off with your mystery man like a lil hussy."

Mae's face flushed.

"Better than that slut from before though. What was her name? Mildred? Unnatural if you ask me. Perverted."

Shame rose up. The hot feeling burned its way from her chest up into her throat. She felt tears in her eyes. "S'cuse me."

Mae managed to reach her bedroom and shut the door behind her before the tears began to flow. She thought of

Nat, how her hands had caressed Mae's curvy hips. The same curves Mae sucked in when she looked in the mirror. And how she'd traced the shape of Mae's bellybutton piercing with her fingertip, love in her eyes. She opened her phone to her contacts, scrolled to Nat's name, and her finger hovered above the call button.

You've got to take steps, Mae.

Nat's words still scorched like they had that day.

You could start working and save up, but you keep making excuses.

The breakup had been mutual. That's what Mae told herself. So why did the memory of that last conversation still roil her stomach?

She closed her contacts and caught sight of the time. Two thirty.

Shit, Feinstein!

Mae's fingers drummed over the armrest. The chair's thick cushion cradled her, and the walnut stain matched the wainscoting, matched the bookcase, heavy with thick, leather-bound volumes. A grandfather clock ticked in the corner, Roman numerals across its face. She watched the brass pendulum swing back and forth. Mae's foot tapped the same rhythm on the thick shag carpet from which no sound escaped. Ten minutes passed before the door opened.

"Ms. Pruitt?" He wore a navy suit and a maroon, patterned tie. His rectangular spectacles framed beady blue irises, dwarfed by his round cheeks, and his salt and pepper hair was slicked back over the thin spots.

"Yep, that's me."

He extended his hand and Mae gave him a firm shake, his palm smooth and soft in hers. "Robert Feinstein, nice to meet you."

Mae followed him down a short hallway.

"You can call me Bob," he said, as he had on the phone. He took a seat in an expensive-looking chair. His desk was neat, the same shade of walnut as the furniture in the waiting room. On the walls hung meticulously framed degrees and a photo of himself with the governor. "As you probably have surmised, I've been managing your father's estate since his death. He was quite the meticulous man and put a great deal of forethought into estate planning, perhaps because his sister, well—he appointed me as the executor and trustee until such time that you turned twenty."

Bob flipped open a manilla file folder and spread out papers dense with writing. "I'm aware that your birthday was some weeks back but seeing as I was on extended holiday in Greece, I reached out to you at the earliest possible convenience. I'm sure you understand."

Holiday in Greece? No, Mae was sure she didn't understand. Bob slid a page in front of her. Her eyes went fuzzy as she scanned it.

"This is paperwork outlining your father's last will and testament. You'll see here expenses and taxes, I have taken care of those up until this point, but you'll want to go over this in detail ..."

The worlds on the page swirled and blurred.

"... line item six outlines his wishes for medical proxy, however, that is not something to concern yourself with at this point ..."

Line item six?

"… nearly the sole beneficiary with the exception of Elizabeth Tompkins, you will see a small collection of items within the addendum of specific bequeaths … "

Mae flipped through the pages, eyes grazing the headings, trying to keep up.

"… most importantly," Mae looked up from the pages, grounding herself in Bob's steady visage. "Please follow along at Roman numeral five." He slid his finger across the page before Mae, tapped the V, and began to read aloud.

"I give, devise, and bequeath unto my daughter, Mae Pruitt, all the rest, residue, and remainder of my estate, whether real or personal, and wheresoever situated. In the event that Mae Pruitt shall predecease me, or in the event that both my daughter and I shall die as a result of a common accident, illness or disaster, then I give, devise and bequeath the residue and remainder of my estate to the New York Philharmonic, the representative of which is named in Paragraph I hereof …

"It goes on this way, but you understand now, I'm sure, that you are the beneficiary of his estate."

Mae blinked. "The house?"

"Yes, the house at 112 Alquist Ave in Landrum, South Carolina as well as his accounts. I can go over those in detail with you if you'd like. I employed a groundskeeper for many years to manage the property, but I'm afraid he retired a couple of years ago. The inside has remained untouched, with the exception of maintenance and a brief police entry after an attempted break-in. Nothing to worry yourself about, however; they determined nothing was taken. In fact, the would-be thief was scared off by Mr. Barlow, our old groundskeeper, before his resignation."

Mae struggled to sort the information in her head. *Accounts?* She'd assumed the house had been foreclosed or knocked down, and that her father's money had gone to some distant relative when she hadn't heard anything on her eighteenth birthday. *How much ...* Her phone buzzed in her pocket.

Carter: Dinner tonight?

"So, the house is mine?"

Bob nodded his head, his glasses sliding down his nose. He offered a silver pen. "Once we get everything signed and squared away. You could move in tomorrow if the mood struck you." He must've noticed the toothy smile encompassing Mae's face when he corrected, "Though I'm sure it's not in any condition. You'd have to fix it up, of course. The remaining account balance should cover a restoration, albeit, not an extravagant one."

Mae straightened her posture. "Of course."

The warm air became thinner, easier to breathe as she distanced herself from the lawyer's office. It was enough to strike out on her own. A deep breath of humid air filled her lungs. The world felt wider.

I'd love to do dinner, she replied to Carter.

Mae felt as if she'd floated all the way home. Even the confines of the trailer's tin walls seemed to expand. Even Auntie Bel, half-spilling from the couch, seemed less sinister. *It's enough,* she thought.

The Bayou's Angel spouted vitriol from Auntie Bel's phone speaker. *"They think I don't know my own damn cat? Like I wouldn't notice he'd been replaced? Don't be fooled, people!"*

"You been out wit' your boyfriend?" Her tone was smug.

Mae considered telling her about the house while the podcast droned on in the background.

"What can you expect from mainstream media, we all know what's goin' on. I just want that golden goose egg that says, yes, but

Hillary, Hillary being there ..." Auntie Bel smacked her lips, nodding at the nonsensical drivel.

"Just out with a friend, planning to have dinner with Carter in a bit though."

"A friend?" Auntie Bel sat up from the couch. "Not—"

"No, not her." Mae didn't want to hear it, not another homophobic jab from her aunt's greasy mouth. "I'm gonna go get ready."

Auntie Bel grunted. As Mae laid out her outfit, an A-line dress with a plunging neckline, she imagined how her old house must look. Crumbling, most likely, dust dimming the shine on the chandelier. She wondered whether her room was still filled with her childhood clothes, her drawings. She shuddered at the thought of the glass shards still littering the floor, but pushed the thoughts away. *I can start fresh somewhere else. Nat was wrong, I know how to take steps, Carter will help me.*

Dressed and ready, she made for the door, taking quick paces to avoid any comments from Auntie Bel. The restaurant was a short walk away, and Carter waited for her at the entrance, linking his arm with hers and escorting her to a lovely corner table with a view of the patio. A lounge singer played piano from a low-lit corner, and oversized wine bottles decorated the window's frame. A single red rose sat in a slender, crystal vase, and she pulled it close to her face, breathing in the floral aroma.

"You look beautiful," Carter said. He wore a brown suit jacket over a powder blue button-down. His almond eyes glittered in the candlelight.

Mae smoothed her dress over the stomach roll that formed when she sat. Her feet already ached in the heels, and she shifted her weight in the chair to take pressure off.

"What's good here?" Mae eyed the prices.

Eighteen dollars for an appetizer!

Carter fiddled with his interior jacket pocket. "I'm sure everything is delicious." His eyes locked on hers and his tongue wetted his bottom lip.

Butterflies as big as birds fluttered in Mae's gut.

"I know just what to order us." He reached across the table and folded Mae's menu closed. "You leave it to me."

Nat had been exciting, in her own way. There was the novelty first off, testing the waters with another girl for the first time. But Carter had the sophisticated allure of experience, nuanced movements and confidence honed by the real world. The waitress noticed it too. Her eyes lingered on him, as if Mae's seat was empty.

Plate after plate arrived on Carter's order, meticulously arranged, including even an orchid bloom as a garnish. First brie, creamy and smooth, offset with raspberry jam which Mae liberally smeared on slices of French bread. Next, the salads. Sliced red apples, yellow raisins, and candied pecans heaped generously over a bed of spring greens, and a dressing so sweet and tart, Mae swore they must've mixed it to order.

Finally, the main course, a tender lamb shank paired with mint jelly. The knife slid through the meat with a gentle nudge, and the rich flavors lavished Mae's tongue, though she did her best to restrain herself from gobbling, conscious of maintaining her sex appeal during the meal.

As they awaited dessert, crème brûlée with sliced strawberries, Mae decided it was time.

"I got something I want to talk to you about." She wiped her chin with the cloth napkin, sat up straight.

Carter raised a single finger, silencing her, and the waitress approached, a slight scowl on her pursed lips. Before Mae, the waitress sat a glass of champagne.

"Thanks," Mae said, with a bit of confusion. "But I didn't—"

She walked away and Mae turned to Carter who smirked and darted his eyes toward the bottom of the glass, a ring rested amongst the bubbles.

"No!" Mae's chest clenched.

She poured the champagne into her mouth, drops streaming from the sides of her lips as she sucked it down greedily. The ring slid forward, and Mae grabbed it between her lips, giggling as she pried it from her mouth and held it aloft. "Really?"

"Mae Pruitt … "

Mae thought he might sink down to one knee, but he remained seated. "Though it's only been a short time, there's something special between us. Something undeniable, once in a lifetime." It was like a movie. Carter, her Prince Charming, here at last to whisk her away. "So, will you?"

Mae pushed the ring over her knuckle, leapt from her seat, and plopped down onto Carter's lap, attracting stares from the elderly patrons to their left. She kissed him wildly, smearing lipstick across his chin. "Of course!" Tears of joy welled in her eyes. "Of course, I will!"

CHAPTER TWO

The sun's welcoming rays poured in through the sheer curtain and bounced off the antique-set diamond on Mae's finger. She stretched, and a delicious morning groan escaped her lips.

"Good morning, Mrs. Duvall," Carter said, gazing from the balcony.

She grinned and stretched as she studied her ring for the thousandth time.

"I could get you a different one," Carter teased.

"Oh God, no!" Mae protested. "It's beyond perfect."

She pulled the blanket from her body, revealing her strappy nightgown, and joined him on the balcony. Her coffee steamed as it waited beside his. She grasped the warm handle of the mug, took a deep breath in to savor the smell. "You're too good to me."

The sun shot red blazes across the sky as it peaked above the ocean. The gentle whoosh of crashing waves caressed Mae's ears. "Isn't it beautiful?" he asked.

"It's like a dream."

"We have our whole lives to be like this." Carter squeezed her hand.

Mae closed her eyes for a moment, absorbing the thought. "Can't we just stay here? I could spend every morning of my life waking up on this beach and drinking coffee beside you."

"We could stay here, we could travel, we could do anything you like, and when you get tired of it, we can change our minds and do something new. The future is ours, Mae."

Mae considered the idea, *Anything I'd like it to be.*

"But what about you? What's your dream?"

Carter stared out into the horizon. His fingers curled around Mae's shoulder. "I've always dreamed of a little farmhouse somewhere. Somewhere quiet. A wraparound porch and a little piece of land."

Mae stiffened.

"What is it, my love?"

"Oh, uh, it's just—I grew up in a house just like that."

"Really?"

Mae chuckled. "Yeah, exactly like that actually. It was an old Victorian house, wraparound porch, white shutters. Out in the South Carolina country. My dad even hung a little tire swing in the tree for me."

"It sounds beautiful."

"It was. It really was, until …" Mae's eyes bounced over the glittering waves. Her face tightened.

"I'm sorry, I didn't mean to dredge up old memories."

"No, no, it's okay. How could you know?"

"Let's change the subject. I saw a flier about horseback riding on the beach, would you want to—"

"It's okay! Really. I want to tell you. You're my husband now, after all."

Carter ran his fingers along her arm.

"My mom ran off when I was little. So, it was always just me and my dad until … I was ten when it happened. Worst night of my life."

Soothing, circular motions from Carter's fingertips drew the tension from Mae's body, urging her to reveal every hidden part of herself.

"I was asleep upstairs when I heard the noise. Glass breaking. It startled me awake. At first, I figured my dad had just knocked over a glass or something, but then I heard a bang, and then a sound that … I just knew he was hurt. So, I ran for the stairs. The guy must've heard me coming because I only saw a flash of him as he ran. But my dad …" She took a deep breath. "My dad was lying on the floor. There was blood everywhere. And shards of broken glass." Her eyes drifted over the lapping waves. "He'd warned me against broken glass. I was barefoot, so I just froze there, on the stairs. The axe, it—well, I knew he was dead. I don't know how long I stood at the foot of the stairs. But I had to call, had to get to the kitchen phone. And when I—it was warm between my toes. My feet stuck to the wood."

"Oh, babe," Carter wrapped her in a forceful hug. "I'm so sorry. I had no idea."

Mae blinked tears down her cheeks, warm like his blood. "It's okay, really."

Carter took her face in his hands, wiped her tears from her beneath her eyes one by one.

"It's good to talk about him, actually. Auntie Bel never would. 'The past is in the past!' she'd say. But, you know, I have a lot of great memories of him too."

"Tell me about those," Carter said.

His eyes traced her as she studied orange patterns in the sky, a smile cracking her cheeks as the memory broke through.

"Well, he always told this story. Any time we had a guest. I must've heard it a thousand times."

"What was the story?"

"Paola's story."

Carter cocked his head to the side.

"Well, you know, I've told you my father was a violinist. World class. Far better than I am or will ever be."

"Don't say that, Mae. You're—"

Mae shooed his compliment and went on. "When my father played, the room listened. It was like he made feelings out of thin air. He played for a little while with the New York Philharmonic. And, as the story goes, during one performance there, some rich Italian heir was in the crowd with his wife. She'd recently had a miscarriage, and supposedly, it had been months since she'd smiled. The heir told my father that after it happened, she'd become a shell of herself. Until that night. She'd heard my father's playing, Glinka's *Rutland and Ludmilla*. The heir told him that his wife became hysterical, first sobbing and then laughing wildly, like some kind of eruption. He told him that after the show it was like a heavy weight had been lifted off her, and she was herself again.

"So, he tracked down my father. Knocked on the door of his tiny New York apartment, and was holding this massive box with an oversized, shiny bow. My father welcomed him inside and unwrapped the gift to find her, Lady Paola. *The varnish looked lit from within,*' he would say. On her tailpiece was a meticulous carving, a woman playing violin. He said it was awe-inspiring. *You didn't have to know anything about violins to know she was special.*' But he knew instantly of course: she was a Stradivarius. One of only about 600 still in existence. It was a priceless gift."

Carter's eyes were deep. "Wow, that is quite a story." He smiled. "No wonder he couldn't stop telling it."

Mae's face radiated a quiet joy.

"So, did he sell it? Is that how he bought the house for the two of you?"

"God, no!" Mae reassured. "It was his prized possession. He had it professionally displayed. It hung in a case above our mantle, sort of smiling down at us, glowing in the firelight, until—" Seagulls squawked in the distance. The beach town was beginning to wake, traffic picking up around the one lane seaside roads. Carter slid on his sunglasses. He leaned back in his chair, soaking in the sun's rays from their place on the balcony. Mae's eyes passed over him. "He left it to me, you know."

Carter sat up; his brow piqued above the rim of his sunglasses.

"The house I mean. We could go there, to live, if you wanted to."

Carter seemed to consider this as a pelican dove into the waves before them. "I dunno, Mae. After what happened … I would never want to make you relive all that."

"It's true, I haven't been back since, but with you I—" She watched another pelican take a daring dive. "I feel like I could face anything. I mean, it's out in the country, just like you've always wanted. We could drive to the beach on the weekends. And we need a home, after all. It seems like maybe it's meant to be."

Carter ran his hands over the smooth railing. "South Carolina would be a perfect place for antiquing. I could go out on my own, build my own business. But only if you're sure. Are you sure, Mae?"

Mae slid her legs out in front of her, slouching down in the chair and casting her face up toward the sun. "I'm sure. Let's enjoy the rest of our honeymoon, and then we'll get settled into our home. Start enjoying life together as Mr. and Mrs. Duvall."

Their honeymoon beach town looked so much smaller from the sky, and the ocean, so much larger. Carter stood, back hunched to avoid banging his head on the overhead compartment. He steadied himself on his headrest, mild turbulence forcing him to bend his long legs for balance. "Be right back."

Recycled air beat down on Mae from the vents above, drying her eyes. She looked toward the middle row to avoid it, and her eyes were caught by the person seated across the aisle. Chunky headphones pushed down their spiky magenta hair.

As Mae tried to snoop at what they might be listening to, they noticed her watching and shot out a hand.

"I'm Ollie, they/them."

Mae thought of how Auntie Bel's mole-spotted mug might twist in horror had she been seated beside her and was delighted at the thought that she'd left her hate-filled diatribes behind. "I'm Mae, she/her."

Teal painted nails, chipping at their edges, grasped Mae's hand with firm confidence.

"Where you headed?" Ollie asked.

"South Carolina."

"Well, duh, you'd better be, or else you're on the wrong plane!"

Mae's cheeks flushed. "Outside Spartanburg, I mean. What about you?"

"No way, same! I live in Landrum."

Mae chuckled. "What are the odds?"

Ollie adjusted their headphones.

"What are you listening to?" Mae asked.

"True crime," Ollie was eager to report. "I'm a true crime fanatic."

"It's always been a little too much for me."

"Well, maybe rethink Landrum, then! You've heard about the famous murder there, haven't you? It's a big mystery in the town. Never solved." Ollie looked pleased.

Mae swallowed her rising nerves. "Famous murder?"

"Yeah, a while back now. But in a town that small, people still talk about it like it was yesterday. Horrible, really," Ollie grinned. "An axe murder of all things," they whispered.

Mae's eyes lingered on the floor. "Terrible."

"And that's not the most fascinating part. This violin was stolen. Turns out, it was worth millions."

Mae nodded.

"But it's never been found. They think the killer didn't know he needed the certificate of authenticity. Nobody knows for sure. But I was listening to a podcast about it a few months back, and their theory is that they never got this certificate thing, so the violin is probably rotting in some storage unit somewhere. Such a waste if you ask me!"

"That would be a waste." Mae scanned the back of the plane. The red bathroom light still lit, *In use*. "So, are you from Landrum?" Mae asked.

"Born and raised." Ollie indicated their short, vibrant hair. "I know, not what you'd expect from a local there."

"From what I remember, Landrum needed a little color."

Ollie's face brightened. "That's what I've always thought."

Carter scooted his way down the aisle, dodging stray legs and carry-ons.

"This is my husband, Carter. He/—" Mae shrunk back so Carter could slip into the window seat. "—him. Carter, this is Ollie."

Carter raised his hand in a subtle wave.

"It was nice meeting you, Ollie."

"Likewise."

"Maybe I'll see you in town."

"I'm hard to miss!" They slid their headphones back on and leaned back in their seat, eyes closed. Mae's eyes passed over their denim jacket and stole glances at their half-shaved head and smattering of freckles. Carter placed a firm hand on Mae's thigh.

"Just another hour," he said.

Mae placed her hand atop his and gazed out the window. Cotton candy clouds whipped around the wing, the sky so blue and brilliant, Mae had to strain her eyes to look. Below was a checkerboard of green and brown, farmland carved into rectangles and squares, patterned and dotted with tiny pricks of red, barns far down below.

"What do you think about goats?" Mae asked.

"Goats?" Carter considered. "Well, I don't think about them often."

"I mean, what do you think about having some? The house has a little barn. It might be fun, a little trial of *kids*." Mae beamed, impressed with her pun.

Carter stared into her eyes with mock seriousness. "There is nothing I want more than to raise a whole mess of *kids* with you." He looked out into the sky. "Just don't let them into the house. I hear they eat clothing."

CHAPTER THREE

Landrum, South Carolina
Early August

The cab ride from the airport stretched on for long, quiet hours across the Carolina countryside. Mae's body, once coursing with excitement at the prospect of beginning her new life, was now perched on the edge of the seat, stiff with unease. The tall buildings and tourist shops of Charleston gave way to small country roads dotted with mom-and-pop cafes, feed shops, and ancient barns that stood on tilted foundations, defying nature's best efforts to bring them down.

Welcome to Landrum, a passing sign read, the *d* punctuated with a dent.

Carter seemed distant and absorbed in thought, like a scientist examining new data.

"Almost there," Mae remarked, cutting the quiet.

"Mhmm," Carter replied without looking. He checked his phone. "Bad signal out here."

The houses were well-spaced, protected by thick hedges and wrought iron fences laced with winding ivy. Mature oaks soared beyond their steeply pitched roofs. The driver took a sharp left, and Mae's stomach nearly leapt from the cab when she saw it. *Alquist Ave.*

The gravel driveway wound past the oak tree, a dangling rope from its bough. She was momentarily transported, picturing her father's face, his head thrown back in a hearty laugh—

"Could use a coat of paint," Carter interrupted.

The pale pink paint, faded by the sun, flaked off in chunks. Its once grand wraparound porch sagged where clusters of rotting leaves weakened the boards. Brakes squealed as the cab lurched to a stop. Carter hopped out and began removing their bags from the trunk. The driver peered at Mae through the rearview.

Got my money? asked his eyes.

Mae dodged his lingering stare and fled the car for the safety of Carter's side. Without being asked, Carter drew his wallet and fingered through a hefty wad of bills, handing a fluffy stack to the cabbie, whose eyes grew wide and a smile crept up as he gripped it. Gravel groaned beneath his tires as he circled around the driveway and left Mae and Carter standing before the creaky Victorian, its finial casting a shadowy line over their tilted faces.

"We'll have to get a car," Carter said.

"I can look through some ads online tonight."

Loaded with their bags, Carter trudged up the steps like a pack mule. The wood whined beneath him, he and the boards bending under too much weight.

Mae trotted up the porch steps and swooped around the corner, avoiding broken ceramic pots and the vines which continued to grow in the spilt soil. A hanging planter clutched at its hook with a single, rusty wire.

"Still can't figure out where Feinstein's got to, but the spare should be in here." She reached into the woven basket from below, her fingertips sinking into the rot. The cool decay wedged beneath her fingernails, and amongst the soft fibers she felt the hard, jagged outline and loosed it from its swampy prison. "Told you we'd find it." Brown smears coated her palm as she held the spare key aloft like a trophy.

Carter eyed her, forcing a smile. "Awesome, but maybe next time you let me hold onto the important stuff so we don't have to go digging through …" He pinched the key with two reluctant fingers, "muck."

Mae wasn't sure whether Carter's harsh tone was judgment, travel fatigue, or stress. Moving was one of the most stressful things a person could do in life. She'd heard that somewhere, hadn't she?

The lock turned with a click, but the door denied them entry. Carter jiggled and shook the knob. "It's just swollen."

Maybe she'd imagined it altogether. Back here after all this time, after—

He thrust his shoulder into the door, backed by his weight, and the door relented, sailing inward as Carter stumbled behind it. Dust rained from the doorframe, sprinkling gray sheen onto Carter's jet-black hair. The musty smell escaping the house pushed Mae back a few steps. She'd half expected it to smell like home, but of course it wouldn't; of course it would smell like decay. She peered through the swinging door at Carter. The textured stained-glass pane warped his features, slouched his figure into some rough beast.

"Place is falling apart," he called from inside.

Mae nudged the door with a fingertip, and it swung open with a creak.

Cobwebs glistened their gossamer sheen in the once grand chandelier. The room was claustrophobic with books. They filled the lower half of every wall in the foyer, a literary wainscoting. The staircase loomed from its place in the corner.

"I'll turn on the gas." Carter disappeared through the back door. A trail of ten-year-old-footprint blotches, now blackish brown, led across the area rug. Mae's eyes darted around the path as a mouse dashed from the fireplace into a small hole at the bottom of the stairs.

The chandelier roared to life, illuminating detritus on the threadbare area rug, and Carter returned, slamming the back door behind him.

Mae's vision narrowed.

"Mae?"

His voice was distant and echoed as if calling from within a tunnel. She grasped at a wall shelf for purchase. His hands were on her now, grabbing her shoulders.

"Are you okay? Mae?"

Her chest seized, words stuck in her throat as if she'd swallowed the resident mouse.

"Mae, look at me."

Carter lifted her chin. Her eyes rolled but steadied on his almond irises.

"Breathe. Just breathe."

A sharp breath wedged into her strangled chest, and Carter ferried her to the kitchen table, swatting away most of the cobwebs before sitting her down. Mae sucked at dense air. It went down thick, like trying to quench thirst by slurping up pudding.

Carter retrieved a bottle of iced tea from his carry-on.

"It's warm but—" He handed it over and she chugged it like a lifeline; missed gulps ran down her chin.

"I'm sorry." She wiped beads of sweat from her brow, leaving a gray streak of grime across her forehead.

"No, I'm sorry. If I'd known it would be this hard for you, I would never have—"

"No, no, it's alright. Really. I'll be fine."

Carter's face twisted.

"It was just a lot to take in all at once. And then that mouse … Would you grab me my vape?"

Carter rummaged through her purse and handed it over. Mae sucked in greedy pulls, her nerves calming which each exhale. The kitchen clouded with vapor that hung in the air with the dust, obscured the light from the antique gas lamps.

"We're gonna need some help getting this place cleaned up. I'll find us a hotel room for tonight and see what I can do about hiring some help to get this place livable."

Mae nodded. "Even the air, it feels hard to breathe."

"Just the dust, I think." Carter swept a finger over the table to show the thick layer. "We'll make it work. You'll see."

Sunlight dappled in from beyond the blinds, stirring Mae, who had a faint recollection of Carter waking her before sunrise.

Gonna get started on the house and find us some help. I'll take care of everything. Don't you worry, she remembered. She stretched and pulled the wool blanket over her shoulders. Mountain birds sang beyond the sliding door, beckoning her onto the porch. Beyond the railing, squirrels chased one another twenty feet below. Her eyes wandered up over the distant, green mountain tops, and she plopped into one of the patio chairs. Her hand hovered over the small table between them, but her steaming latte was missing.

It was a short walk to Main St, which was small-town-bustling. The smell of roasted coffee beans enticed Mae into *Brewed Awakening*, a café where pastries tempted from beneath the glass. Pushing past a tightly packed friend group who, from the abundance of pink and blue cookies, appeared to be celebrating a pregnancy, Mae landed at the counter. She ordered her staple: vanilla latte, Splenda, not sugar. Warm caffeine in hand, she traversed the uphill climb back to the lodge. Leaves crunched underfoot, and Mae slowed her pace. *Look for white tails,* her father had said. He'd fed the deer in the winter, and Mae had the sudden, illogical thought that one might remember her. She reached a dip in the trail and movement passed between two branches, a snapping twig. Mae froze, her eyes bouncing over the landscape in search of a cottony tail, but instead she noticed an orange flash. Curiosity turned to caution. She called out.

"Hello?"

Leaves shimmied nearby and a head of spiky hair poked out of the brush. "I love that place!"

Mae stumbled backward a few steps, catching herself and her latte before both tumbled down a steep incline to a rocky ravine.

"Didn't mean to startle you."

A familiar pattern of freckles framed by chunky headphones stared back at her.

"Ollie?"

"Ah, Mae from the plane! Right. Great to see you. Sorry again about the mild heart attack." Ollie used the sleeve of their button down to wipe sweat dripping from their temple, their hair now a vibrant, citrus shade.

"That's okay, just caught me off guard, that's all. Didn't expect to see anyone back here. The lodge is pretty slow."

Mae noticed the axe dangling from Ollie's fist, stopping her heart with a jolt.

They must've noticed her startle and leaned the axe against a tree. "Slow, yeah, been slow the past few years. I've had to pick up odd jobs along the way. Not enough to do around here for full-time."

Mae blew the steam off her latte, imagined her nerves wafting away on the wind.

"And what do you do? Mostly axe things?"

Ollie chuckled. "Axe things, hammer things, nail things. Pretty much all the garage type things."

Mae couldn't help but smile.

"Hey, speaking of, did you hear? Someone is staying at the murder house."

"Oh?"

"Yeah, it's a real mess I guess. My boss asked this morning if I had time to help get it cleaned up. Should be a big project, been sittin' a decade."

Mae sipped. Tried to conjure an explanation that wouldn't transform her into some victim to be pitied, but nothing came. So, she sipped again.

"Good work for me though. Should keep me busy a month or so, I'd guess."

A month. Surely, I'll be able to move in before then. Mae scratched at her coffee cup. "That's great, Ollie. I'm sure it's not easy to find work in a town this small."

"Not always! And hey, while I'm there, maybe I can look for clues." Ollie winked.

"Well, I'd better …" Mae shifted her body away.

"Yeah, yeah, of course." Ollie picked up their axe. "And I should get back to it."

The twinge of embarrassment followed Mae all the way up to the cabin.

They'll realize it eventually. Maybe I should've just told them.

Upon entering her temporary home, the red blinking light on the nightstand distracted her from her shame, and she pressed the answering machine button. Carter's voice emanated from the speaker.

"Hey Mae-by, oh gosh. I mean Mae. Started to say baby and Mae. I actually kinda like it. Mae-by. So, Mae-by, I've got some good leads on help for the house. Tried you on your cell but couldn't get through. I'll be out a while more, just wanna get everything squared away. Don't worry yourself about it, okay? Gonna go check out a truck for us. You just relax, enjoy a quiet day in the mountains. Love you, bye."

Message deleted.

Mae checked her cell.

No missed calls. Strange.

She shrugged it off, remembering the romance novel in her backpack. After a quick dig through tangled wires, she found it. The scantily clad woman on the cover arched her back, obscuring the male character except for his boulder-like biceps. Mae pulled back the curtains around the sliding glass door, letting light pour in and warm her from afar. She slipped off her shoes, pressing on the pillowy duvet before snuggling under the covers. Her latte perched on the nightstand at arm's length; she wriggled her legs beneath the comforter, birdsong from the forest the only sound.

I'm sure Carter will be back soon, but until then …

She flipped the book open to the dog-eared page, ready to pass the time.

CHAPTER FOUR

By the time Carter returned, the sun was retreating behind the mountaintops, painting him red.

"Hey Mae-by! You get my message?"

"Yeah." Mae twiddled the fibers of her shirt between her fingers. "Why didn't you answer my texts?"

Carter flipped a set of keys around his finger. "You know how the service is around here. And look"—he held the keys aloft—"I was taking care of stuff for us." He eyed the book on the nightstand. "At least you weren't lonely."

Mae's eyed the steamy hero on the cover, and her anger dissipated.

"Well." Carter radiated the excitement of teen. "Don't you want to see it?"

Popping up from the bed, she slipped her shoes on. "Duh!" She trailed Carter down the stone stairway and into the gravel parking lot, her feet sinking into the pebbles with each step. A matte green truck waited in the spot assigned to their room. Carter's brows danced around his face.

"Eh?" He beamed.

"It's—"

"A '77 Ford 250. A classic."

Mae circled the truck, smearing aside kicked up dust to peer into the windows.

"It'll come in handy for moving our new furniture."

Mae nodded. *Not what I had in mind but* ... "Can I take it for a spin?"

Carter tossed her the keys and hopped into the passenger seat. Mae slid inside and stretched her legs, but her feet barely touched the pedals. She struggled to adjust the seat, which resisted her before careering forward.

Regaining her composure, Mae turned the engine over and the old beast roared to life, snorting out a tuft of exhaust from the tailpipe. Mae flipped on the lights and looked down at the stick shift.

"Oh."

Crickets trilled all around.

"Can't you drive stick?"

Mae shrugged. "Never learned."

"Aw, dammit." Carter looked out the window. "And it was such a great deal. I'll call the guy about bringing it back."

Mae reached across the console. "No, no. It's great, I mean, we're movin' and all. And you can teach me. It'll be fun."

Carter turned back to her, a glint in his eye. "You want to be my student?" His gaze penetrated.

Mae blushed, frozen to her spot.

"I should've known with our age difference 'd have to teach you a few things." He reached across and cut the engine. "Get back up to the room. Lessons start tonight."

The Victorian seemed less beastly in the bright light that day, four walls and a shoddy roof. Plenty of practical concerns to be sure: the plumbing, the spiders, the lifetime of belongings crowding every room. But the dense memories seemed tucked away with the afternoon sun shining in, and panic didn't chase Mae inside. Carter adopted the kitchen table as his work station, the only area emancipated from dust.

"Why don't you do a quick once-around, make sure there's nothing you want to keep down here," Carter said without looking up from his phone.

"You sure about cramming all this up there? Seems like a waste."

"Mae-by, we've got our hands full. Two full floors to move and sort and clean. It's just the two of us. What would we even use it for?"

Mae eyed the stacks of books along the walls, the stained chaise, the china cabinet stuffed to the brim. "I suppose you're right."

"A third floor really isn't practical anyway. It's a lot of stairs."

Knock, knock.

"That must be Eva." Carter checked the time on his phone. "And Ollie is late."

"Ollie?"

Carter paused with his door on the handle. "Yeah, I hired her to fix up those baseboards and repair the door frame."

"It's *them.*"

Carter scoffed. "Whatever."

Mae's intestines coiled. The heavy wooden door opened with a creak; two figures stood at the entryway.

"Oh great, you're both here."

Yup, here in the Murder House. Mae made a mental list of ways to busy herself, to avoid explaining her … omission.

Ollie's citrus hair poked out from behind a voluptuous frame. Eva, Mae presumed, wore a tank top cut down the middle creating curtains for her cleavage that distracted from her perfectly symmetrical face. Hands rested on her hips, her spiraling blonde locks draped over her shoulders and kissed her elbows.

"I'm Eva," she said.

Carter returned her coy smile with one of his own.

Of course you are.

She thrust out her manicured hand for shaking. "You must be Mae." Her smile revealed braces-aligned teeth.

Must be veneers.

"Sorry I'm late," Ollie chimed in, scooting inside.

"I—" Their congenial expression dropped when they saw Mae.

"It's fine. Come on into the kitchen, we'll discuss work for the day." Carter's left hand led the way, but his right landed on the small of Eva's back. Mae had to keep from yelping as if struck, and lingered in the living room, hiding her scowl. From there, she watched them settle at the kitchen table. Carter doled out instructions, Ollie taking vigorous notes. But Eva's eyes were fixed on Carter. Like the girls at the roller rink, like the waitress, like—Mae pulled her vape pen from her pocket and closed her eyes as she drew in.

"You ever wonder what that's doing to your lungs?" Carter interjected.

Mae eyed the pen, a flutter in her chest. "I mean, I'm sure it's not great."

"If you've got to use that stuff, you should at least go the natural route."

She tucked it away. "The smoke wouldn't bother you?"

Carter crossed the room, abandoning Eva at the table, and smoothed a stray hair away from Mae's face.

"It's not about me. It's about your health and it's important." He planted a soothing kiss on her lips. *Take that, Eva.*

"I wouldn't know where to get it. Don't think it's legal in South Carolina."

"Leave it to me. I'll find some for you."

"Oh actually," Ollie called from their seat. "I can hook you up if you need." They tapped an implied bag in their chest pocket.

"Great," Carter said. "It's settled then."

Carter returned to his meeting, and Mae busied herself sorting through tchotchkes on an antique desk while lingering within earshot of the kitchen. Her father's collection of ceramic frogs began with a vague mention of her liking them. Then, year after year, from hobby shops and second-hand stores, they'd filled the shelves.

"Come to me with any questions," Carter said. "I don't want you bothering Mae with anything."

The emerald one in a straw hat, the lime one atop a strawberry, the spotted one with the chipped eyeball.

"Understood," Eva said.

Mae pushed dust from the face of one with painted blush that held a flower. His yellow eyes were a comfort. They whispered of her father's love. "What if you're not h—"

"My wife gets very anxious. I don't need you adding to her stress. Got it?"

"No problem," Ollie said.

Mae hoped Ollie wasn't insulted by Carter's taking charge. She had half a mind to join the group in the kitchen and reassure Ollie they could come to her with any questions, but it was a relief to not be a caretaker for once, especially in the face of needing to sort through her childhood home. So, she stayed in the living room and slid open a desk drawer. It overflowed with papers. A letter addressed to her father sat on top. She lifted it, the paper edge cutting into her finger. "Shit."

"What is it?" Carter called from the kitchen.

"It's nothing," she said, sucking a drop of blood from her fingertip.

"Ollie, go ahead and get started on the door frame. You can invoice me for the materials."

Quiet footsteps signaled Ollie's departure, and Mae snuck in a small wave, which they returned with a cautious smile.

"Eva, I want you to get started cleaning the second floor today. Mae and I will be sorting through things down here."

"Should I start with the bedrooms?"

"Yes, please."

Eva sauntered up the steps with dramatic swishes of her hips like Lola Bunny, at least, Mae imagined she did. Relieved that Eva's curvaceous figure was no longer in her husband's sight, Mae freed the letter from its casing.

Mr. Pruitt,

Apologies for using such an outdated form of communication. I am overseas at the moment, and internet access is spotty at best. I wanted to confirm that I am still interested in completing the appraisal as we discussed. The photos you provided were a great help, but I will need to perform a thorough inspection in person to provide an accurate estimate and verify authenticity. I plan to be in town in the coming weeks and will reach out by phone to arrange a day and time which suits you.

Best,
Brooks Babineaux

Mae looked back at the envelope. "Hey, babe?"

"Yeah," Carter replied with a tone.

"Come look at this." She held the letter out and he scanned it. "It was written right before he—"

Carter cleared the distance between them in a flash and snatched it away. "Dammit Mae!"

"What?" Mae took a step back.

He circled the room, letter in hand. "This entire room to sort and you're getting lost in old letters! Are you kidding me?" He crumbled it up and threw it into the kitchen.

"Why are you freaking out?" Mae gestured at the filled boxes. "I'm making good progress."

Carter slumped down onto the sofa, dust motes rising up around him. "I'm sorry." He hung his head in his hands. "It's just, I'm worried. I'm doing everything I can to get things squared away here and you're just …"

Mae felt a pang of guilt as he shook his head.

"… I thought this house would be a fresh start for us, but you're so focused on the past. Maybe this was a mistake."

Mae sat beside him, placing a tentative hand on his thigh. "I want to start fresh too, I—you know what? Let's just put it all up. We can sort through what we want to keep later on. Let's focus on us."

"Are you sure?"

"Yeah, bring it all up to the third floor. We don't need it, and it's less cleaning for us to do anyway."

Carter wrapped his arm around her shoulder. "I love you, Mrs. Duvall."

Mae nestled close, letting the heat from his body warm her. "I love you too."

A little box waited for Mae on the kitchen table, adorned with a rose-colored bow. Carter shouted instructions at the furniture delivery men outside, barely audible over the sputtering truck. Mae placed her bag on the newly cleaned floors.

She ran her fingers over the satin ribbon, careful not to tug at the magazine-perfect curls.

Carter staggered in. "Ah," he huffed, "you found it." He caught his breath.

Mae held up the box, "What's this?"

A few drops of sweat fell from Carter's nose, gobbled up by the new welcome mat. "Open it."

Mae pulled at the ribbon, and the package eagerly undressed itself. She popped off the lid and let it hit the floor. Inside was a bronze barrel key topped with three, intersecting loops.

"I had it specially made."

Mae held it up, the weight substantial in her hand. "What is it for?"

"The house. A house this special deserves an ornate key, don't you think?"

Mae skipped to the door and inserted the fantastical key into the lock. *Click.* "

Wow! I've never seen anything like it."

Carter moved to the sink, splashed some water onto his face. "I'm glad you like it. Maybe put it away for now though, until you have a key ring. You have a tendency to lose things."

"What?" Mae asked over the sound of the running water.

Carter blotted his face with the hand towel. "Oh, nothing Mae-by. Just teasing you."

Mae dropped the key into her purse.

"I've got to get back out there," he said, moving away. "We've got an entire house to unload."

Mae called after him, "Need any help?" but he was already well into the yard and didn't hear. She stood in the foyer, now stripped of the sofa, chaise, and china cabinet. The room dwarfed her small frame. Cobwebs in the ceiling crannies and wafting off the chandelier threatened to reach down and tickle the top of her head.

Some cleaning lady Eva is.

Colored light dappled in from the stained-glass windows and patio doors. It drew her closer. The vibrant panes bent daylight around her, and she stepped through the rainbow exit to the expansive yard, hugged by towering oaks on all sides. The uncut grasses caressed her bare legs as she passed the greenhouse, its glass walls opaque with water stains.

Before her eyes, a decade was stripped away. The greenhouse came alive with herbs and veggies, a private jungle to explore. Her father handed her ripe tomatoes which she stashed in her purple bucket until it weighed down her thin arms. He wore his wide-brimmed hat and hummed while he plucked.

She approached the crumbling barn.

Not big enough for horses, but perfect for goats.

Splintering wood nicked her palm as she forced the barn door open. It groaned as it granted her entry. Light wriggled its way inside from holes in the roof. A single leaf floated in from the largest cavity.

Hope Ollie can fix that.

Her father's ride-on mower was parked in its final resting place, a small stall in the far side of the barn. She knew it was green, but only from memory. Ten idle years had not been kind to it. She remembered being five years old and riding on the front, her father steering from behind. Her legs dangled over the sides as she pretended to steer. *Faster, Daddy, faster,* she would squeal.

She could still hear his lectures, *Never go in the barn alone,* and eyed the hanging rake, the shovel, the machete. An uncomfortable stir. She stepped slowly around the corner, which she knew concealed a tree stump. It was bathed with light pouring in from holes in the roof. Highlighted, a mockery of that night, the axe still wedged in the center.

Mae backed away, stumbling in the process. She tumbled onto the scratchy hay floor and smacked her head on the wooden railing in the process. Timothy strands scattered over her face like confetti. One poked her eye as she laid there, dazed. Opaque circles obscured her vision. The barn around her doubled, then came into focus, then doubled again. She rubbed the spot on her skull which was already starting to swell, and inched herself backward like a worm until she could sit up against the wall. Of course it wasn't the same axe. Of course it wasn't. Her fingers searched her pocket for her vape pen but found only fabric.

Shit, did I lose it?

Heaps of surrounding hay needles left little hope for finding the slender device.

"Ugh."

From her spot on the floor, Mae's eyes traced the walls to the gas lamp. She heard her father's voice again. This time describing the gas lines he had repaired throughout the property. *It's gotta be gas. It's the only way to get that Victorian feel.* Mae didn't know what it meant back then, *Victorian feel.*

"Creepy feel is more like it," she grumbled. Using the wall to hoist herself up, she turned the lamp knob, rust flaking off on her finger. The ignition switch clicked, and Mae gazed in childlike wonder as the gas light erupted with flame.

Still working after all these years.

The spark danced within its glass prison. Something inside her awoke from a deep internal spring.

Maybe we can make this place something after all.

CHAPTER FIVE

Four specialty museums sat on opposite corners of Buncombe Street: one for children, one for art, one for history, and, the jewel in the crown, the Sigal Music Museum. In a former life, it was a Coca Cola plant, regal brick with rectangular glass windows from which passersby could watch the bottling process. Now with a new name and purpose, it rose from lush vegetation atop a hill, purple exterior lighting casting an otherworldly, neon glow.

"Did you come here as a kid?" Carter asked, taking Mae's hand.

"No, but we always meant to. I remember my dad talking about it."

As they crossed the threshold, they were greeted by the stale smell of history and a list of exhibits including the 1761 Double Manual Harpsichord, 1785 Demi-lune Piano, and the 1860 Vielle a Roue.

"Can you believe they've been preserved so long?" Mae asked.

"I come across a lot of old things in my profession, Mae-by."

Mae shuffled her feet. "Of course, yeah."

Carter led her to a cluster of banjos and ornate guitars hanging on display. Mae focused on a banjo with opal lining that seemed to change color under the light. "Beautiful."

Carter keyed in on it. "Valuable too."

Mae watched his face as he dissected the pieces with his eyes.

"These aren't just instruments, Mae. They have a whole history, a whole life of their own."

"Is that why you got into the antique business? The nostalgia?"

Carter scoffed. "*Nostalgia.*"

Mae fiddled with her buttons, suddenly feeling childish in her overalls and white Keds. Through the glass she saw two young boys in the next room. They pawed at the glass over an old recorder, winced then smiled at one another when their father chastised them. They shoved their hands into their pockets and twisted their mouths into exaggerated pouts. Their mother, a bit older than Mae, ignored the scuffle. She stared at Carter through the glass.

Mae nudged him with her elbow.

"What?"

She gestured at the woman with exaggerated eyes. "You know her?"

Carter cocked his head to see over the hanging instruments. The woman turned abruptly and walked through a neighboring exhibit.

Carter's expression was vacant. He watched the children toddle behind their father, who took long steps to keep up with his wife.

"Well?"

"Never seen her before."

Carter moved in the opposite direction. "Let's go see the nineteenth century clarinet."

Mae struggled to keep up. "She was really staring."

Carter whipped his head around. "Well, *Mae-by* she thought you were flirting with her." His eyes narrowed to slits.

Mae's cheeks flushed. *He must be hangry.*

Carter bounced from room to room, professed obscure facts, and made estimations of worth. Mae echoed his compliments, agreed with his critiques, hoping he'd agree to stop for lunch before the long drive home.

As they approached the final exhibit, Mae said, "Why don't we cut this short and grab a bite?"

Carter rolled his eyes. "Is this boring you?"

"No! I just thought maybe you could use some food. You seem a little ..."

"A little what?"

"Nothing." Mae smoothed her brows and forced a smile. "I'm just hungry."

"No problem," Carter said, his tone sharp. "Let's get you something to eat."

As Mae suspected, Carter's mood improved after lunch, and the animosity at Sigal was forgotten in Mae's belting of show tunes on the drive home. Her rendition of *The Wizard and I* earned an enthusiastic round of applause from Carter. And though his voice was less than virtuoso, Carter's commitment to Sweeney Todd made Mae sit up in her seat and watch, entranced. He bared his teeth, his eyes bore holes as he sang, transformed before her into the demon barber himself.

Mae overflowed with giggles. "I didn't know you were such a performer!"

"Well, you've got a lot to learn about me." Carter sported his usual, self-assured look and fixed his eyes back on the road. The miles passed and the turn onto Alquist Ave came quicker than expected. From the driveway, Mae spotted a light in an upstairs window, her chest tightened.

"Is someone there?"

Carter put the truck in park. "Just Eva, I asked her to do some cleaning while we were out."

Mae sucked down the last dregs of her vape oil.

"Thought you lost that," Carter said.

"It turned up." Mae cringed at the embarrassment of finding it in the kitchen sink all over again.

"Think that stuff is making you paranoid."

Mae bit back a retort as Carter jogged around the truck to open her door. She softened when he clasped her hand like a turn of the century gentlemen, guiding her hop down from the vehicle. "Why, thank you." She curtsied.

As they climbed the steps, Carter tapped his pockets. "Got the key?"

Mae plunged a hand into her purse and shuffled it around. "Of course." She placed it on a step and opened it wide, letting the fading sunlight pour in. Her fingers flipped through the contents. "It must be here."

Carter watched her from above, eyes like a judge or a hawk.

Mae dumped her purse out on the steps. Her wallet, lipstick, and coins tumbled out, but no key. "I don't understand." She outturned the inner pocket. "Where could it have gone?"

"Ugh, Mae." He rubbed his temples. "I knew this would happen. Say what you want about that"—he gestured at the vape pen—"stuff. But it makes you forgetful."

"It doesn't make me paranoid or forgetful!" Mae sounded more defensive than she meant to. "I just mean, I've always been a little anxious. This helps."

Mae scraped her fingers along the lining of her bag. "I don't get it, I swear, it was in here. I guess I'm a little more scattered than I realized."

"*May-be*," Carter said with a sneer. "No big deal, I guess I can get you another one. Eva!" he called, ringing the bell. "Just never thought I'd be ringing my own doorbell."

Dusk fell around the old Victorian, orange light filtered through the property's border of Eastern Hemlocks, their bristly branches casting spiny, creeping shadows on the walls. A flash of red through the window, then muddy brown, a cardinal and his mate. Mae curled up in bed with a book, doing her best to ignore Eva's puttering downstairs.

Carter emerged from the bathroom, dressed.

"Going somewhere?"

"Yeah. I took the day off so we could go to the museum, but I still have to work, don't I? I've got a client to meet about a sale." He straightened some wrinkles from his button-down in the mirror.

"When will you be back?"

"Could be late. This guy, Peter, he's a great buyer, but always asks me out for drinks after a big sale, and he's a talker."

Mae's forehead creased. "Thought you didn't know anyone around here."

"I don't. He drove down from North Carolina." He bent over the side of the bed and planted a kiss on Mae's forehead. "Been in this business a long time Mae-by. Lucky to have contacts all over, otherwise we couldn't make this move work." He winked and Mae nodded. She watched him polish his outfit in the mirror's reflection, admiring the outline of his pecs as they pressed against his fitted, collared shirt. He turned and faced her. "Well, how do I look?"

Affection warmed Mae as her eyes passed over his angular jaw, jet black hair tousled just so, his flashing almond eyes. "Tragically handsome."

His laugh was hearty. "Tragic, eh?"

He gave himself a final once-over. "I'll take it."

"Hope it goes well," Mae said before reopening to her page.

"Thanks, don't wait up."

Carter's steps grew faint as he moved down the stairs. She heard some exchange between him and Eva, and then the door creaked open and closed. She lost hours in her book, another sensuous romance, a skulking hero, a damsel in distress.

Night fell, inky black beyond the window. The warm glow of the gas lights set a moody vibe in the room, but as she neared a chapter ending, her eyes squinted.

Is it darker in here?

She crept down the stairs, her footsteps dampened by the carpet and her yellow socks. Unease prickled at her, but she assured herself it was just because she'd run out of THC oil. On the couch, Eva scrolled through her phone, not cleaning, as Mae suspected. Mae paused on the landing.

"Eva."

Eva glanced up, the light from her screen illuminated her emerald eyes. "Yes?"

"Were you turning on some lights down here? Or maybe using the stove?"

Eva's face twisted before she could correct it. "The stove?"

"The lights dimmed in my room, just wondering if you were using the gas down here."

Her lips puckered and her brows piqued. "No, Mrs. Duvall. Just like I wasn't the last time you asked."

Mae's ribs constricted. "Last time I asked?"

An exasperated sigh escaped Eva's full lips. "Yes, ma'am." She checked her phone. "Maybe thirty minutes ago. You stood right there" —she pointed a manicured nail —"and asked me the same thing."

Mae struggled against her memory.

I was in bed, reading. No, I haven't been down here since Carter left.

"Anything else, Mrs. Duvall?"

Mae backed up a stair. "No, no. Sorry." As she closed the distance to her bedroom, she replayed the evening in her mind. *Carter kissed me goodbye. He left. And I've been reading. That bitch is screwing with me.*

Her chest clenched as she rehearsed in her mind how she'd tell Carter about Eva's games when he got home.

I need something to take the edge off.

Climbing back into bed, Mae pulled the covers over her head.

I'll call Ollie tomorrow, see if they can get me something.

Mae read a few more pages until she heard Eva call from downstairs.

"I'm heading out, Mrs. Duvall. Come lock up behind me."

Before Mae could answer, she heard the front door open and shut. *Bitch.*

She descended the stairs, relieved to see her new couch unoccupied, and turned the lock.

Some tea might help calm my nerves.

Mae loosed her father's old teapot from a high cabinet, one of the few things not ushered into exile on the third floor. She rinsed off the dust and filled the kettle. When she flipped on the burner, the kitchen lights dimmed. She remembered her father explaining, *Anytime another light gets turned on or an appliance, it pulls some gas away from the lights that are running. Can't have everything all at once, can we? Like having our cake and eating it too.* Mae had joked, *I want cake! And bright lights!* He'd smiled his warm smile and patted her head. *I'm sure you do.*

She leaned against the olive cabinets, felt the smooth brass hardware as she waited for the water to boil.

Clunk.

Her head darted up toward the sound.

Clunk. Knock. Clunk.

Mae's blood pulsed in her neck. She froze to her spot. Her fingers tightened around the knob.

Clunk.

Her nails dug divots into her palm as the house seemed to exhale, walls leaning concave around her. Cicadas trilled a violent symphony beyond the backdoor's reach, a fragile, stained-glass barrier between Mae and the wild, stretching yard.

"Hello?"

Dread settled upon her shoulders like an itchy blanket. She strained her ears, the chorus of insects playing forte, staccato, in harmony with ancient boughs groaning grievances to invisible wind. Clammy sweat leaked from her hand, slicked her grip on the brass knob.

Screeeeeeeeeeech! The teapot whistled an insufferable tone.

Jolted from her position, she snatched it from the heat. Hot metal singed her fingers. She dropped it, let it clang against the counter. "Shit!"

Her thrumming heartbeat stabilized as she ran cool water from the faucet over her taut, burned skin. She shook her head, mocking herself.

'So, you're gonna freak yourself out and break Dad's tea kettle. Very smooth."

She slung her pinky through a lavender teacup, freed it from its glass shelf. Hand towel wrapped around the kettle handle, she poured boiling liquid, steam enveloping her face, and plopped in a chamomile tea bag.

"It's an old house. Probably just settling,"she told herself as she stirred.

CHAPTER SIX

Late August

Anxiety floated around Mae's chest like helium as she peered through the bedroom window. Between the odd noises and Eva's presence, saltier since their run-in while Carter was out, a low hum of fear seemed to be her constant companion. In the yard below, she spotted Ollie's vibrant hair, a clementine spot amongst the pale green grasses.

"Babe, Ollie's here." The billowing grass swayed and folded around their hips, encircling them, and Ollie ran their fingers along the pointed tips as if fingering a piano arrangement.

No response from Carter. Mae glanced around the room to find it empty.

Has he gone to work already? Her phone told her it was noon, later than she'd thought.

Mae pulled on a lacy beige dress and smoothed her flyaways beneath a braided headband. She trotted down the stairs and found her boots by the door, scooting them over bare feet. The last warmth of summer still embraced Alquist Ave, and she followed Ollie's trail through the long grasses to the barn. With nerves on fire and feeling more scattered than ever, Mae hoped against hope that Ollie had some weed with them.

"Ollie!"

A defined arm poked through the barn door, followed by a freckled cheek.

"Good afternoon, Mae."

Ollie wore a teal cutoff, their muscles defined by the strenuous work. A thin dew of sweat coated their forehead, making their smooth skin glisten in the filtered light.

"Whatcha workin' on?"

Ollie pointed up at the conspicuous tatters in the ceiling. "Can't keep goats through winter without a roof."

"Oh good, Carter told you about the goats." Mae was unsure of what to do with her arms and pressed them against her side at awkward angles.

"Yeah, and I gave him my honest opinion." Ollie turned from Mae and fiddled with a box of nails atop a hay bale. "They're a nightmare to keep, Mae. You should really think twice. I watched a few some summers back; they get into everything."

Mae frowned. "Thanks, I'll keep that in mind."

Ollie glanced back over their shoulder; their typical, wide smile dampened to a courteous grin.

"Everything okay, Ollie?"

Ollie scratched their head. "Yeah, it's just …"

"What?"

"Why didn't you tell me you were living here? When I brought up the house before."

Shit.

Mae pressed her lips between her teeth. Though she knew this was coming, she hadn't prepared a convincing excuse. "I guess I was just embarrassed."

"When I saw you that first day on the job, I felt like an idiot." They combed their hair with their fingers. "I'd been blabbering on about the Murder House and looking for clues. I had no idea—"

"I know. I should've told you. It was stupid. I'm sorry."

"It's okay." Ollie shrugged and tossed a playful elbow into Mae's ribs. "You must be a bigger true crime fan than me."

"Actually," Mae said, stepping back. "I'm kind of the story."

"Huh?"

"I inherited this house." Mae dug the toe of her boot into the hay floor. "It was my dad who, uh, you know. I hadn't been back since … well, I just wanted to start fresh. Didn't want to be the sad story all grown up. You know?"

They extended their arms. "Do you hug?"

Mae accepted their embrace with a coy smile. It felt warmer than it should have to a married woman.

"What would make you want to come back here after something so awful?"

Mae sighed and plopped down on a nearby hay bale. "Life with my aunt—she took me in after my dad died—was … not great. She's one of those, you know, tin foil hat types. I think she had this fantasy that I would become a prodigy violinist, earn enough money to buy her a big house. And, don't get me wrong, I love playing, but I was never gonna be *that* good. More than anything, I want to live for myself. Not base my life around someone else's dreams for me, or what I could do for them. You know what I mean?"

Ollie nodded and sat down cross-legged beside her. "Yeah, I know what you mean. My mom wanted me to be a pageant queen." They looked down at themself dramatically. "Clearly that didn't happen."

Mae chuckled. "I think you turned out pretty awesome."

Ollie's wide grin exposed their dimples.

"So, anyway, when I met Carter, it was like love at first sight. And he wanted to run away together. I wasn't sure at first, but he's so handsome and smart and successful, and he's good to me, so I decided to take a chance. The house was just sitting here. So, here we are."

"Wow." Ollie's expression was muddy. "I have so many questions."

"I thought you might." Mae blushed.

"Do you mind if I—"

"Shoot!"

Ollie's eyes opened like scrolls as they shot off rapid-fire questions. "Any idea who did it? Did your dad have any enemies? Anyone who would want to hurt him?"

Mae shook her head. "I've gone over it so many times in my mind. But I was young. I didn't know much about him outside of being my dad. He was so generous and kind. Can't imagine anyone would want to hurt him."

"And what about the violin?"

"Lady Paola."

"*Lady Paola,*" Ollie repeated, their eyes wandering the barn like they were digesting this new bit of information. "It had a name."

Mae's eyes drifted shut. She imagined the warm wood tones. The robust melody Lady Paola produced. "She was really something."

"How would you sell something like that?"

"At auction, I'd think. But a stolen one? I don't know, you'd need connections."

Ollie leaned in and lowered their tone. "And that certificate, right? Do you have it?"

"To be honest, I'm not sure where the certificate got to. Probably tucked away in my father's things. Could be lost. It was so long ago, who knows."

Ollie nodded their head, taking it in.

The quiet settled uncomfortably in Mae's stomach, and encroaching nerves urged her to change the subject. She rose and glanced up at the Swiss cheese roof, the grime settled in heaps at the barn's corners.

"Mind if I take some before pictures?"

Ollie cocked an eyebrow.

"It's gonna look so different once you're done with it." Mae drew her phone from her pocket and framed the shot, adjusting her position to get as much of the barn in frame as possible. "Come on." She waved Ollie into frame.

"Oh, no," Ollie said, pushing their hair around.

Mae reversed the camera to forward facing. "I'll get in it with you." She extended her arm and let it hover, leaving an open space for Ollie to join beside her. They shifted their weight, wiped beneath their lashes, then joined Mae in frame. Through the screen she watched Ollie lean to get centered in the shot, such a narrow frame, they had to press their ear against Mae's. It was warm and slick with sweat. Above their heads and out of focus was the shredded roof. Mae clicked, eyes fixed on their beaming faces. Suddenly self-conscious about their touching bodies, Mae broke the pose and inspected the picture. "I'll send it to you."

Ollie brushed a bit of straw from their shirt and glanced at their shoes. "Thanks."

"I've got a question for you too," Mae said, helium in her chest reminding her why she came.

"Shoot."

"You mentioned you could get me something for my nerves." Mae tapped an imaginary chest pocket. "I'm fresh out."

"Oh, yeah!" Ollie fumbled around the hay bale and located their leather wallet, which had toppled onto the floor. From the cash fold, they pulled out a baggie filled to the brim with green and purple nuggets coated in fine crystals and handed it to Mae for sniffing. "Fifty bucks for an eighth."

Mae cracked open the bag and inhaled the aroma. "Follow me inside."

They traced the path through the grasses and Ollie tailed Mae through the multi-colored glass door.

"Just a sec," Mae said. "Let me grab my purse."

Ollie stomped mud from their boots on the welcome mat as Mae tore around the house like a tornado, overturning couch pillows and bopping from room to room.

"I know it's here somewhere." From the kitchen counter to the coat hanger, the roller desk in Carter's office to the coffee stable, Mae searched.

"You can get me back next time." Ollie's leg bounced as they leaned against the door frame.

"Ugh, I'm sorry. Seems like I can't keep track of anything these days. Are you sure? Let me at least get you some water before you get back to work."

She moved into the kitchen and opened the fridge. Staring back at her was her pale pink purse, between the butter and the eggs. She pulled it from the shelf, the cold zipper chilling her hand.

"That's one place to put it," Ollie joked.

Mae shook her head. "I swear, I'm all over the place. Between losing things and the footsteps at night …"

"Footsteps?"

"Yeah, so Carter goes out at night a lot for work dinners and stuff. And when I'm alone in the house I hear noises. I can barely sleep." Mae fished the cash out of her wallet and handed it to Ollie. "I'm sure it's nothing to worry about."

"What kind of noises?"

"Like footsteps or something moving. From the attic, I think. Or the third floor."

"Aw, damn." Ollie stroked their forehead and scrunched their freckled nose. "You know, I was worried about that."

Mae shot them a questioning look.

"I saw a family of raccoons in the barn the other day. Scared them out, but it got me thinking, they could be in the house too. When they're nesting they look for some place warm and quiet."

Mae erupted with tense laughter. *Raccoons. Of course.*

"You think you could check out the attic for us? And the third floor? I don't want them living up there."

Ollie tucked the money in their pocket. "Well, I'd be happy to, except Carter had me board up the third floor, and that's the only way to access the attic."

"He had you board it up?"

"Yeah, the other day."

"Why?"

"Didn't say." Ollie shrugged. "Not my job to ask too many questions."

"Well," Mae held up the baggie, "thank you for this."

Ollie reached into their pocket and handed over some rolling papers. "On the house."

"I appreciate it."

"Better get back to the barn. That roof ain't gonna secure itself."

"Enjoy!" The words escaped Mae's throat on their own accord, and as the stained-glass door clicked into place behind Ollie, Mae went hot with embarrassment. *Enjoy?* Her eyes lingered on Ollie as they passed through the yard, and while Mae wondered whether they thought she sounded stupid, she could've sworn Ollie took a peek at the picture Mae had sent before disappearing around the greenhouse.

Darkness pressed against the sealed window, confining Mae to the four-poster bed that had been her father's. Her vague memories of him sitting amongst its carved acorn posts as he read in the evenings made it strange for her to share it with her husband. On the first night, after Carter struck dust from the mattress's innards, it felt as if his ghost rested between them. And not even Carter's flashing eyes or electric touch could lull Mae into feeling sultry there. But nights passed and the strangeness became familiar. She didn't expect to see her father's spectacles on the nightstand, or his pajamas folded over the side. On the nightstand drug from the guest room, she scattered bits of the pungent bud as she tore, a pleasant stink that calmed her nerves already.

Good stuff.

She loosed a rolling paper from the pack and flattened it out next to the pile of weed debris, hoping she remembered how to do this.Lovingly, she sprinkled the sticky pieces along the paper's crease and lifted the drug taco with pinched fingers on each end. With a steady grip, she worked the sides of the paper, pushing the bits of bud back together into a cylinder. They clumped happily, reunited. When she had a cohesive strand, she rolled the paper in her fingers, twisted the ends. A loose but smokable joint, she thought, inspecting her work in the lamp light.

With a flame held to one end, her lips pulled on the other. The fire arched and ignited the thin paper. Smoke filled her lungs and clawed at the bottom of her throat. She erupted in a coughing fit, dug her fingernails into the comforter for purchase.

Carter scooted around the corner and poked his head through the open door. "Jesus, Mae. You okay?"

Mae glanced over at him, through quaking eyelids, eyes already burning. "Yeah, I'm good," she choked out. "Just got a little more than I bargained for." She eyed the ember, which stared her down. A challenge.

Carter sucked his teeth and disappeared into the hallway.

She took another puff, smaller this time, and held it in her chest. Smoke danced inside her and she straightened her back, blew it out about her head like a dragon, victorious. Two tiny puffs, then another two. Sensuous smoke like a masseuse vibrated her body from within. Her shoulders fell. Her mind was allowed to wander.

I wonder how Auntie Bel is doing. Been a few weeks since I've called.

Mae slid her phone from the nightstand to her lap and sent the call through.

"Hello?" Auntie Bel croaked on the other end.

"Hey Auntie, how are you?"

"Hah!" she scoffed. "How'd you expect me to be?"

Carter poked his head back into the room. "Mae-by, I've got to run. Don't wait up, okay?"

"Auntie, hold on." Mae looked up from the phone to answer Carter, but he was already gone. "Never mind."

"Enjoying the haunted mansion?"

"Uh, it's not really a—it's good."

"Ready to run back home yet?"

Her aunt's words tasted sour, and for once, Mae didn't have to hide her grimace. "No, Auntie. I'm good."

"Well, when you realize you can't hack it on your own, you just let me know."

Mae let her eyes roll.

"You been practicing?"

She pictured her violin, still packed in its case from the move. "Yeah."

"Good. Anyway, honey, my show's back on. Gotta run."

"I lov—"

Click. Call ended.

"Great."

The roach burned at Mae's knuckles as she took a few more pulls, moving across the room to the open window. Cool night air floated inside. An unseen owl hooted from a distant Hemlock. Mae flicked her joint to the yard below, watched the ember weaken and die out a story below.

A walk would be nice.

She descended the stairs, each step in slow motion. The carpet fibers massaged her toes. Her nose caught a whiff of the banana bread Eva cooked earlier, and she followed it into the kitchen like a cartoon drawn around by a visible, hovering smell. Imagining blue teardrops of drool falling from the corners of her lips, she was startled to find Eva gathering her belongings.

"Oh, Eva! Didn't know you were still here."

Eva scarcely looked up. "You're having a good time, from the looks of it."

Mae swallowed a laugh. "I'm headed out for a walk." She felt the redness in her eyes but refused to be embarrassed by it. Instead, she tossed open the front door and stood in the open doorway, taking a deep breath of dark air and feeling the cool reach under her clothes. Eva had scrubbed the wraparound porch so hard, it was like no one had ever died there.

"I don't think that's a good idea," Eva said, coming up from behind and pushing past. She stood on the white painted boards, doe-like eyes illuminated by the glowing gas lamps. "I'm leaving, and you don't have a key, remember?"

Mae deflated.

Eva trotted down the steps. "See you tomorrow, Mrs. Duvall."

Her red taillights glowed like a pair of monstrous eyes, and Mae watched with envy as she pulled down the driveway. Her tires screeched as she lunged onto Alquist Ave. Feeling like a caged thing, like a doll in a box, Mae took one step backward, then another, closed the front door and turned the lock.

"Just me and you tonight," she said to the old Victorian. *I'm talking to myself.* Mae giggled. *I'm very high.*

She looked up. "Enjoying your night, Mr. and Mrs. Racoon?"

Mae waited for an answer, then forgot why she was waiting, and approached the stairway.

Clunk.

Her hand hovered over the banister.

Clunk, clunk.

Imagining an animated racoon family, knocking on the attic floor wearing hats and bows and big smiles, she called, "Enjoy the attic!" But as she climbed the stairs, she heard something new. She brushed it off at first. So soft and low, barely audible. But as she climbed, the sound became clearer. Notes. Chords. Harmony. Kavakos's *Paganini Caprice No. 5.* There was no mistaking it, the screaming strings as the bow sawed through the arpeggio. Seamless execution. Mae's heart pounded in her chest, no helium, just a beating drum. It had to be him. Him or Kavakos himself.

"Dad?" she squeaked out. She strained her ears, half expected his tenor voice to waft from his rightful bedroom, to answer, *Mae?* But as suddenly as it started, the playing stopped. Only the trilling of crickets kept her company on the landing, the sound of their tiny insect strings drifting downstairs from her open bedroom window.

CHAPTER SEVEN

Early September

The passing weeks turned the bags under Mae's eyes a purplish gray. She hunched in the corner chair, her empty gaze channeled toward the open window. The long grasses outside were turning brown and chafed in the wind.

"Dammit, Mae!" Carter flew into the room and slammed the window shut. "How many times have I told you? The heating bill will be enormous."

He waited for her to make eye contact, but her pupils floated aimlessly and made their landing on the greenhouse below.

"You've been hearing it again, haven't you?" He knelt down to intercept her eye-line. "You've got to get some sleep."

"Why don't you believe me?" she snapped.

Carter smoothed back the wispy hairs around her face. "How about a shower today? *Mae-by?*"

The blanket around her shoulders fell to her waist. Carter extended a hand to help her out of the chair, walked her to the bathroom, and started the hot water. Mae straightened her arms above her head and he lifted off the ratty T-Shirt. She scooted off her underwear and stepped into the steam. Carter sat on the edge of the tub. "I thought today you could look into enrolling in school. It would be good for you to get out of the house."

Mae let the scalding water sting her back. "Maybe I'd get out more if you got around to teaching me how to drive the truck."

Carter sighed. "Is it not enough, Mae? For me to provide for us? Be the *only* one providing for us? I'm trying to keep food on the table. Sorry I haven't had time to be your driving instructor." He shook his head.

Mae turned her back to him. "And yet you somehow afford to pay Eva. She's here every goddamn day."

Carter jumped up from his seat. "You know, we're all doing our best. I've kept Eva on because you've been a wreck! Leaving messes all over the house, leaving things in the weirdest places; you barely get dressed anymore. We need Eva. Who else would cook? Who would clean, Mae?"

It's true. Mae's eyes began to water, hidden beneath the shower stream.

"I need you to believe me." Her voice cracked.

Carter pressed his hands against the glass shower. "Tell me what you need, Mae. You need me to believe that your father's ghost is haunting our house? Do you hear how it sounds?"

Mae shrank down to a ball, grasping her knees in her arms. She let the hot water trickle down her spine and felt Carter leave the bathroom. She could sell the house, she thought. But for what? It was all but crumbling around her. Barely enough money in the accounts to restore it.

Steam clouded the mirrors and the shower walls. Water beaded on the black lacquer tiles. Floral wallpaper gawked at her from above. In her head repeated the melody from the night before. And the night before. A song played so many times it rang in her ears even when she didn't hear it. And Carter never did. Never heard it. Never heard *her*. It played now, again and again. Forte, mezzoforte, then the measured, andante cadence. The hiss, the pull, the scream.

I'm not crazy.

I'm not.

Mae was awakened by a distant clamoring. And when had she slept? Time, lately, seemed to buck and fold like an untamed thing. Her nights and days were distinguished only by the dim light that crept in from her window. The window where she spent her waking hours, trying to spot the source of the banging, clanking noise. If not for Carter checking on her, bringing her Eva's cooking, she thought she might've withered away to nothing.

A dream faded from her consciousness, the sensation of kissing Carter, his arms around her tight and then claws sinking into her flesh, his tongue turned to ash in her mouth. She returned to the window seat. Ollie's toned figure hammered pieces of tin over holes in the barn's roof. Mae pushed up against the window frame, winded by the effort. Every piece of the house seemed to resist her, plot against her. From the floorboards that groaned to make her every movement known, to the window, now unwilling to rise. She braced, used her feet as leverage, and the pane whined as it rose several inches.

"Ollie!" Mae called, her voice cracking.

Ollie took uneasy steps back and would've toppled off the side if not for using the hammer as a counterbalance.

Mae cringed. "Sorry!"

Ollie descended from the roof, grasping the gutter and using the door frame as a foothold.

"Meet you at the back door."

Ollie's head bounced in acknowledgment. Mae jogged to the landing at the top of the stairs, but the sudden movement made her head swim. She placed a hand on the banister and took a deep breath. The stars obscuring her vision rolled, expanded, then jettisoned. Her stomach grumbled, but the passing thought of food was driven back by fatigue-induced nausea. Using the railing as a brace, she plodded, hunched, like a three-legged creature, to the backdoor and unclicked the lock for Ollie, who waited behind the shimmering glass. Cold air pushed its way inside behind them, uninvited, and Mae noticed that the slow passing of weeks had sapped the color from Ollie's mane.

"What's up, Mae?" Sweat leaked through the white cotton of Ollie's shirt.

"Oh, uh—" Mae glanced around. She hadn't thought this far. "Just wondering how the work was coming. Been getting a little lonely in here."

Ollie frowned as they took in Mae's sallow appearance. Mae watched their eyes linger over her now protruding collar bones. "Everything okay, Mae? You seem a little … fraught."

Mae's balance began to waver, and she collapsed into a kitchen chair. "Since you brought it up, there was something I'd like to get your thoughts on."

Ollie settled in a neighboring chair. "Shoot."

"Well, it's not just the noises anymore, the raccoon noises I mean. There's been something else. It comes at night, only when everyone else is out."

Ollie raised their brows, urging Mae to continue.

"It's gonna sound crazy, but it's music. And not just any music. It's my father playing. I'd know the sound of his strings anywhere. It's got to be him. There's just no doubt in my mind."

Ollie nodded.

"You must think I'm nuts. Carter does. I wouldn't blame you." Mae slid her head into hands for support.

"Have you been eating, Mae?"

"I can't eat anything that witch cooks." Mae shook her head. "I'm sure she's spitting in it."

Ollie placed a gentle hand on Mae's thigh which bounced like a rubber ball from her jittery foot. "You don't look well. Maybe you should get out of town for a few days. Visit family?"

Mae chewed a hangnail on her thumb.

"I think maybe coming back here, maybe it's been too much on you all at once. No one could blame you for taking a little break."

Her teeth snagged a thin strip of skin, pulling it away from her finger and leaving a long thin strip of blood in its wake. Ollie hugged her bleeding hand in theirs. "I think some comfort food, some sleep, might do you a world of good."

Mae's head bobbled in agreement. "Hey, you think you could take down those boards? I'd like to check out the third floor. Maybe scare the raccoons off. Make sure it's secure up there, no open windows." Her eyes ping-ponged off the walls.

"Mae, I …" Ollie rose slowly. "I don't think that's a good idea. Can I walk you up to bed?"

Mae acquiesced, following Ollie up the steps like a stray animal, and climbed onto the floral comforter.

Ollie hesitated in the door. "You have my number, right?"

Mae nodded, glancing back out the window.

"Take care of yourself, okay?"

Their steps grew quiet, and Mae heard the clinking door. From the window, she watched Ollie traverse the now worn path, pull their sweater closer as wind ripped across the yard.

Mae pressed her palm against the glass. The cold permeated and crept into her hand as Ollie disappeared into the barn. Maybe they were right. Maybe the house had been too much. A break. A break would do Mae a world of good. Just a little break, and she'd come back recharged. Ready to enroll in school, learn new recipes, finally get that herd of goats …

Mae pulled out her phone and dialed Auntie Bel.

Of course, she'd welcome a visit. She must be terribly bored with no one to boss around, starved thin with no one to do her bidding.

"What?" Auntie Bel answered.

"Oh, uh, hi." Mae adjusted her tone. "I was thinking, might be time for a visit. What do you think? Could you stand to have me for a few nights? I could make your favorite, pot roast."

"Eh, hold on."

Mae heard rustling in the background.

"Would you get a handle on those fuckin' mutts!"

"What?" Mae asked.

"Nothin'. Not you. Anyway dear, it ain't gonna work out for a visit, unfortunately. Had to rent your room. Got this idiot here with a whole pack of tiny stinking dogs. But at least I got him to overpay." She cackled. "But how's married life? Must not be too good if you're lookin' for an out already."

Mae saw Auntie Bel's smug expression in her mind. "No, actually, it's great. He's just about to head out of town on business. Things have been really picking up for him. So, uh, just thought it would be a perfect time for me to come out. But no problem, really, I understand. Maybe we can work something out over the holidays."

"Sounds good, fuck, GET BISCUIT, HE'S ABOUT TO EAT MY DAMN CHIPS! Sorry honey, I've gotta run. You take care now."

Click.

Carter's chest rose and fell evenly as his breath slid in and out his nostrils. From the chair by the window, Mae watched him, one eye on the clock. 3:27 a.m. Only a few more hours. 6:30, that's when his alarm would sound. When she stared straight up, she could hear it better. She had it down to a science now.

Listening was key, and if she could figure out the pattern, she could figure out the mystery. Kavakos's *Paganini Caprice No. 5*, Biber's *Mystery Sonatas*, Tchaikovsky's *Violin Concerto*, Kremer's *Spiegel im Spiegel*, Wieniawski's *Romance*. No repeats so far. Carter had rolled into bed late, and when he'd bundled himself up in the covers, Mae had stirred. She'd tried to drift off to sleep, but then she heard it. Soft and menacing. Scraping at the edges of her mind. So she'd sat up. Listened. She'd moved to the window chair. Listened harder. If she could just figure out the pattern, then maybe … and he'd believe her then. He'd have to. So she listened. And she waited. And she watched him. Breaths in and out, in time with the adagio tempo.

Then the coda. The winding finish, the way only her father played it. She waited for the next piece. Nothing. Silence.

She stood up in the chair, lifted her chin. If she could just get her head closer to the ceiling, she'd hear it. She'd have to. Legs wobbly with exhaustion, her knee buckled. The chair leaned and Mae grabbed at the curtain to steady herself, but it was too late, the angle too drastic. The chair tumbled into the bedframe with a crash, Mae crashing with it. Carter jolted from the bed.

"Mae? What the fuck," he rubbed at his eyes, disbelieving, "are you alright?"

She stumbled to her feet, smoothed the hair away from her face. "You've got to come with me, now."

Grabbing Carter's hand, she dragged him from beneath the covers. He followed her to the stairs, his steps heavy with sleep. As she began to climb, he pulled against her.

"What's going on, Mae?"

"It's coming from up here." Mae grabbed at his arm. "Just come. You'll hear it. You'll see."

Carter climbed the flight leading to the third floor, and Mae stopped when she reached the wooden boards nailed across its entry. She pressed her ear to the splintering plywood.

"Mae—"

"Shut up!" She leaned in hard until a tiny spike of wood drove itself into her earlobe, but she heard nothing, only the muffled sound of her veins pumping blood. "It was playing! It played for hours. *Paganini Caprice No. 5, Mystery Sonatas, Violin Concerto, Spiegel im Spiegel, Romance.* Carter, it played them all!"

He twisted his hand away. "Mae, I've gotta get some sleep. My trip is in the morning. Just a few hours from now."

"Babe, please. I swear." She grabbed at the plywood board, dug her fingers into the wood and pulled at them.

"Mae, stop."

She yanked at the corner, but the board wouldn't give.

"Mae!" Carter placed his hand on her shoulder and Mae spun, pushed his shoulder with both hands. Carter stumbled back a step, almost fell down the flight, but caught himself with a lucky grab at the banister.

Mae's eyes peeled like she'd seen a ghost. "I'm sorry." She jogged down the steps and grasped his arms, but he shook her off.

"I don't know what to say, Mae." He rubbed at his temples. "I've got to get some sleep." Carter turned and descended the stairs, Mae tailing him to the guest room where he stretched out on the couch, his feet hanging over the side. "Please, Mae. You need sleep too. Just go to bed."

Hours later, in the meek morning light, Carter's sleek travel bag waited for him at the door, bulging with clothes. Mae wilted beside it over the arm of the couch, her hip bones protruding over sagging shorts.

"It's just a couple weeks," he said.

It shouldn't have been a big deal. Mae knew that. But two weeks alone evoked dread like a prison sentence, like being buried alive. Her forehead was greasy with unrest, blemished from days between showers.

"I left cash on the kitchen counter. Remember to eat, okay? I had Eva stock the fridge and that Chinese place delivers, if you don't feel like cooking."

Mae glared. *When do I ever feel like cooking?*

"Hey, maybe while I'm gone, you'll research some schools?"

"With what Wi-Fi?"

"You could walk down to the library."

"It's too late for the fall semester."

"Well," Carter grabbed a banana from the counter, "pick up your violin at least. Playing always helps you center yourself, right?"

Mae nodded but didn't hide her disdain.

Carter hunched over her and pinched her cheeks. "Can I get a kiss before I go?"

Mae pursed her lips, accepting the kiss like a back-handed compliment.

"I love you." He opened the door and lifted his bag. "Remember, I left the house key on your nightstand. Don't forget to lock up if you go out."

Mae nodded. "Call me every night, at least."

Carter smiled. "Of course, Mae-by. Be safe, okay?"

Safe.

Mae languished on the couch for thirty minutes or so, hoping Carter would realize he forgot something and return. But the door remained shut. Her stomach growled. Begrudgingly, she moved into the kitchen and opened the refrigerator door. The uncut veggies mocked her. The milk and eggs conspired. The scent of fish filets bullied her nostrils. She slammed it shut with a vengeance.

The next day, a polite high school girl delivered boxes of fried rice and crab rangoons with a demure smile. Mae shoveled scoop after scoop of rice into her mouth with a plastic spoon. Grains scattered around her one by one, taking residence on the area rug and between sofa cushions. Mid-shovel, Mae heard a knock at the door. Her neck curved so she could see out the arched window. An empty porch.

Knock, knock, knock.

Mae's head whipped around, and she spotted a distorted figure through the curved, rainbow glass at the rear exit. She crept closer, wary of who might be knocking. She crouched down. *Knock, knock.*

Mae dashed behind a protruding wall.

"Mae! I know you're in there. It's Ollie."

A wave of relief let Mae unclench her jaw, swallow the bits of rice in the pouch of her cheek. "Coming."

The opened door revealed a different Ollie. Mae had only seen them in their work or travel clothes, but tonight Ollie wore a fitted jacket and shiny loafers, hair combed back just so.

"What's up?" Mae asked, feeling slightly under-dressed.

Ollie flicked a bit of fried egg from Mae's top and smiled. "Want some?"

They happily accepted the plastic fork from the to-go pack and sat beside Mae on the couch, doing their best not to create further rice confetti.

"I just wanted to check on you," they said through chews. "I remembered you mentioned Carter going out of town."

"I appreciate it," Mae said, crunching a crab rangoon.

Ollie snapped a pair of chopsticks and rubbed them against one another. "You know Mae, it's probably not my place, but I want to tell you something."

Mae cocked an eyebrow, folded the top of the to-go container and tucked the pieces together to reform a box.

"I think I saw him."

"Who?" She pushed the cardboard container away.

"Carter. Driving around town with some woman. Couldn't tell who."

Mae's face darkened. "What?"

"I was headed into town for a d—well, it doesn't matter—and I spotted him, well, his car really."

"I'm sure other people have old green trucks, Ollie."

"It looked like him. And there was a woman in the passenger seat. It happened so quick, but I wouldn't say anything unless I was pretty sure."

Mae disregarded them with a wrist flick and rose from the couch. "My husband is out of town." She dropped the remainder of the Chinese food into the garbage. "I dunno what you saw, but he'd never lie to me."

Ollie eased the unused chopsticks onto the coffee table and made their way to the back door. "Yeah, I'm sure you're right. I'll just ..." Eyes cast down, Ollie stepped through the door. They closed it gently behind them as Mae watched, arms crossed, from the kitchen.

Some people just need drama.

Still, Ollie's words played on repeat in her mind and nagged at her gut well into the night. The house was quiet. No singing strings from sealed rooms to haunt her, and yet, without the music, she felt alone. Tempted to resent Carter for leaving her, Mae reminded herself that if not for his work, they'd barely be able to afford groceries. She'd certainly been no help past getting them this crumbling house which needed enough work to drain the little money she'd inherited.

Mae thought of her lonely violin, no doubt coated in dust by now. Perhaps if she played, she would feel a little more useful. Perhaps if she played, her father would answer back. Where had she left it?

In the study? No. Maybe the guest room?

Flames from the gas lamps cast a warm glow over the halls, poor lighting for a proper search. She strained her eyes in the shadows, scanning for the black case. From room to room she went, checking inside old trunks and under stacks of empty boxes.

The library was mostly untouched since Mae and Carter's arrival. Eva's cleaning hadn't made it there, and the floor to ceiling shelves towered over Mae much as they had when she was a child. A black, spiral staircase stood in the room's corner, its steps adorned with ornate swirls. She ignited the sole lamp, causing the light in the hallway to dim. The flame cast a meager penance of aid in her search, and she fumbled over an object in the dark, losing her balance and catching herself on the edge of the bookcase. *Shit.* She pulled her phone from her pocket and clicked on the flashlight, shining it toward the floor to identify whatever delinquent object had nearly caused her to fall.

She gasped. Three steps backward. Her phone shook in her hand, causing the light beam to leap around the room, illuminating cobwebs and the odd spider.

On the floor lay her violin case, spotted with a red spray. Spotted with blood.

She'd kicked it open in her stumbling, and lying inside was not her secondhand Cremona. Her eyes passed over the radiant varnish, the golden strings. The unmistakable figure carved into her tailpiece.

Lady Paola.

Her image was burned into Mae's mind. Whether ten years or ten moments, she would recognize Lady Paola in an instant.

Her pulse raced, beating allegro in her ears. Mind emptied of thought, her feet carried her into the living

room, then flew up the steps. Gasping breaths, she reached her beside, steadied herself with her hands.

It's not possible.

There's no way.

She thought of calling Carter, but the tall tale would only worry him further, convince him that her sanity was failing.

And Ollie?

After their presumptions about Carter's infidelity, she couldn't face them.

I've got to handle this alone.

CHAPTER EIGHT

The dark hours offered little rest, and Mae welcomed dawn, snatching the key from her nightstand and slipping on jeans and a T-Shirt for her trip into town. She knew the psychic's shop wouldn't be open, but the café would.

Caffeine would do me good.

Mae scurried down Alquist Ave and looped onto Main St. Town was still sleepy, only a few construction workers grabbing their morning pastries as she made her way to the cafe. She passed the shop on her way.

10 a.m. - 7 p.m.

Mae checked her phone.

Three hours to kill.

A sole barista worked behind the counter, her sugary drawl a warm comfort.

"What can I get you, sweetie?"

"Vanilla latte, please. And a cruller."

"Comin' right up!"

She was awfully cheery for the early hour. Mae watched her bop around behind the counter, frothing milk and swirling in syrup.

"Big day?" she asked.

Mae shrugged. "Not really." The cardboard cup warmed her hand, and Mae tossed a few dollars in the glass tip jar.

"Thank you!"

The corner table was a perfect hideout. Mae picked apart the cruller on her napkin, watching the town awake from behind the picture window. If she dozed off in her seat, she couldn't be sure. Her waking and dreaming bled together, equal parts nightmare and mundane, but the hours passed with a hazy quickness, and she knew the psychic when she saw her.

Her white hair defied gravity in tufts, constrained by a patterned headband which was tied at the nape of her neck and streamed down her back. Her bohemian skirt trailed behind her, and she walked with both urgency and calm. Mae discarded the remnants of breakfast, left the cafe, and followed at a distance.

Psychic Readings, Tarot, Walk-ins Welcome.

A bell jingled as she entered, and Mae was instantly overwhelmed by smoky frankincense. The shop was dim but colorful. Myriad patterns and florals draped over shelves and counter space. Plants clung to life near the covered windows.

"Just a minute," the woman called from the backroom.

Mae ran her finger over book spines, *Psychic Growth, Healing through Tarot, Surpassing the Veil.* She spied a small table in the corner with two chairs and took a seat.

"You're looking for answers," the woman stated as she emerged from the fabric draped over the back-room doorway.

Aren't we all?

She sat across from Mae. "What can I do for you, my love?"

Mae fanned crumbled bills in front of her. "What can you tell me for forty bucks?"

The woman cleared her throat and shuffled a deck of illuminated tarot cards.

"Ask the cards your question."

Mae grimaced, unsure whether to direct her question to the woman or to the deck itself. She settled on halfway, striking an awkward gaze at the woman's neckline. "What is happening in my house?" She winced at hearing the question aloud.

The woman tossed the cards back and forth, arranging and rearranging them in her palms.

"Cut the deck with your left hand," she instructed, "and pull the top card."

Mae obliged and repeated the action twice more. Three cards embellished in gold leaf and illustrated with pastels lay before her.

"Ah, the five of cups." She gave Mae a sympathetic smile. The card depicted a young man who knelt down, his head cradled by his arms, spilt cups at his feet. A distant tower loomed behind him atop a grassy hill. "You've lived through grief."

Mae nodded.

The psychic pulled the center card, on which a nude woman was swaddled in a beige sheet at her waist. Her flowing hair bounced around her in wild curls as she gazed into calm water below. She bore a contented smile. "And the Star, upright, which tells me something changed. You were feeling hopeful that things would be different. The sadness would end."

The woman ran her finger over the final card. "This is your future card." Her face was grim. It showed a tower, not unlike the distant one which stood in the background of the five of cups, but here it took center stage. From it a nude man fell, clutching at the air with flailing limbs. He wore a white mask, like a theater mask, though Mae was unsure whether it was the one for comedy or tragedy. "The Tower. You're in danger, my sweet."

Mae's heart moved into her throat.

"What do you mean? From who?"

The woman closed her eyes and drew the card close to her chest. "I see—I see a woman. She is not what she appears to be. She means to do you harm." She coughed out a dramatic breath. "I'm sorry"—she shook her head, absolving herself of responsibility—"I wish I had better news for you."

Mae handed over the cash and lifted her purse from the chair to leave. She thought of returning to the old Victorian, alone. Of a female phantom lurking in the library, or the attic, or the sealed third floor. Of Eva. "Is there any way … do you do home visits?" The words sprung from her throat uninvited. "I think, if you came to my home, you might get a little more."

The woman's eyes grew. "Well yes, but it's quite costly. Two-hundred per hour."

Mae thought back to where Carter stashed a wad of bills, in the kitchen drawer, in case of emergency. "It's no problem. I can pay."

The psychic gathered her cards. "Generally, when someone asks me to come to a home, it's an attempt to reach to the other side. Is that what you're looking for? Do you need to speak with someone who's lost?"

"Yes." Mae's voice caught in her throat. Gnawing at the base of her skull was *Paganini Caprice No. 5*, a bow sawing with speed enough to ignite the strings. "My father. He died, uh, suddenly. And there've been some strange … things in the house."

"How's seven?"

Having never conducted a seance, Mae was unsure how to prepare. She lit every candle in her possession and placed them around the living room, clearing a space on the floor where she and the psychic could sit. The house, embarrassed for her, moaned at her efforts.

Winding her shirt around her fingers, Mae fiddled around the living room, adjusting a crooked mirror, straightening the accent pillows, going over what she might need in her mind.

A picture. They always need a picture.

The only photo of her father left after the scourging was a black and white portrait in the library. She hadn't faced the stacks of books, the gossamer strands linking them to the spiral stairs, since the night before, and dread curdled the air as she approached the doorway.

She peered inside, her feet planted firmly in the hallway. Through the shadows she discerned the black violin case, closed and resting beside the spiral stairway. Mae shook off the thoughts that Lady Paola rested inside.

It had been her imagination. Lack of sleep, transfiguring the Cremona in the dim light. Richard Pruitt's portrait stared back at her from a shelf, veiled in a fine layer of dust. She balled her fists like a runner crouching in the blocks. A glance behind her revealed no villain, no ghost. So, with long, quick strides she closed the distance between herself and her father's image. She snatched it from the shelf, a speck of dust wafting up and digging into her eye, and clutched the portrait close to her chest. Tears welled, and as the dust dislodged from her cornea, she made out the warped, black shape of the violin case. Curiosity tugged at her. She snuck a glance. It was the Cremona inside. Had to be. A tear rolled down her cheek, restored her sight. Perhaps just a peek. It was right there, after all.

She tiptoed to the case and crouched down beside it. Her thumbs unfurled the clasps and she whipped it open, as if to frighten off the past. Lying humbly inside was her Cremona, not grand enough for a name. An unexpected sinking feeling drew her shoulders down. Her eyes passed over the case in search of bloody specks.

There were none.

Lack of sleep, she told herself. Lack of sleep and lack of light. The weed, maybe. Anxiety and missing her father. That was all. Mae abandoned the library, retreating to the living room where she placed her father's portrait on the mantle overlooking the cleared space on the rug. She stared into his gray face, his plump cheeks. "Do you think I'm crazy?"

Knock, knock, knock.

Mae popped up and glided to the front door. On her welcome mat was the psychic, dressed in dark wash jeans, a simple top, and a chunky necklace. Mae swallowed her disappointment before it showed itself. She couldn't expect the woman to show up in starry robes. Right?

"Thanks for coming, uh—I'm sorry, I didn't catch your name before."

The woman plunged her hand into her deep, patchwork bag and handed Mae a business card. *Evangelina the Ethereal,* it read. "But you can call me Joanne."

"Well, Joanne, thanks for coming." Mae gestured to the open space in the living room. "Please, come inside."

Joanne obliged, sitting crossed-legged on the area rug. Mae was pleased with herself. She'd judged the sitting arrangements right at least.

Mae settled opposite her as Joanne pulled object after object from her seemingly bottomless bag: placards with odd symbols, numerous crystals, and a blue candle. She spread them across the coffee table and struck a match.

"You've created a serene space," she said gazing at the flickering candlelight. "That's good. Bring the photo here."

Mae rose and handed the portrait to Joanne.

"Do you have anything that belonged to him?"

"He owned this house. Is that enough?"

Joanne nodded and placed the picture in the center of her arcane objects.

"Your phone. Turn it off."

Mae retrieved her phone from the kitchen, noticing two missed calls from Carter on the screen. She cleared them and turned it off. When she returned to her spot on the rug, Joanne was holding a pendulum, a metal chain with a large white quartz on the end.

"I want you to take some deep breaths in and out."

Mae aligned her breathing with Joanne's. Self-conscious at first, several long breaths helped her to settle, and warm peace took hold. Joanne extended her hands and grasped Mae's.

"Close your eyes. Focus on your purpose."

Mae straightened her back. Was Joanne watching her? *No, focus. Okay, okay. Dad, please help me. Tell me what's going on in this house.*

From a deeper place, the real question came. *Am I safe here?*

"We welcome peaceful spirits into this circle. Please make your presence known."

Mae's stomach clenched.

"Dear, what's your father's name?"

"Richard," she whispered. "Richard Pruitt."

"We call on you, Mr. Richard Pruitt. Please join us in the circle when you're ready."

The hairs on Mae's arms stood upright. She squeezed her lids to keep them shut. A crow cawed from the ledge outside, making her jump.

"I feel him," Joanne said. "He's joined us, and he's heard the question from your heart."

Mae gripped Joanne's palms harder than she intended. Sweat leaked between her fingers and they threatened to slip away, but Joanne held them in place.

"He has a message for you."

Wind whipped at the windows, howling as it passed. The crows screamed. The front door blew ajar, and Mae's eyes shot open. Footsteps on the landing. She expected to see him, the age he was when he passed, returning to the home they shared. It was the figure of a man, but as the shot of adrenaline dissipated, and the figure became clearer. It was Carter's face she saw.

"What the fuck is going on here?" His eyes bounced from the lit candles to the table covered in archaic objects. "Mae, what are you doing?"

Joanne popped up from her seat on the floor. Her hands quaked as she ushered her belongings back into her sack.

"Babe, I—"

He threw his hands into the air. Joanne rushed out the door without a word, extinguishing the candles she passed with the fervor of her exit. Carter locked it behind her.

Mae was ten years old again. Defenseless. Humiliated. "You wouldn't believe me!" She yelped.

Carter covered his face with an arched hand. "I can't deal with this right now." He climbed the stairs, lugging his baggage behind him, leaving Mae alone in her spot on the rug. She rose, knowing she couldn't leave the remaining candles burning through the night, but hesitated before she directed her breath at the flame.

"Dad," she whispered, "what is it? What do you need me to know?"

Goosebumps covered her body and a chill crept up her spine. She waited expectantly, but the only answer she heard was a final shriek from the crows on the porch. A puff of air from her lips extinguished the flame, and a curl of smoke wafted up from the smoldering wick, painting ornate patterns in the air.

CHAPTER NINE

Carter tossed crumbled clothing into the laundry bin, shoved folded shirts back into drawers. Mae pretended to read while she waited for the argument to start. Feet curled beneath the comforter, at least she'd be comfortable. When he ran out of clothes to stash, she knew the question was coming. Knew he'd ask, despite knowing the answer.

"Did you look into school?"

Mae cascaded the pages of her book back and forth in her hands, watched thousands of words fly by.

"Did you practice?" he pressed. "I saw your violin on the floor of the library."

The rush of air from passing pages pushed the familiar book smell into Mae's nostrils. "Ollie said she saw you. In town."

"What?"

Mae felt his eyebrows raise, though she didn't look up to be sure. "With a woman."

"What's happening to you, Mae?" Carter paced around the room, the thin floor shuddering beneath him. "I'm starting to think—"

"What?"

"You need help!" His words were sharp. His mouth hung open.

She ran a finger along a bundle of pages.

Maybe he's right. Should I tell him about the—No.

"I'm calling the doctor in the morning. I've heard that around your age …"

"You think I'm crazy," Mae said. Strong in the words, she rose from the bed, stood shoulder to shoulder with Carter. "You've been implying it for weeks now."

"Schizophrenia, Mae." The force of the words launched droplets of spit onto Mae's upper lip. "That's why you never knew your mother. They talk about it in town, not that you would've heard, locked up in here day in and day out." His eyes were cold, empty.

Something icy crept around Mae's ribcage.

"She started getting sick when you were a baby, and she ran off. Nobody knows where, but what they do know, what they gossip about at town barbecues, is how she complained about weird noises, music playing, and then voices. How she locked herself away. In this house, Mae! The groundskeeper would see her staring from the window. Doesn't that sound familiar?"

That's not true. Can't be. Dad would've told me. Auntie Bel would've told me.

"It's genetic, you know. And you're around the age she was when—"

"Stop!" Silent tears streamed down Mae's cheeks and over her trembling lips.

Carter stepped back. "I'm going to sleep in my study. Tomorrow morning, you're going."

Mae passed the first few hours of Carter's absence occupied by smoldering resentment. He'd slid her dinner through a crack in the door, and unspoken jabs about being a prisoner rolled through her mind with every chew and swallow. The last of the weed she bought from Ollie was already rolled into a misshapen joint. It bounced around in her unsteady fingers, resisting the flame. A few lungfuls of smoke steadied her hand, but the news of her mother's condition still rattled around in her head.

Why wouldn't he have told me?

She took another long drag.

Why wouldn't anyone have told me?

Her window-side chair was a familiar comfort. She ran her hands over the carved wood and watched crows land atop the greenhouse. First two, then four, then twenty. More and more landed and she feared the glass roof might crack under their collective weight. The heavy navy curtains diminished the fall chill but offered little comfort to her fragile mind. Around her the lights dimmed, as they did every night. She knew better than to mention it. And it seemed that outside darkened too.

The horde of crows blended together in the blackness, now a looming shadow, a thick cloud atop the straining glass. Mae swore she could hear it splinter and crack between whistles of the wind. And above those distant sounds rose harmonious tones, one of Biber's *Mystery Sonatas*. Her father's artful playing bolstered the mounting dread. Shadows cast on the red and gold wallpaper by twisted curtain rods doubled in size. The walls themselves seemed to bend and press with her breathing, now strained, as if her neck was gripped by some unseen force.

"Like mother like daughter," she heard. It was faint but clear, a voice emanating from the rippling wall. She pressed her ear against it. Held herself steady with her hands, the floor rolling like a gentle wave.

"A seance, hah!"

Mae's heart dropped through the hardwood, and she tossed the smoldering joint into the ashtray.

"Stupid little girl," the voice hissed.

She pushed off the wall and dashed around the corner, whipping the door open to the neighboring room. Her eyes passed over the empty guest quarters: the four-post bed meticulously decorated with eight pillows in varying shades of green, the yellow tasseled rug beneath, pale squares on the wall where long hanging art had been removed. Exiled to the third floor.

"Who's in here?" she demanded.

But the empty room refused to answer, the furnishings dead and quiet before her.

She slunk back to her quarters and locked the door behind her. The *Mystery Sonatas* droned on. She climbed under the covers, dwarfed by the king-sized mattress, the looming walls around her. Tiny, like Tinkerbell. Like Thumbelina. The lights brightened once more, and she drew the comforter over her head to escape them. Her closed eyes conjured images of her mother, dressed in a torn hospital ground and screaming from her shackles. They were too bright, too vivid. It set her teeth on edge.

Two puffs of a joint? Mae had smoked much more than this before. It couldn't be that, despite Carter's incessant suspicions.

Tomorrow morning. The doctor.

"It's a bit of trial and error," Doctor Levine said, scribbling orders on his prescription pad.

Mae stared at the crumpling paper sheet beneath her, pressed down on it to create a tear.

"Thank you," Carter offered for her, accepting the paper on Mae's behalf.

"You may experience some side effects," Doctor Levine continued. "Weight gain, dizziness, nausea …"

His words droned on and on as Mae inspected the vintage advertisement framed on the wall.

Electricity, A Natural Cure!

"Dry mouth, headache, occasionally vomiting …"

No more use for crutches or drugs.

"But call me right away if you see any signs of seizure …"

Take a Treatment for Free

He directed his warnings to Carter, because, Mae presumed, he was the only non-crazy adult in attendance.

"Any questions?"

Mae shook her head.

Doctor Levine left the room, and Carter stared at Mae like an alien species, some experiment gone awry.

"What do you think?" he asked.

Mae shrugged.

"Worth a shot, right?"

"Yeah," Mae hopped down, the tile cold on her bare feet. "Worth a shot."

She told herself she should be grateful, that at least Carter cared enough to try. Her mind wandered back to the image of Lady Paola in the darkened library, the low toned voice that mocked her through her bedroom wall, sending a shudder through her body as she slipped on her shoes. As much as she hated to think it, maybe they were right. Maybe the medication would help.

A sea of staring eyes focused on Mae in the general store. She thrummed her fingers over the hard plastic countertop, watched the pharmacist dip in and out of tall aisles stacked with bottles of drugs. She imagined hers might reside in a cartoonish jug marked with a skull and crossbones.

Maybe, somewhere in that mess, there was a bottle filled with tiny violins.

There she is, the nut, the mother in the red romper must've thought as she pulled her child close.

A real loon, echoed the elderly man sorting through diuretics.

Do you think she knows where she is right now? the trainee questioned, stocking pantyhose.

Their eyes were cold rods in her back. Carter might've heard them too, driving him to pace in front of the counter.

"Duvall," the clerk called.

Carter received the folded brown bag before Mae recognized her new name. He pushed his hand into the small of her back, ushered her past an elderly woman in a church hat who thought, *I'll pray for you, dear,* on their way out of the store.

He cracked open the passenger side door of the truck. "I'll hold onto these."

Mae climbed inside.

"You'll take one each morning with food. I'll make sure Eva has breakfast ready."

Eva. Perfect Eva.

Mae's stomach coiled. She envisioned Eva adding a hefty dose of rat poison to the eggs, whistling as she stirred. Mae watched the town roll by as Carter piloted them through Main St. The episcopal church flurried with activity. Was it Wednesday already? Time had slipped from her grip. It couldn't be Sunday, right? They'd just been to the doctor, after all. Aren't doctors closed on Sunday? Mae had decided on Wednesday when the truck pulled into its spot. The Victorian stood grim and tall, and Mae thought the winding ivy that curled up the siding looked much like barbed wire in the low light.

Through the picture window, her nemesis tried to look busy in the kitchen. Eva's blonde hair curled around her ears just right today, her dress, impractical for cooking and cleaning, hugged her curves like a '50s model. Mae rubbed at her stomach without thought as Carter moved around the side of the truck. The roll of flab about her hips had thinned into loose skin she could pinch. Her husband eased her down from her seat like you might a child. As they climbed the porch steps, Mae heard voices, Eva's sharp tone and a warmer one, Ollie's. In her periphery, Carter's brows furrowed as he listened.

He hears them. Good.

Greeted by the smell of ham in the frying pan, Carter looked enthused.

"Smells great, Eva. Maybe you can teach Mae sometime."

Mae did her best to ignore the subtle dig, looking to Ollie who was fumbling with their pockets. She had a strange thought, an uncouth hope that Ollie preferred her over Eva.

"How'd it look up there?" Carter asked.

Ollie wore time-worn overalls, demin made soft over years of repeated washes. Mae wanted to ask where they came from, whether they were handed down, wanted to touch them, feel the threads between her fingers. "Bad news, I'm afraid. The roof here is compromised too. Wouldn't be surprised if the weather weakened the third floor. Good thing we boarded it up. Probably not structurally sound."

"Shit." Carter smoothed his black hair. A careful eye could see it was thinning about the top of his head. "Sounds expensive."

"Yeah," Ollie agreed. "You'll need to get an engineer out here. It's out of my scope."

Carter ripped open the brown pharmacy bag and placed the pill bottle on the counter. "Make sure Mae gets one of these with breakfast," he told Eva.

Ollie offered a sympathetic half-smile as they made their way to the back door. Mae jogged several steps to catch up, following them through to the backyard where Eva's green eyes couldn't follow. Shutting the door with a gentle nudge, Mae stopped Ollie in their tracks. She spotted pity in their face.

"I shouldn't have said anything about Carter. It's none of my business. I'm—"

"Actually, I was wondering if you had any more weed. I'm fresh out."

"Oh," Ollie tapped their pockets, one of which emanated a crinkling sound. "I think I stashed some in the barn."

Brown grasses crunched under the weight of their steps, and the barn door sailed open with Ollie's light pull.

"You fixed it," Mae remarked.

"Just needed a little grease is all." Ollie flipped over a hay bale, exposing a baggie like the one Mae had purchased before. They passed it to Mae, who cracked the seal and inhaled the scent deeply.

"This doesn't ever make you …" Mae thought better of asking. "Never mind." But the door was open now.

"I don't wanna overstep, Mae." Ollie's eyes wandered the barn as if searching for the proper words. "But I'm worried."

Mae was suddenly aware of her disheveled hair, the stain on her blouse.

"Do you feel"—Ollie twiddled a strand of hay between their fingers—"safe here?"

Mae remembered the psychic's words, *A woman means to do you harm.*

"I know I'm …" Mae spun a strand of hair around her finger tight. "But the psych—Eva. I don't trust her."

The pity in Ollie's expression mixed with intrigue.

Mae eyed the tip of her finger, now white, strangled by her own, dirty hair. "What do you know about her?"

Ollie's lips turned inward. "She's new in town. All I know is she's staying at the Extended Stay on Shamrock. Seen her car parked in the lot."

"The Extended Stay?" Mae did mental math, tried to justify the cost against Eva's wage—

"Maybe I can ask around town," Ollie offered.

Mae tucked the baggie of weed into her bra. "I would really appreciate it. Yeah, thanks."

CHAPTER TEN

Mid-September

Ollie felt their bulging pocket and drew out the crumpled paper they'd rescued from the Duvall's kitchen floor, tracing their fingers over the lettering for the hundredth time that day.

Mr. Pruitt,

Apologies for using such an outdated form of communication. I am overseas at the moment and internet access is spotty at best. I wanted to confirm that I am still interested in completing the appraisal as we discussed. The photos you provided were a great help, but I will need to perform a thorough inspection in person to provide an accurate estimate and verify authenticity. I plan to be in town in the coming weeks and will reach out by phone to arrange a day and time which suits you.

Best,

Brooks Babineaux

A clue like this could crack the cold case wide open.

'Authenticity.' It has to be about the violin. Only one reason to discard something like this: to keep it from police. Someone knows something.

Ollie's loft apartment was a one-story climb up from a boutique shop in town—the one with very few visitors thanks to the overpriced garments and Linda, the grouchy shop owner—and just two blocks from the police station. They slid on their headphones, switched their playlist from true crime to alternative hits, and swaddled themself in a thick hoodie to protect from the chill.

Ollie's boots on the stairs stirred Linda, who rose to greet what she thought was a customer, but grimaced when she saw Ollie.

"Good morning!" Ollie chirped.

"Mornin'."

No one had informed the wind that the official start of fall was still a week away, and the sun hid behind a blanket of clouds. They took the turn onto Shamrock Ave, walking amongst the flock of shining police cars which waited to ferry a town drunk or goat thief to a holding cell.

"May I speak to Captain Williams?" they asked the uniformed trainee at the front desk. Ollie spied a framed photo of Jesus behind the desk.

"The Captain is busy," she said through gritted teeth. "Something I can help you with?"

Ollie pulled a chain from beneath their hoodie and settled the cross on their chest. *See, I'm one of you.*

"I really need to speak with Williams, he knows me."

Confusion rattled the trainee's expression. "Just a minute." The trainee dipped behind the desk and through the door which led to the offices. Ollie scanned the various flyers on display. *Housing Resources, Shelters, Domestic Abuse.* They lifted the Domestic Abuse flier and flipped it open.

Break the silence.

Ollie skimmed the 1-800 number and a few bullet points.

A plain clothes detective rounded the corner, his eyes narrowed and fixed on Ollie. "How many times I gotta tell you, Alden, your application was denied. It's a small force for a small town. No openings."

"I'm not here about that, Ruthers, but it's great to see you too."

Captain Williams poked his head out of the door and spotted the flyer in Ollie's hand. "Shit, Ollie, something I should be concerned about?"

Shoving the flyer in their pocket, they scrambled to clarify. "No, no. Was just wondering if I could talk to you about something." Ollie glared at Ruthers. "In private."

Captain Williams gestured for Ollie to follow and led them into his plush corner office. Ollie took a seat in an overstuffed leather chair studded with brass. The view from the window let Captain Williams spy on the town through the blinds, only intermittently disturbed by the ringing of his landline phone. "If someone is hurting you, Ollie—"

"No, seriously. I'm fine. Single and ready to mingle!" Ollie hoped their joke would lighten the mood, but it only confused Captain Williams further. "It's about the axe murder."

Captain Williams sighed, "Oh, dammit Ollie, not again."

"Seriously! You said to come back if I find something significant. And well, I've found something. Significant."

Ollie rifled through their pocket and retrieved the crumpled note, flattening it out with their palms on the desk. "It was in the house. Tossed on the kitchen floor like trash."

Captain Williams studied the page. "*The* house?"

"Alquist Ave, the very one."

The Captain drew the letter close to his face. "I've been doing some work on their barn, and I'm telling you, something strange is going on there."

"Brooks Babineaux," Captain Williams mused.

"Mae Pruitt, well, Mae Duvall now, she was totally fine a month ago. A pothead, sure"—Ollie grinned—"but who isn't." A wink.

Captain Williams shooed the information away.

"I know, I know, but anyway, now she barely leaves her room. She's scared. Might be paranoia, but something's up with her husband, Carter. He's shady."

Captain Williams raised an eyebrow and Ollie realized how flimsy their explanation sounded.

"He told her he was traveling for two weeks on business. But I saw him in town with some woman."

Williams shrugged. "So, he's cheating. It's not a crime."

"I think it's more than that."

Williams sighed. "Based on?"

"A f—"

"Ollie, you had a *feeling* about the old groundskeeper. You had a *feeling* about frazzled Joanne, who was just trying to make a few bucks off the ghost story. You have lots of *feelings*, and I know you mean well but ..."

Ollie felt blood rush to their face. "Can you at least look him up? This Brooks character?"

Williams let out a heavy sigh.

"And Eva, the housekeeper. Mae doesn't trust her, and I promised her I'd—"

"The case is dead, Ollie." He removed his glasses, a sure sign the discussion was over. "As much as you'd like to resurrect it, there just isn't enough here to suggest we should reopen it."

"But—"

"I was there that night, Ollie. I carried Mae away from her dead father's body. You're not the only one who wishes this case was solved, but we're a small department. We just don't have the resources to chase our tails on this."

Ollie felt the familiar sinking feeling return and rose to leave but paused in the door. "But you'll let me know—"

"If there are any openings. Of course."

On the way out, Ollie diverted to Brian's desk. He flipped through photos of his wife and sons on social media and jumped when Ollie placed a hand on his shoulder.

"Workin' hard or hardly workin', Jenkins?" Ollie joked in their most deep throated voice.

"Your Williams impression needs work," he said, closing the page. "What brings you to the station? Trying your hand at bribing the captain into creating an opening?"

"Geez, no," Ollie said, shaking their head. "I'll just apply for your spot after you get canned for bullshitting on the job."

Brian ran his finger over the brass placard on his desk. "De-tec-tive," he enunciated.

"No shit." Ollie eyed the family photos Brian was scrolling through on social media. "Is Steph some kind of person of interest?"

Brian's mouth hung open.

"The boys then? They headed to juvie?"

Unable to think of a snappy comeback, Brian settled on, "Alright, alright. Point taken."

Ollie pulled up a chair next to his. "Actually, I was wondering if you could help me with something."

Brian opened a game of solitaire on the screen. "Can't, busy that day."

Ollie punched him in the shoulder. "Come-on!"

"Jesus! Fine. What is it?" He rubbed the spot.

"You seen the new housekeeper on Alquist Ave? The one carting her cleavage around town?"

Brian chuckled. "How could I miss her? She's got my wife all stirred up, asking all kinds of hypotheticals. *Would you still love me if I got burned in a fire? If I cut off all my hair? If*

I transformed overnight into a praying mantis?" He exhaled stress through his nose. "What about her? She doesn't strike me as your type."

"It's not that. Actually, I was wondering if you could tail her."

"Tail her?" His smile swallowed his face. "Like an old noir film?"

"She's shady, Jenkins. I'm tellin' you. Just for a night or two. Please?"

"Ah, ya say she's shady, eh? I ain't yer errand boy though, see?"

Ollie's mouth was a flat line. "You too busy with playing security for the high school play or something?"

A guttural sigh escaped his throat, though Ollie knew the reluctance was only for show. "Alright."

Ollie curled their hand into a fist, which Brian tapped begrudgingly with his own.

"She gets off around six, six-thirty. Alquist Ave. Assuming you know the place?"

Brian rolled his eyes. "How could I forget?"

"Let me know how it goes," Ollie said, sliding their chair back to its place.

"Oh no. You're coming with me."

"Seriously?"

"Hell yeah. Meet me here, five forty-five. Every stakeout needs a partner."

Disbelief turned to excitement.

A real stakeout.

Ollie's amateur sleuth heart sang. They floated through the rest of the day, preoccupied with picking out their most noir outfit, landing on a duster jacket and a thrift store fedora that both made Ollie feel like an old-timey detective and obscured their vision.

What if she sees us? What if there's a chase?

Their insides pitter-pattered as the minutes ticked closer to go-time, and by the time Ollie rounded the corner to the police station, bag of snacks in hand, Brian was waiting in his sleek Crown Victoria. The engine hummed as Ollie plopped into the passenger seat. The stale scent of French fries did nothing to dim the thrill.

"You ready, Detective Poirot?" he asked.

Ollie ignored the dig, opening the plastic bag full of chip bags and juice boxes so he could see they came prepared.

"Apple juice?" He crinkled his nose.

"It was all I had."

"Toss me a box."

Ollie freed the straw and punctured the top for him. He sucked at it, air bubbles gurgling in the tiny straw.

"Hits the spot."

Ollie had crunched halfway through a bag of cheese doodles by the time Brian parked at the end of the avenue. He shut off the lights and killed the ignition.

"It's gonna get cold," Ollie complained.

Brian eyed them with reproach. "It's a stakeout, Ollie. Not a sleepover."

Ollie flushed. "So now what?"

"Now we wait," Brian said, lowering his seat to a near horizontal position.

CHAPTER ELEVEN

Night chill crept into the car, spurred on by whispering wind. Twin gaslights glowed beside the front door, but Ollie's eyes wandered up the ball and spindle woodwork to the vacant stare of the third floor windows.

Why did Carter ask me to board it up? He didn't know about the rot then.

During the day, the property felt expansive, spacious enough to easily accommodate the greenhouse, the barn in back, and the private drive in front. The three-story Victorian felt dwarfed by the five-acre yard, which gave it a wide berth on all sides before breaking into the forest of Eastern Hemlocks. But once the sun dipped below the horizon, the trees seemed to hunch inward. Silhouettes pressed against one another, encroaching on the house, claustrophobic. The flickering flames of the gas lamps gave life to every shadow. They'd dart across the corner of Ollie's vision, making it impossible to settle. Always a movement just out of sight. Always a feeling of being watched.

"Weird, isn't it?" Brian mused. "Like the house got stuck in time."

"Creepy more like it."

Tonight the lights were more ominous than quaint, glowing eyes daring them to get closer. Ollie stared at the slouching porch. Moss crept up the handrails, carpeting cracks in the soft wood. Tangled vines choked the support beams, clawing away the rose petal paint. They tried to imagine the Victorian newly built, standing straight and strong and proud. They struggled to picture the hanging tire swing and a joyful girl swaying on it through a spring breeze, now a frayed rope that twisted and jerked at the groaning bough from which it hung. But the specter of death shaded the property from levity, even that conjured from imagination. Ollie shifted in their seat, crinkling the empty snack bags around them.

"How long has it been?" Anxiety threatened to take hold.

"Not long enough." Brian focused on the front door. "Just wait."

Dried leaves rapped the sides of the sleeping vehicle and were carried down the street in a swirling gust. It didn't feel as Ollie thought it might. Pouring over the old news articles in the library and stealing opinions from townsfolk who remembered the ghastly crime had been exciting, an awakening of Ollie's investigative spirit. But the reality of the house steeped in shadow, its oppressive presence thickening the air sapped enthusiasm even from Ollie. If the house was stuck in time, then Ollie was stuck within its gravity. They imagined themself as a rat, feet pinned to a glue trap, clicking its teeth and eying its ankles.

It seemed that dawn should be approaching, despite Brian's reminder that it had only been two hours, when a strip of light escaped the door frame, outlining a curvaceous figure. *Eva.*

Ollie tensed.

"Just wait," Brian said.

She stepped onto the porch, Carter behind her, his head thrown back in a hearty laugh. His arm circled her waist and she spun to meet his face. Ollie watched their lips, wishing they could read the words they exchanged. Carter grabbed both of her hands in his and lifted them above her head. His foreword steps pushed her back until she was pressed against the siding. Brian sat up in his seat.

"Br—"

His hand shot out to silence Ollie.

Carter collected Eva's wrists in his fist. They were eye to eye like animals. His free palm grazed her neck, then clamped down. Eva's eyes bulged.

"Should we—"

"Shh!"

Seconds limped by and the veins in Eva's face bulged. Just as Ollie thought Eva would collapse, Carter's hand relaxed around her throat, and he pulled her mouth to his, wrapping both arms around her back. She embraced him, her fingers digging into his shoulders.

Brian was transfixed. "Holy shit."

"See?"

"Just watch."

Carter escorted Eva to her car and gave her one last kiss through the open window.

"Can you make out the license plate?"

Ollie squinted but the distance and the dark made it a fuzzy rectangle. They shook their head.

"Let's follow her."

Brian started the engine as Eva pulled onto Alquist Ave. Ollie's eyes lingered over Carter who paused in the doorway. His eyes passed over Brian's car.

Shit.

"I think Carter saw us."

Brian snatched a notebook from his center console and pulled a pencil from the spiral binding. He cruised several car lengths away from Eva, jotting down the license plate, then made a right turn, letting Eva slip out of sight.

"That's all for tonight," he said, circling back to Main St. "If Carter gets suspicious, he could tip her off."

Ollie's head swam. The violent kiss played on a loop in their mind.

"What was that all about?"

"Well, he's clearly cheating," Brian said, shaking his head like he was throwing off the same images in Ollie's mind. "But that's not a crime. *Kinky* cheating. But still, not a crime."

Ollie nodded, still seeing Eva's bulging eyes. Landrum's Main St was a ghost town. No such thing as nightlife there. The darkened shops were quiet and still, save for the orange tabby cat who trotted around looking for scraps.

"I'll run the plate in the morning, see if anything interesting comes of it."

The Crown Victoria sailed into the street parking in front of Linda's boutique, the shop beneath Ollie's apartment. Brian placed the car in park and sat in silence for a moment, studying the picture window. Linda had displayed a Fall Festival sign between two gaudily dressed mannequins. It was hand drawn. Craft leaves of orange and brown pasted in the corners.

"You going?" Ollie asked, desperate to shake off the diseased feeling infecting the car.

"Every year." Brian's stoic stare lifted, revealing the smile of a consensually chained man. "Family tradition."

Ollie's mouth watered as they remembered the syrupy sweetness they'd gobbled up the year before. "Is Steph making her famous pecan pie?"

Brian shrugged. "Most likely." He eyed Ollie with a smirk, no doubt remembering when they'd showed up at the Jenkins family's door asking for seconds.

"Well then"—Ollie cracked open the door and stepped onto the curb—"I'll see you there."

As Brian's taillights disappeared around a corner, Ollie wondered if the chill that raised the hairs on their arms came from the early fall wind or from the Old Victorian. The orange tabby bopped across the street, its light steps silent on the brick. Ollie knelt down.

"Psst, psst, psst." They rubbed their fingers together.

The cat galloped up and arched its back as it rubbed on Ollie's leg. They stroked its eager head and it purred with gratitude. Ollie unlocked the boutique door, and the cat cocked its head to the side. A kissing sound was all the convincing it needed to follow Ollie up the stairs.

No pets, Ollie heard Linda say in their mind. But they enticed the tabby into their apartment nonetheless. A can of tuna and saucer of milk made for a gluttonous feast, and Ollie stroked the tabby, glad to have company after the jarring night.

"I don't want to have to tell her," Ollie told the cat, who responded with a curt *Meow.*

Ollie sighed and pulled the phone from their pocket. The call to Mae went straight to voicemail and, unwilling to leave such news in a text message, Ollie typed an ambiguous urging.

Call me when you get this. It's important.

The bubble struggled to send and promptly turned green.

Great, her phone is off.

Relieved for the moment, Ollie stretched out onto their pull-out couch, which squeaked under their weight. The coils pressed through the thin mattress into their back, but the lackluster accommodations did nothing to dampen the alley cat's spirit. It leapt onto the lime-colored sheets with another *meow* and plopped down onto a pillow, eyes shut and purring. Ollie caressed its head as they drifted into sleep, the intermittent flashes of Eva's bulging eyes jolting them into a stir several times before unconsciousness fully took hold.

When Mae woke, the sheets were still tucked in on Carter's side. Dazed, she dragged herself from the bed and checking her phone, despite knowing the familiar *No service* message meant she wouldn't have any waiting messages.

I'll have to walk around the property at some point, see where I can get a signal.

The cell service had turned from spotty to nil as the last warmth of summer was blown away by autumn breezes. The wood floors were cold on her feet, and the house was quiet as she rounded the corner to his study. Blankets were strewn across the tufted couch inside, and Mae noticed a crusted spot on the crushed velvet where his drool had collected and dried.

"Good morning."

The abrupt greeting startled Mae, who didn't expect to see Carter emerge, fully-dressed, from the closet.

"Why'd you sleep in here?" Concern furrowed her brows.

Carter scoffed. "You don't remember?" He turned his head to the side, revealing a sizable scrape, bordered on all sides by a swollen green bruise.

Mae cocked her head, confused.

Carter beckoned her to follow, leading her to the stairs. She remembered what Ollie had said about rot and hesitated as he began to climb.

"Come on," he urged.

With uneasy steps, she followed. The stairs spiraled higher, only nailed plywood boards at the top, and Carter slowed to a stop. He pointed at the wooden railing, a portion broken off at the landing, splintering into a menacing stake and leaving a gaping hole. Mae eyed the distance between the broken banister and the second floor below, a hefty fall though not a deadly one.

"You seriously don't remember?" His eyes narrowed.

Mae's gut urged her to descend the stairs. Her vision wobbled, and the house around her began to spin in slow circles. She grabbed the broken railing to steady herself.

"I found you up here last night," Carter said, placing his hand on the small of her back.

Mae searched her memory with each step down.

I read. I blew out the candle. Then nothing.

"What?"

"You were grabbing at the boards, yelling about your father."

No.

"I tried to get you down. The third floor is compromised, remember? I tried to reason with you but ..." He shook his head and his mouth twisted into a frown.

"Did you fall?"

Carter eyed her. "You pushed me, Mae. You're not well."

Mae waited for the shameful recollection to strike, but found nothing in her memory, and no twinge in her body told her this was the truth. There was only the empty black of sleep. Still, she allowed Carter to lead her back to her room and sit her on the bed.

"I think we need to take some measures. For your safety." Carter ran his fingers over his swollen face. "And mine."

"Measures?"

"I can go into town today and pick up a new lock."

Thin lines appeared in Mae's forehead as she tried to understand.

"For your room. I know it seems extreme, but I think it'd be best."

He means to lock me in. From the outside.

Mae shook her head and extended her arms in a full stop motion. "Carter, no, that's—"

"Look at my face, Mae!" His eyes were wild and words were sharp. "And it could've been much worse. We're lucky I didn't break an arm or a leg."

Mae studied the painful looking bruise. Already it seemed to grow.

"If I'd landed just a little bit differently ..."

Mae remembered her father's body lying at the foot of the stairs, his head caved in around the axe blade. How the blood pooled and threatened her from the stairs. She was frozen again.

"Just think about it. For my sake." He rose and shut the door behind him. The message was clear.

Stay in there.

Mae slid open the nightstand drawer. Inside she found her leather-bound journal. Its blank pages, striped with gold lines, welcomed the first entry.

September 17

Last night I read The Flames in our Hearts. I marked page 164, so that's where I stopped. I blew out the candle, the red one that smells like candied apples. It was Kremer's Spiegel im Spiegel *then Wieniawski's* Romance. *I went to sleep. Carter slept in the other room. He told me I pushed him off the stairs by the third-floor landing. I don't remember doing that. I don't think I did.*

She marked her page with the attached brown ribbon and slipped it beneath her pillow. The satin pillowcase was smooth against her hand as she pulled it back into view. She inspected her hands.

Fingernails are clean. No splinters.

She rose from bed and checked her nightgown. The thin fabric pilled from careless washing but was otherwise unmarred. Mae flexed her ankles so she could inspect the soles of her feet. She leaned in close and ran her finger gently across the exposed skin.

Nothing. How could I not have a mark on me?

Chapter Twelve

Vague memories of the Fall Festival were a precious comfort. Mae could recall being perched on her father's shoulders, watching the sea of orange and yellow pumpkins carried by dads and grown sons. Baked brown sugar had permeated the air as Landrum's housewives offered up slices of pie and caramel apples on sticks to passersby.

The year her father won the carving contest, Mae tunneled into a pile of hay with a neighbor kid.

Was Katie her name? Sarah?

Mae's memory felt clouded. But she latched onto the hope of joy that morning, used it as a shield against Eva's glares over breakfast. Mae didn't mention her plans to Carter, unsure how he might react. Still, the hope that they might have a normal day out together led her to dress in denim overalls, to fasten her hair into low, braided pigtails. She painted orange circles on her cheeks, a dotted, exaggerated smile, and strung a few pieces of hay she'd collected from the barn into her braids. Satisfied that she had captured the perfect balance of cuteness and scarecrow, she descended the stairs, pausing near the landing where Eva swept.

"You're all dressed up," Carter said from the sofa.

Eva raised a single brow at the sight of her and went back to sweeping.

"Fall Festival is today," Mae said with false confidence. "The one I told you about. We could pick out some pumpkins together."

Carter barely suppressed his reluctance. "You really think you're up for that, Mae?" He tilted his head, exposing the green bruise and scabbed scratches on his cheek.

Mae winced but steadied herself with a deep breath. "Yep. I've been looking forward to it."

Did Eva scoff?

Carter glanced down at his T-Shirt and pajama pants. "I'm not even dressed, Mae. And I don't think it's a good idea." He glanced back down at his phone, intending to dismiss her, but Mae continued moving toward the door.

"Okay," she said, grabbing the handle. "I'll walk over myself." Crisp breeze rushed inside as she swung the door ajar.

"Wait." Carter popped up from the couch, encircling Mae in his arms. His eyes were bottomless pools of love. "You look great." His warm smile returned. "I didn't realize how badly you wanted to go." He planted a peck on her lips and tweaked a piece of hay from her hair between his fingers. "I'll get changed. Give me five minutes."

Mae watched Carter jog upstairs and caught a glimpse of Eva leering from the sitting room.

"Hey Eva," Mae called, puffing out her chest.

Eva cocked her head to the side.

"I noticed there's still quite a bit of dust on the chandelier. The ladder is in the barn, I think. You aren't afraid of heights, are you?"

Eva's lips tightened around her teeth. "Not at all, Mrs. Duvall."

"Wonderful." Mae's smile widened. "Then you won't mind taking care of that while we're out."

Eva's lovely face turned a pleasing shade of red.

"And please be careful. The crystal is fragile, it's antique after all."

Carter returned wearing a pressed pair of jeans and a long-sleeve crew neck, the cut of which accentuated his broad shoulders. Mae extended her hand for him to grasp. As they made their way toward the door, Mae glanced over her shoulder to deliver one last parting smile to Eva.

A hand-painted wooden sign greeted them as they left the truck and walked through a cobblestone alley onto Main St: *Welcome to Landrum's Fall Festival.*

The town was alive with the laughter of children, solicitation of street vendors, and the auctioneer rattling off dollar amounts for a particularly fat hog. On the corner, a group of kids waited in a circle to have their faces painted, and stacks of pumpkins lined the street, marked five dollars each. Mae felt her phone vibrate in her pocket and reached for it but was distracted by the maple scent of fall pies.

"What's your favorite?" Mae asked, beaming. She hoped the day could be like it was when they first met, before the past had crept between them.

"Pie?" Carter dodged a bunch of balloons bouncing in a passing child's grip.

Mae pulled him to a table filled with a dozen tempting pies. "They've got cherry, apple, pumpkin of course, and pecan." She looked up at him. "So?"

Before he could answer, a familiar voice chimed in from behind.

"Mae?"

Mae turned to see Ollie's freckled cheeks. "Ollie! Perfect. We were just deciding on pies. What do you think?"

Carter stepped back to allow Ollie into the discussion, but his body tensed, and his smile faded.

"Oh, pecan pie, for sure." Ollie's eyes bounced over Carter. They leaned into Mae and whispered, "Did you get my message?"

Carter reached across Ollie, blocking them with his body, and grabbed a pecan pie. "Excellent, thanks." He blocked Mae's view and grasped for his wallet to pay. "Come on Mae-by, let's go pick out a pumpkin."

Carter passed off the pie to Mae and ushered her through the crowd, leaving Ollie in a sea of faces drowned out by a cacophony of sound. As Carter pulled Mae to the opposite end of the street, Mae felt her pocket buzzing once again. She ignored it for the moment in favor of Carter's attention, a rare commodity in recent weeks. Turned hay bales became a square of benches, where families sat amongst pumpkins and gourds of all sizes. Traditional orange made up the better part of the haul, but speckled throughout were spotted, twisty gourds ranging from light yellow to pale green. Carter lifted a massive pumpkin with one arm. It nearly equaled his torso in size. He spun it around, inspecting it for defects and pressed his finger into a soft spot in back. Discarding it, he repeated the process with another and another.

"Only the best for the Duvall home." He winked.

Mae sat on a hay bale, doing her best to ignore the spiny strands sticking into her butt through the denim overalls.

She picked out smaller ones in a variety of colors: white, marigold yellow, a rusty shade, and a gourd in Frankenstein green. When she glanced up from her gathering, she noticed a group of young girls, high school age, had gathered around Carter. They forced laughter and flashy smiles, fiddled with their hair. A midriff-baring brunette spun her bellybutton piercing while she spoke.

Mae sighed and drew out her phone, greeted by message after message.

Auntie Bel: Where'd you leave the orgone? Can't find it. Call me ASAP.

Ollie: Call me when you get this. It's important.

Auntie Bel: Ain't heard from ya.

Ollie: You okay?

Ollie: ??

Auntie Bel: Still kickin?

Ollie: Come talk to me! I'm by the apple bobbing.

Carter now inspected the pierced brunette, suggesting adjustments for the perfect selfie. Mae abandoned her circle of colored pumpkins, leaving Carter with his admirers in search of apple bobbing. She passed a scarecrow holding signs.

Spooky Corn Maze, arrow right

Face Painting, arrow right

Pumpkin Carving Contest, arrow left

Apple Bobbing, arrow left

Mae jutted to the left, weaving into the thick crowd. She first spotted the barrel, then Ollie's faded citrus hair. Ollie gestured for her to come, winding between the local art gallery and the fudge shop. The small alley was paved with bricks like the street and strung lights hung overhead.

Potted plants sprouted in every corner, blooming pansies in shades of purple, pink, and yellow.

Mae sat beside Ollie at the patio table beneath a navy umbrella. The buildings shielded them from the raucous in the street, a private haven amongst the festivities. Nerves tightened in Mae's chest at Ollie's somber look, a dramatic departure from their usual effervescence.

"I have to tell you something."

Ollie picked at a worn spot on their jeans, separated the fibers and pulled out a thread. "I know you don't want to believe this but …" Ollie's teeth tightened around their lips.

"Out with it already!" The sharpness of the words surprised even Mae, whose tolerance for stress was thinner than she'd hoped.

"I saw them kissing. Carter and Eva, on your porch. Clear as day, Mae." Ollie's eyes filled with grief as Mae tried to digest the words. "I'm so sorry."

The news was like trying to swallow a brick. Mae pushed it away at first, but the idea sunk in, the image of Eva's cleavage pressed against Carter's defined chest, him holding Eva the way he used to hold her. It made sense. Eva's ire. Carter's distance. A wave of nausea hit. No doubt it was true. Mae's hand trembled as she placed it on the concrete table to steady herself.

"I've been trying to reach you but—"

"No service," Mae's voice cracked. "I—" Tears streamed down Mae's face, boring channels into the orange circles painted on her cheeks. Despair turned to embarrassment, and Mae rose from the table, feeling a sudden urge to escape.

"'Scuse me."

Ollie half stood to pursue her, but Mae shot them a wild look and they sat back down. Fleeing into the stream of festivities, Mae's humiliation turned to rage. She wiped the wetness from her face, smearing orange paint beneath her eyes in horizontal lines, from scarecrow to war paint. Carter was no longer under the pumpkin tent; the high school girls had shifted their attention to a group of boys their own age. Mae scanned the crowd for his maroon crewneck. A young boy atop his father's shoulders obscured her view, but as he passed to the right, she spotted Carter at the apple cider stand, sipping a frothy cup with smug enjoyment. Mae rocketed through the crowd, the pecan pie turned roughly on its side in one fist, bouncing off the legs of people she passed.

Carter's eyes met hers.

"You fucking asshole!"

He froze, as did all the families in a ten-foot radius.

Mae snapped open the plastic pie container and launched it at him. It smacked his chest, tearing apart and coating him in sweet brown filling.

"Mae, what's wrong?" Like he didn't know. He extended his palms as if to hold her, but she smacked them away.

"What's wrong?" Mae gritted her teeth. "THEY SAW YOU!" The burning shame of the past weeks and rage at the image of Eva in his arms erupted from Mae in a guttural scream. Parents shooed their children from the scene. A man beside Carter picked a chunk of pie from his shoulder, a man Mae recognized, Doctor Levine.

"Mae-by, let's get you out of here," Carter said, calm and innocent as a lamb.

Doctor Levine lent a sympathetic hand, helping Carter to block Mae from the horrified stares of onlookers. Together Carter and Doctor Levine circled Mae and she realized the scene she had caused. More hot shame poured over her, and she allowed the men to guide her away from the gathering crowd. The festivities thinned and Carter reached to place his hand on the small of Mae's back as they walked. She twisted her body away, and caught sight of Joanne, draped in a richly colored boho scarf and lugging a stack of books to her psychic shop.

"Joanne!"

She turned her hunched frame in Mae's direction, tilting her chin upward to listen. Doctor Levine continued his hurried pace toward the parking lot, Mae's arm firmly in his grasp.

"What did he say?" Mae yelled as the gap between them widened.

Joanne hugged her books tightly as Carter grasped Mae's other arm.

"What was my dad trying to tell me?" she demanded, her voice high and cracking.

There were a hundred yards between them now, and Joanne's whispery tones would've never cleared the distance, but Doctor Levine and Carter continued to pull Mae toward the muted green truck. The doctor helped Mae inside and gave Carter a sympathetic look as he shut the door behind her. Mae watched them exchange words in hushed tones.

"Mae-by," Carter started as he crawled into the driver's seat, but Mae whipped her head away and stared defiantly out the window. He took the hint, continuing the drive home in silence. As the yellowing trees rolled by, Mae felt a wave of regret for the all the kids who'd witnessed her outburst. She pushed away a collection of images of Eva and Carter, their bodies wrapped around one another in contorted poses, and the stabbing feeling that accompanied them. Gravel crunched under the tires as they rolled up to the old Victorian, and Mae watched her phone blink from two bars to *No Service*.

CHAPTER THIRTEEN

Mae took the stairs two at a time, slammed the bedroom door and locked it behind her, though Carter hadn't tried to pursue her. The throbbing ache in her gut threatened to overwhelm her, so she whipped open her nightstand drawer and snatched a joint from her stash.

Inhaling the smoke burned away the sharp edges of the pain inside and left a nagging throb. The dull soreness of Carter's betrayal radiated through her nervous system, pounding like an infected tooth. She stared at the red and gold patterned wallpaper. The pressure of her beating heart made her vision skip in rhythm, her eyes twitching in time with each thud. The floral shapes surrounding her seemed to widen and shrink, bend and warp. She heard the pumping of her blood, and then a ringing in her ears. Mae clutched the bedpost, her head swimming as she tried to stand. She saw a flash of the ceiling and black spots trailed across her vision.

Mae awoke. She had no memory of lying down to sleep, and yet here she was, tucked beneath the covers. Her door was cracked open, and she heard Carter rustling around his office.

I thought I'd ...

Night had fallen. Mae had twisted memories of unsettling dreams, and she rubbed the sleep from her eyes trying to orient herself to the present. The confusion of losing time evoked a primal urge for Carter's company, safety in numbers, despite his unforgivable transgression. She sat upright and pulled the covers over her goosebumped shoulders, the wooden bed frame creaking beneath her.

"You up?" Carter asked from down the hall. His steps drew closer, and she felt both relieved and repulsed as his chiseled face emerged through the crack in the door. He studied her. "I thought it was best to let you sleep."

Mae pulled the comforter tighter around her shoulders, and Carter sat at the foot of their bed. Despite herself, she was grateful to see him in their room. Since Carter had taken up residence in his study, it felt like hers alone.

"Doctor Levine said you had an episode."

The details of the incident at the Fall Festival came creeping back. Had she really screamed at him in public? Thrown a pie? Mae's throat clenched.

What must they think of me?

Then the images returned. Carter and Eva's perfect, naked bodies, tangled up with one another. Her chest threatened to rip in two. The surface of rage parted and the ocean of grief beneath flowed through the cracks in Mae's defenses. Her lip quivered. "How could you do this to me?"

"I'd been meaning to talk to you about this." He looked at the ground as if it might spell out the words for him to say.

Mae braced for the admission of guilt. The description of how it started. The answer to the unavoidable question: Does he love her?

Carter cleared his throat. "I should've brought it up sooner, but you've been—" His piqued brow told Mae that he thought better of ending the phrase and continued without it. "I've seen the way Ollie looks at you."

The tension released. He wasn't confessing. Mae's brows knitted together in confusion.

"I thought it was harmless, your little flirtation, but …"

Mae blinked hard. *Our flirtation?*

"Don't worry. I'm not angry." He said it simply and gave a reassuring smile, resting his hand on Mae's leg over the blanket, as if to show all was forgiven.

Mae spoke slowly, sorting out her own thoughts one word at a time. "So, you think Ollie made this up? To drive a wedge between us?"

Carter gestured for Mae to go on.

"Because they have feelings for me?"

"And?"

"And they think I have feelings for them?"

Carter's shoulders relaxed. "You can't put all the blame on Ollie. You've been giving signals, after all." His hand caressed Mae's shoulder. "But I'm not upset." His almond eyes locked onto hers. "You've been struggling, and I've been so busy with work."

Mae thought back to her conversations with Ollie.

Have I flirted?

A pang of guilt tickled her abdomen, the memory of watching Ollie work on the barn's roof, noticing their defined figure. Had her eyes lingered too long over Ollie's freckles? Had Ollie seen?

"Ollie's known for starting trouble." Carter stood up, as if making his closing arguments. "I've heard around town they went around accusing the old groundskeeper of your dad's murder. That psychic too, what's her name? Justine?"

"Joanne," Mae corrected.

"Ollie's a bit of a joke down at the police precinct. She—"

"It's they." Mae's tone sounded sharper than she intended. Carter eyed her as if this gesture of defense was a small proof of Mae's prior indiscretions, the *signals* that made Ollie believe Mae shared their feelings.

"*They* practically begged for a job down there. One of those armchair detective types who thinks they'll put on a uniform and solve every cold case on the books. Wouldn't be surprised if all this"—Carter made a dismissive gesture, —"drama was them trying to get close to you because of, you know. What happened."

It was a lot to consider.

Ollie had been pretty obvious about their interest in her father's case. And it wasn't the first time they'd tried to drive a wedge between her and Carter. *Could Carter be right?*

He passed the window, no doubt thinking of Ollie on that barn roof and how Mae could see. He settled beside Mae on her side of the bed. His thumb brushed cheek, sending warmth from the spot he touched deep into her chest. "Doctor Levine called," he said, gazing into her eyes like he had when he first asked her to run away with him. "He thinks you're getting worse. He recommended a," in finger quotes, "higher level of care."

Mae's chest tightened. "What's that supposed to mean?"

Carter shook his head.

"Does he mean, like, an institution?" Mae's eyes narrowed as she pumped Carter for more information. *He couldn't possibly think that I ...*

"Don't worry Mae-by. I won't let that happen to you." He wrapped his arms around her tight, and it felt like safety. And the feeling of safety, that felt like shame. "I love you, Mae."

On his way out of the room he called back, almost an afterthought, "You missed dinner. I'll have Eva heat something up for you."

The realization that Eva was downstairs, that she had been the whole time, was like a kick in the gut. But Mae couldn't argue. She didn't have the energy. Instead, she retrieved her journal from the nightstand drawer. Marked the day in the upper lefthand corner. And detailed the Fall Festival, to the best of her recollection, quoting Ollie's words and Carter's where her memory would allow.

September 20th
I saw them kissing.
> *You had an episode.*
Clear as day, Mae.
> *Your little flirtation.*
I've been trying to—
> *Institution.*
> *I won't let that happen to you. I love you.*
I threw a pie. He held a pumpkin.

Brian parked just outside of town, near the rest stop where truckers pulled off to spend the night and working girls tried to solicit them before they dozed off. Three tractor-trailers aligned in spots next to one another across from the convenience shop, aptly named *Food Store*. The area was known for petty crimes, and Brian had made an arrest here just a week prior when the gas attendant called about an overweight naked man running circles around the pump, chased by a hollering working girl brandishing a high-heel. It was a long walk for Ollie, who was breathless by the time they slid into the passenger seat.

"Wh—" they caught their breath, "Why'd you make me haul ass all the way out here?"

Brian raised up his hand, pointed subtly at a bottle-blonde in a leotard resting her back on the shop. "Wanted to make her jealous."

Ollie threw a soft punch in Brian's shoulder. "You're a real shit, Jenkins."

He pulled a folder from between his seat and door and scanned the top page. "Well, it ain't her car."

Ollie straightened up, tried to peer over the center console, but couldn't make out the writing on the page. "Is it stolen?"

Brian snapped the folder shut. "Nope. Not reported stolen anyway."

"Well, who's it belong to?" Ollie tried to lift the folder from Brian's hand, but he snapped it away.

"Can't give this to you, Ollie. In fact, I can't do anymore diggin' around for you either. Captain Williams saw I accessed the system runnin' that plate for you, he reamed my ass over the coals."

Ollie slumped down in their seat. "That why we're out here?"

Brian nodded.

"Well shit …" Ollie's eyes darted back to the bottle-blonde, who turned in their direction. Ollie ducked behind the door, sending Brian into a fit of laughter.

"Chill!"

Ollie straightened a bit but still held their head at an awkward angle to avoid being seen through the window. "Don't want you getting canned over this."

"Look, I really doubt blondie over there is keeping tabs on us."

"Guess you're right."

"And I'm sure everything's fine over on Alquist. If anything, I think Mae's a little," he whistled and drew circles around his temple with his finger.

Ollie scowled.

"Lots of guys cheat. It ain't a crime." Brian chuckled, "I'm sure you heard Mae screaming her lungs out at him yesterday at the Fall Festival. I don't know if I blame him for lookin' elsewhere, to be frank."

"Don't fuckin' do that." Ollie's voice was a low grumble. "She was upset. Imagine how you'd feel if it was Steph."

Brian shrugged. "If you say so."

Ollie opened the Notes application on their phone. "Can you at least tell me who the car's registered to?"

"Nobody from 'round here."

Ollie's eyes widened. "A name, Jenkins. Please."

Brian let out a deep-chested sigh. "Alright, alright." He cracked the folder back open. "Babineaux."

"What?" Ollie's ears perked.

"Brooks Babineaux. You know him?"

Ollie's hands thrust into their pockets, turning them out, but all were empty. "Shit, I left it back home."

"What?" Brian pressed.

"Brooks Babineaux. That's the same name that was on this letter I found in their kitchen, all crumpled up. I showed it to Williams. Something about an appraisal, written right before the murder. I fuckin' knew it was connected. Goddamnit!" Ollie beat their closed fist on the dashboard. "I mean, this changes things, right? There's obviously something going on here, and it's connected to what happened back then."

Brian's finger and thumb smoothed his brows, and he rested his hand in his palm. "Ollie, I can't. Captain Williams was straight up with me. If he catches me digging around on this, you really will be applying for my spot at the precinct."

Ollie huffed. "Does he know?"

Brian's head wobbled. "Know what?"

"What you found?"

He shrugged. "I dunno, I don't think so. He didn't mention it." Brian caught Ollie's eye-line. "Ollie, look at me. This is serious. You can't bring this to Williams. If he knows I shared this with you … I'm on thin ice with him right now."

"Fuuuuuuuuuuuck," Ollie groaned.

Across the lot, the blonde left her spot against the brick wall. She trotted up to the window of a semi, hopped up onto the step and leaned inside. A raccoon scuttled out from behind a tire, startling her, and she had to cling to the grab handle to keep from falling.

Brian started his engine.

Ollie popped open the door.

"I'll give you a ride back into town," Brian offered.

Snapping the door shut, Ollie said, "Fuckin' least you can do," with a smirk. "You can drop me by … Dalroy Circle."

"Two streets off Alquist Ave, very smooth." He rolled his eyes.

CHAPTER FOURTEEN

The west side of the Alquist Ave property backed up against a heavily wooded area, accessible from Dalroy Circle if you cut through the Huddleston's land. It was only 4:00 p.m., but the thick canopy of tree cover blocked most of the remaining daylight, creating a contained, artificial dusk. It'd been years since the last controlled burn, and the brush was two feet high in places. Ollie slogged through the detritus, rogue branches stealing strips of skin where they could.

This would be easier if he'd return my calls about the greenhouse job. Wouldn't have to sneak up from behind like some pervert.

Ollie knew Mae's bedroom window looked out onto the yard. They'd caught glimpses of her while they worked on the barn roof, unsure of who was catching who staring.

Just gotta pray he's not in there with her.

A quick internet search on Brooks Babineaux hadn't revealed any results, but the connection was worth sharing. If they could just get to Mae, she would know that she wasn't crazy to think something was up with Eva. And since Mae's phone always went to voicemail, and the texts to her always turned green, Ollie couldn't think of any other way. So, through the woods they trudged, leaves crunching and branches snapping under their steps. Ollie tensed as the silken hold of a spider's web wrapped around their face. Common enough for a maintenance worker.

Just back away.

But the sight of spindly legs on their cheek made them flail, taking haphazard steps sideways and backwards, turning and swatting the strands away. The wild movement tumbled them out of the dark, and Ollie felt the parting rays of the sun break through the tree line. They froze. Standing in the wide-open space between the woods and the barn, in a clear line of sight from Mae's bedroom window, Ollie heard their heart pound. They shot a look upward.

A shadow lurked behind the framed glass. It could've been Mae. Logically, it could've been. But instinct drove Ollie into the barn.

Walls on all sides provided an illusion of safety. Ollie's pulse slowed, the familiar scent of timothy hay was a comfort, but they knew Carter might be on the way. He'd be angry after what happened at the festival, and something behind his eyes unsettled Ollie from the day they met. Something, or an absence of something. The figure beyond the window had moved quickly, an unidentified shape. Ollie looked for a place to hide. There was a cramped room within the barn, an old feed room where roaches and silverfish feasted on decades old scraps. Ollie had never braved it. They weren't a maid, after all, but now seemed like an appropriate time to make its acquaintance. The plywood door caved as Ollie pulled the rusted knob.

Steps outside pushed Ollie to yank, sending a wedged rock careening across the barn as the door flew open. Ollie dipped inside. Plastic garbage bins wore dusty coats. A gaslamp hung from the wall, but Ollie knew that light flooding out from beneath the door would be a beacon to their location, so they pulled it shut, swallowed by the windowless dark.

The barn door opened with a creak. The hay floor rustled. Ollie backed away from the source of the sound, feeling more spiderwebs wrap around their head. They willed themself to be a statue.

There is no spider. Just stay still.

Ollie hoped to hear Mae's voice call their name, but the only sound was the rustling of the hay underfoot. Reaching arms found a trunk behind them, and Ollie lowered themself to a sitting position, silken webs stretching across and tickling their skin.

You're a statue. A gargoyle. Made of stone.

Their hands flitted around behind them, reaching for rescue, for a weapon, for anything, and their fingers wrapped around a small cube. Hard plastic. Not heavy enough to use as a weapon, if it came to it. The box was smooth on three sides, but from the fourth shot long, smooth antennae, like stiff tendrils. Ollie rubbed at the dust on the side and squinted.

Syntova 476.

The door whipped open, a sudden rush of light obscuring Ollie's vision. Hands gripped their shirt collar, yanking them from their sitting position and tossing them onto the hay-strewn floor. Ollie's eyes adjusted and traced the black running shoes up to sweatpants-clad legs, over the black T-Shirt, and settled on Carter's gritted teeth.

"You know—" His face was unlike it had been before. "South Carolina is a stand your ground state." He hocked a loogie and spit it inches from Ollie's hand.

Ollie sat up, but their gut told them not to stand.

Carter took slow steps in a semi-circle, eyes wandering

from Ollie just long enough to let them know he was not afraid. "I think your work in here is done. Isn't that right?"

Ollie thought of the greenhouse job but knew better than to mention it. They nodded instead.

"So, I take that to mean that if I find you on my property again, the only rational explanation is you're trying to steal from me, maybe somethin' worse."

Carter's irises seemed to expand, shrouding his eyes in black. Creeping dread raised the hairs on Ollie's neck.

"It would be well within my rights as a citizen to take lethal action against you." He smiled. "Ain't that right?"

Ollie nodded, diverting their eyes, and spotted the axe, poised in its tree stump.

Carter crouched, resting his elbows on his knees. "You think I'm blind, you little freak? Like I can't see the way you look at my wife?" *Wife* came out as a hiss. His hot breath condensed on Ollie's cheek.

Their organs squished together, hiding from Carter within their body.

"I'm gonna count to ten." He stood upright, assuming the full breadth of his height and weight. "I suggest you run."

Ollie hesitated. It was a threat out of a slasher movie, too dramatic to be real. They half expected Carter to burst out laughing, apologize for a prank gone too far.

"One."

But he didn't laugh.

"Two."

Ollie staggered to their feet.

"Three."

His expression was stoic, his pupils a void.

"Four."

Ollie's steps threw hay strands behind them as their shoes struggled to find purchase.

"Five."

Their hand found the rear door handle, threw it open.

"Six."

His voice barely cleared the distance between them, but as they passed the greenhouse they heard—

"Seven."

Ollie broke for the woods. The clawed branches were a meager threat in comparison.

"Eight."

He'd raised his voice. It echoed over the grounds, bounced off the greenhouse glass to catch Ollie's ears.

"Nine."

They ran blindly, swatting at low limbs which tore bits from their palms. Ollie considered looking back, convinced Carter had freed the axe from its stump, was chasing them, holding it aloft like a crazed animal. But they didn't dare break their pace to check.

Their feet disappeared into brush as they launched themselves forward, and an unlucky step twisted Ollie's ankle, sending searing pain up their calf. They hobbled a few more feet, but the spiraling sting brought Ollie to their knees. They spun around, fearing this misstep would provide the extra seconds Carter needed to close the gap between them, but Ollie found themself alone but for the company of looming trees. They strained their ears against a whistling wind. *No ten.* The counting had stopped. Their ankle puffed up a bit, but not enough to indicate a break. They massaged it, leaving small streaks of blood from the lacerations in their hands.

I need help.

They pulled the phone from their cargo shorts, but their heart sank when they read *No service.* Using a fallen bough as leverage, they staggered to their feet. A little pressure on the ankle punished Ollie with throbbing discomfort, but they found they could take hopping half-steps. In this slow and tedious manner, they reached the break in the trees before collapsing on Dalroy Circle, huffing to catch their breath.

Vivid images of Carter and Eva together had wriggled into Mae's skull like an earwig. They buzzed deep between her ears, intermittently throughout the day. She watched Eva with a close eye. Waited for the slightest reveal, the most minuscule evidence of indiscretion, but she found none. In fact, Carter had taken to ignoring Eva. And Eva, who must've despised very idea of a Mrs. Duvall, resigned herself to cooking and cleaning the old Victorian five days per week without much more than the occasional word. A week passed. Carter returned to their shared bed and paused his evening business meetings. Mae, at first, made the cynical judgment that he stayed home to babysit her, his invalid wife. But the warmth that won her heart in the beginning returned. A bouquet of flowers. An antique bracelet. Offers of back rubs. He stayed up late into the night, even when he had to work early, asking intimate, probing questions.

What do you admire about me?

What was your first memory?

When are you most at peace?

The Victorian felt warmer too. The lights remained steady, even after dark, and the whispers from the neighboring room had ceased. Even her father's playing was silenced, though the melodies had dug so deeply in her head, it was as if they played for Mae regardless.

Carter fumbled around in the kitchen below. She had time before the water boiled and the tea steeped, so she pulled out her journal.

September 24

The nights are different now. I don't know if it's knowing Carter is here with me, but I don't feel afraid anymore. In fact, I feel so silly for my paranoia before. If my father's ghost ever was in the house (which I doubt), he must be at ease knowing that whatever woman who threatened me has been thwarted. I thought it must have been Eva. I was sure her revealing clothing and obvious contempt for me were because she was jealous. Of course, I've noticed how Carter captures attention in a room. I'd be blind not to. But maybe I judged her? Did I look at her clothes and assume she was a home wrecker? Shame on me. Maybe I'm a bad feminist.

I haven't seen Ollie since the Fall Festival. It's probably better that way. Looking back, I guess I fell for their act. Told them too much about my dad early on. Always blinded by an attractive face. But who would've thought they would make up such a crazy story? They never struck me as someone who would do something so high school. What kind of friend would do that? Not to mention they promised to look into Eva, and I haven't heard a word. They completely ghosted us on the greenhouse project. Carter was furious. He'd already paid a deposit on it, but I convinced him not to turn it into a scene. If they want to take our money as some kind of consolation prize for not being able to steal me away from him, or solve a case or whatever, then so be it.

Anyway, I'm glad things are back to normal. A new normal that is. One with Carter and me, husband and wife, in a home of our own. I think I'll start looking into school again. It would be good to get out of the house. I'm a bit cut off from the world here, but at least I have Carter. I found the perfect photo for the silver locket he got me. It's an old print of dad, black and white, so it matches the style.

Carter and I had a rocky start, but it's smoothing out now. And THANK GOD. I can't imagine what I would've done if Ollie's lie had been true. Alone in this house with no money, no car, no friends. Ugh! Not to mention, I was beginning to think my mind was going the way of my mother's.

Carter returned bearing two cups of steaming tea and a warm smile. This was their new nightly ritual. Heat passed through the ceramic cup, a pleasant sensation on Mae's palm. Carter's boxer briefs hugged his body, and Mae couldn't help but stare as he nestled under the sheets. She took a long, indulgent sip. Mint tingled on her tongue, and she inhaled the sweet aroma.

"We're in a good place, right Mae-by?" His arm reached around the small of her back and he pulled her closer to him. His body was tight. It called to her.

"A great place." She wanted him to put his tea down, to lift her nightdress over her head.

"The past week has been so great, spending all this extra time together." The way he tightened his lips alerted Mae that he was couching something. "But I've been putting off meetings, and I really need to get back to work if we want to keep the bills paid."

Mae knew this moment would come. She could only steal her husband away from the world for so long.

"I'm gonna have to start up again. Will you be—"

"I'll be fine." Mae felt a little embarrassed by his concern. If she couldn't bring in any income of her own, the least she could do was free up her husband to work. "Really, don't worry about me. I think all the changes, and coming back here, it just ..." She looked around and sighed. "Had me rattled, that's all." She squeezed his thigh. "I feel much better now. Don't feel like you have to cater to me."

Carter gently lifted Mae's teacup from her grasp and placed it on his nightstand with his own. "I'd like to cater to you, though." A smirk curled his lips. "In another way."

CHAPTER FIFTEEN

Only a yellowish bruise remained on Ollie's ankle, a tender reminder of their encounter with Carter in the barn. They'd sequestered themself to their apartment, afraid they might run into him in town, but only a packet of instant noodles remained in their pantry, and no tuna left for Hobbes, as they'd come to know the orange tabby cat.

"How would you feel about some actual cat food?" they asked.

Hobbes ignored the question, spotting a lizard outside the window, and chattering at it through the glass. Staying inside for a week had a number of consequences. Dirty laundry was piled high in stacks around the small studio. Tissues stood in as a substitute for toilet paper. And Ollie's stomach growled at them incessantly like a territorial dog. Ollie clicked their phone to life. It still read, *No Service*. The day after the barn incident, Ollie tried to call the phone company about the issue, but, *No service*. There was a small cellular store ten minutes outside of town, but that would require a ride and leaving the safety of home, concessions Ollie had not been prepared to make until today. Sorting through laundry mountain, Ollie located a less dirty top (determined by a rigorous sniffing process) and an only marginally stained pair of slacks.

Wallet, wallet …

Ollie scattered unpaired socks and felt beneath the pile for the rectangular lump which held their cash and cards. What their fingers located, however, was a decidedly unfamiliar rectangular lump. Harder than the faux leather, it had smooth edges and long, tentacle-like outcroppings. They pulled the mysterious object free from the stack of clothes.

Syntova 476

Oh shit.

In the scuffle and ensuing escape, Ollie must've stashed the plastic black box in their oversized pockets without realizing it. Their eyes narrowed as they scrutinized it. The finger-like pieces moved a bit, but not in every direction, just splayed out like a fan. On the back side rested a tiny screw. Ollie tapped their fingers in cascading, rapid succession.

Tiny screwdriver … tiny screwdriver.

They rummaged through a kitchen drawer and located a small screwdriver with a blue handle.

This might do it.

Ollie twisted the mini Phillips head into the slot and the screw happily unfurled.

No rust, must not've been in that barn for long.

With a nearly inaudible ding, the screw bounced off the tile floor, and Ollie popped open the compartment, hoping to uncover its secret purpose.

Standard battery case.

Ollie sighed.

When I get my phone working, I'll search the name.

They dropped the device onto the couch, and the force of the fall popped a battery out of its holder.

"Ugh!" Ollie dropped to their knees and reached beneath the couch where the battery had rolled. They felt around, trying not to imagine what sort of filth had escaped the vacuum down there. They strained against the couch's edge, but the battery lay just out of reach.

"A little help here?" Ollie asked Hobbes. But Hobbes didn't help.

"Ah, fuck it." Ollie grabbed their phone, prepared to use the flashlight to locate their wallet when they noticed, *three bars?* A serenade of dings erupted as texts and voicemails popped up in quick succession. *No shit.*

Ollie pulled open an internet tab and ran a search on *Syntova 476.* The first result confirmed their suspicions.

"The Syntova 476 is the most powerful jammer on the market! Guaranteed to block cell phone signals, GPS, and Wi-Fi with an unparalleled range of 400 meters."

Ollie pictured Mae checking and rechecking her phone, asking Carter why he thought they'd become so cut off from the world. *That sick fuck.*

Ollie scrolled through their phone to Captain Williams's number. Their thumb hovered over the screen. *What would I tell him?* They could hear his response from the other end. *It's strange, Ollie, but not illegal to block signals on your own property. For all we know, Mae knows about this thing and they just don't want people making calls when they come over. Evidence, Ollie. We need evidence.*

They clicked the phone, closing the app. Brian wouldn't risk his job for a hunch, and Ollie knew better than to press him.

"Come here, Hobbes. Let's talk this through."

Hobbes trotted over and rubbed his head against the back of Ollie's hand.

"What we need is a theory. Right now," Hobbes gently bit the meat of Ollie's palm. "Ow. Right now, we have a bunch of strange things, but can't see how they fit together."

Another bite.

Early October

The voices downstairs were too muffled to discern. At first, Mae assumed Carter and Eva were discussing payment, or schedule, or the deep cleaning of the library planned for the weekend. She nestled her nose between the pages of her latest romance, *The Hero's Bride*. The hero, John, had finally gotten Margret alone. His fingers teased the flesh beneath her blouse, and he was leaning close for that first, steamy kiss when Mae heard it.

"It's too much!"

Eva's voice carried up the stairs and Mae thought she heard Carter shush her. She dogeared the corner of her page and rose quietly from bed, taking careful steps to press her ear against the door. She couldn't make out words, but she detected the low register of Carter's tone. It was the same one he used when she'd found that letter, when he'd walked in on the seance, the sense memory made her stomach flip.

The sound warbled through the heavy wood. Mae sealed her other ear with a fingertip, hoping to channel the sound. Desperate whispers and the odd word, "we could … don't". She heard a thud. Flesh against plaster. Then a shuffling, feet sliding on tile.

Mae's hand trembled as she reached for the knob, adrenaline surged. And she wondered, as her fingers gripped the brass, why her body would respond this way.

The knob twisted and the hinges groaned as she pulled it open, just a foot, so she could slip through.

She took four silent steps into the hall, bare feet on the carpeted runner. The ground floor was quiet. Daylight poured through the stained-glass window crowning the stairs, painting her toes yellow and red. From the landing she spotted Carter taking brisk steps toward the study with hands in his pockets. He passed from her view without seeing her. She descended the stairs and wandered from the empty living room into the kitchen. Eva spotted her and smoothed her hair. She straightened her back from its hunched position and took in a deep breath that puffed her chest.

"Mrs. Duvall," she said, louder than necessary. "What can I do for you?" Her voice had a strained quality.

"I, uh," Mae took steps closer and heard Carter's footfalls approaching from the study. Eva's eyes were swollen, bloodshot.

"Hungry?" Carter asked, now directly behind Mae.

Mae jumped and Carter placed a heavy hand on her shoulder.

"Jumpy tonight?" He chuckled and sailed past her into the kitchen. Eva rubbed her right eye, wiped it on her apron.

"I made muffins," Eva said, turning from view and opening a cabinet door. "Orange cranberry." She pulled out a small plate.

Carter passed close behind her and she twisted her body reflexively, like she'd been poked by a phantom finger. The eerie exchange soured any appetite Mae might have had, but she accepted the offer, nonetheless. The muffin gleamed with sugar crystals, and its fat top threatened to topple it over. Mae balanced it on the small plate and took a seat on the couch. Eva's demeanor strengthened, her posture returning to its usual arch, but she avoided looking at Carter, like one might avoid looking directly at the sun. She regarded him with peripheral glances and shuffled around him with shallow breaths.

Carter joined Mae on the couch, a muffin of his own in hand, and took a generous bite out of the top. Crumbs avalanched from his mouth and toppled over the cushions. When he placed it down on the coffee table, they scattered over that too. Mae snuck glances at Eva over the countertop as she removed her apron, revealing leggings that hugged her firm curves.

"I'll be back Saturday," she said, slinging her purse strap over her arm.

"Saturday?" Carter questioned.

"For the library."

Mae heard unspoken words between them.

Eva's keys jingled in her hand as she took brisk steps to the door. Her path exposed a side view of her face and a rosy red hue on her cheek and temple. "I hope you enjoy the muffins." Her words were cold, and Mae sensed they were less for her than for her husband. The door closed with force, and Mae watched Eva's car light up and pull away through the window.

"I see the way you look at her," Carter said as her taillights disappeared from view.

Mae gave him a puzzled look.

"You don't like her. That much is obvious." Carter scowled.

"What were you arguing about?" Mae asked, placing her muffin onto the coffee table and turning to square her shoulders with her husband's.

"We weren't arguing." Carter took another careless bite of his muffin. A cranberry wedged between his front teeth, and he fiddled with his tongue to dislodge it.

"I heard from upstairs, and another sound, like—that's why I came down."

Carter let out an exasperated sigh. "I was trying to spare your feelings but," he tossed the muffin onto the table, the force clanging the plate against the wooden tabletop, "it's your attitude."

"What?" Mae scoffed. "I barely see Eva. And when I do, she barely speaks to me." Mae threw her hands in the air. "If anything, it's her attitude that's the problem. She's never liked me since the day she first came through our door."

"She feels uncomfortable working here, because of the tension you've created."

Mae's mouth hung open. She searched for the words.

"And she's not wrong. Maybe you believe Ollie's drivel after all." His posture was resigned, his arms folded neatly in his lap.

"I do not!" Mae felt the blood rushing to her face. She stood and looked down her nose at her husband.

"You'll have to work on being more friendly to her. She might quit, and where would we be then?" He shook his head and added under his breath, "living in filth, that's where."

Mae stomped a few steps away. "You're an asshole."

He rose and caught up with her. "Oh, calm down. You're just bent out of shape because you ran out of your stash."

Mae whipped around. For a moment, she thought she might slap him, but she was greeted with an uncanny smile that disarmed her. He pulled a baggie out of his back pocket.

"You can thank me later." He winked.

The bag burst at its plastic seams with succulent buds adorned with purple hairs and crystals like the ones that topped the muffins.

"Where did you get this?" Mae held the bag to her nose. The scent snaked inside her nostrils.

Carter grinned. "I have my ways." He wrapped an arm around Mae's reluctant shoulder. "Let's go out back, light up the fire pit. You can test out my present."

Mae's anger fizzled. "Fire pit?"

He ushered her to the backdoor. "I picked one up earlier and got it set up. Another little surprise for my Mae-by."

Mae fetched her rolling papers from her nightstand drawer and joined Carter in the wicker loveseat on the back patio. His skin was warm, a haven against the whipping wind. The sun was beginning to set, orange rays backlighting the trees, turning the leaves to black specks.

"Do you ever find the property a little spooky?" Mae asked as she molded the sticky bud into a cylinder between the sides of the thin paper.

"That's what I like about it."

Mae finished rolling the joint, twisting the ends. "Does Eva really not like me?" she asked as she lit it. The hit was strong, stronger than what Ollie had sold her. The smoke scraped her lungs.

"Ah, she's just jealous."

Carter watched her inhale like a scientist. Mae offered him a puff with an extended hand but he declined. "Makes me paranoid," he said.

The fire crackled in the metal basin, and the odd mosquito hovered above the flames. Mae blew her smoke in their direction for Carter's amusement. She sucked down half the joint and her vision began to spin. She held it away from herself and her face twisted into a frown. Carter took what remained and smothered the embers in the dirt. He laid the smoldering roach on the firepit's rim.

Mae rubbed her temples. "I feel a little dizzy."

"Yeah, the guy said it was strong."

Mae felt Carter's hand on her thigh, but even with her eyes closed, the blackness spun. From behind her closed eyelids, danced white light. It broke into patterns and exploded with vibrant colors: red, purple, and navy.

"Can you help me upstairs?" Mae reached for Carter's hand. Maybe the weed was a problem after all, but she couldn't let Carter know that. He'd demand she stop, and Mae wasn't ready to let go of her crutch.

"Of course."

He let her rest her weight on him and guided her inside and up the stairs. She cracked open her eyes when she crossed her bedroom's threshold, but the room tipped over and made her squeeze them shut again.

"That stuff is no joke," Mae said, feeling a wave of both nausea and embarrassment as Carter tucked her under the covers.

"Would some food help?"

Mae covered her eyes with her hands, but it couldn't block the light that radiated from beneath her eyelids. Usually, smoking sparked her appetite, but the mention of food filled the back of her throat with burning bile. "No, thanks."

"Do you think that stuff had anything else? Like mixed?" From Carter's tone, Mae knew he was worried, worried he'd been right about the weed being a problem, that his wife might return to her instability. "Is this normal? Should I—"

"No, I mean, yes, it's normal. Just very strong and I haven't eaten much today. And no, thank you, I don't need anything. I'm sure I'll feel better in fifteen minutes or so."

Mae watched patterns of squares morph into pyramids behind her shut eyes. Her stillness helped the nausea subside.

"I'll let you rest." Carter tucked the comforter closer around her sides. "Check on you in a few minutes."

CHAPTER SIXTEEN

Ollie's bike popped and jerked over the rocky trail, rattling their headphones around their ears. It came into view over the top of a hill, and Ollie had to stand and pump the pedals to work the bicycle up the incline. Ahead, a small house tucked into dense overgrowth appeared bit by bit. A rusted-out corvette rotted in the yard atop cement blocks, and a German Shepard pulled at its chain, snarling, spitting foam as it watched Ollie bump into the driveway. They'd heard plenty about Charles Barlow, the old groundskeeper. Rumors circled in town that he was a recluse. Kids dared one another to run up and touch the old corvette in the yard, but rarely was one brave enough to make the sprint.

As Ollie swung their leg over the side of the bike, a grasshopper landed on their calf. Startled, they hopped from one foot to the other, dropping the bike, which bounced off a nearby rock with a clang.

Dammit.

They shook their leg and righted the bike, letting it rest on its kickstand, then hesitated in the driveway.

Just rumors, they assured themself. *He's probably a nice guy.*

Cracked ceramic pots littered the porch, some host to yellowed vines. A rocking chair creaked in the wind; its red cushion stained with mold. The air was still as Ollie moved up the weedy drive, as if prepared to bare witness. But to what? They tapped the door with their fist, a tiny rap over the dog's throaty barking.

The door's orange paint flaked off in chunks. Ollie noticed the shell of an old doorbell, a stray wire escaping from the top. They raised their hand to press it when the door whipped open. Their body clenched. Charles stood inside a tattered screen, towered over them, wearing faded overalls and a plaid button down. His long, unkempt beard matched his wiry gray hair, his tongue pressed the inside of chapped lips, pulled tightly over his closed mouth.

"Can I help you?"

His heavy accent was like all the older folks' in town. The ones who watched Ollie from inside shops as they passed the windows, from safe distances as they turned their grandchildren away. Like the Preachers, who never said it outright, but whose Sunday morning glares sent Ollie back home to pray from the relative safety of their loft apartment.

"You're Charles, right? The old groundskeeper for the Victorian on Alquist?"

Charles scrunched his mouth. His eyes narrowed.

"Not sayin' you're old. Just that, you're not the groundskeeper anymore." Ollie heard their accent mimicking his and winced. The German Shepard's barks became hoarse.

"Shad'dup, Lady!" Charles yelled in its direction.

Lady whined, circled, and laid down on a nearby blanket.

"I worked the property, that's right. And what of it?"

Ollie shifted their weight from foot to foot. "I was hopin' you remembered the break-in," they said, embarrassed about the twang and praying he would think they always spoke this way. "The one after—well, after Mr. Pruitt was gone."

He looked at Ollie from shoes to headphones. His wrinkled nose suggested he was trying to decide what to make of them, and he remained silent.

"There's some strange stuff going on over there," Ollie added.

He lifted his hand, and Ollie thought he might close the door in their face, but instead he opened it, screen blowing free of its frame as it swung.

"Come in."

Ollie stepped inside, although their good sense told them not to. The wall to their right held shelf after shelf of ceramic carousel horses. To the left was a battered couch and straight ahead a pinewood kitchen table and two matching chairs. Ollie followed Charles across the peeling linoleum floor and was relieved when he headed to the kitchen instead of the couch. Beyond the table was another door leading to the backyard, and sunlight poured in through its dingy window. An escape route if it came to it.

Charles pulled the ashtray close and reached into his chest pocket, drawing out a pack of Marlboro reds. He stuffed one into his mouth, and as he lit it, Ollie feared his untamed mustache might catch ablaze.

"What sort of strange things got you askin' bout the break-in?" Smoke tufted from his mouth and punctuated his words.

Ollie reached into their back pocket and Charles tensed, gripped the table. Ollie's free hand shot up, showing their palm, and the other showed they were just reaching for their cell phone. Charles relaxed. Ollie clicked the phone to life and scrolled through their photos until they found the somewhat blurry shot of Carter they'd taken through their bedroom window while he was shopping in town.

"Do you recognize this man?"

Charles eyed the photo. "It's a lil' blurry. Far off too."

"Could he be the one who broke into the Victorian those years ago?"

His face clenched. "Ain't you heard the story?"

Ollie widened their eyes and stayed quiet, hoping to lure him into telling it. It was one thing to hear a story secondhand. Another to hear it from the horse's mouth.

"Well, I'd been workin' the grounds at Alquist Ave since I was a teenager. When the Pruitts bought it, Richard kept me on. Said he could use the help. I was prob'ly in my fifties around then, was lookin' toward retirement but didn't quite have the funds, so I was grateful to keep the work. He was a decent man. I was sorry about what happened to him." Charles took a long drag that turned half the cigarette to ember. "So, after that," he exhaled, "I stayed on still. Got paid through the estate, Pruitt must've set it up before … well, you know."

Ollie focused on his eyes, blue and clouded with cataracts.

"It wasn't too long after that, maybe a couple years, I was workin' in the greenhouse. Nothin' growin' in there, just keepin' up with the glass, when I heard somethin' shatter. I thought maybe I'd knocked over a pot or somethin', but then I heard another shatter and could tell it was farther off, comin' from the house. I couldn't tell ya what I was thinkin', to be honest. I wasn't paid to be no kinda crimestopper, but I chased after the sound all the same. He was standin' by the side window, clearin' glass shards from the window frame. I yelled out. Prob'ly shouldn't of, lookin' back. No tellin' what folks might do to ya these days, desperate folks that is. But I was lucky. He caught sight of me and run off."

Charles sucked the cigarette down to the butt and stamped it out.

"Did you see his face? Any distinguishing features?"

"Nah." Charles shook his head. "He was about average height, average build. He wore a mask over his face, so I couldn't tell much to the police when they asked."

"And what happened after that?" Ollie leaned in, hoping for something they hadn't heard before.

"Well, after that I repaired the window. Kept on with my work several years more. And then in 2017 I retired. Overdue, if you ask me."

Ollie offered the picture again. "Can you take one more look?"

Charles looked over the picture again. Ollie zoomed in on Carter's face, blurring the picture to wide pixels.

"Coulda been. Coulda been Captain Williams. Coulda been me had I not been standin' where I stood. Coulda been almost anybody."

Ollie sighed. A wave of disappointment crashed through.

"Can I offer ya anything before ya head out?" He rose from his chair and motioned toward the fridge. Ollie rose too. They'd worn out their welcome.

"No, thank you."

"You don't pay no mind to Lady, now. She's all bark, no bite."

Ollie nodded and made for the door. "Thanks again," they said. The loose screen brushed their ankle as they closed it gently behind them. On the ride home, their tongue dried, and Ollie regretted not taking Charles up on his offer of a drink. Despite the rapidly cooling autumn air, sweat leaked through their pits, drawn forth by stress and effort. Charles was their only idea for another piece of the puzzle, and that had been a bust. They carried their bike up the steps to their loft apartment, shoulders hunched with exhaustion and defeat. Passing through the door, they set the bike upright, careful not to scratch the walls, and as they shut the door and moved past the hallway, they froze.

Ollie wasn't generally a tidy person, but the flipped sofa cushions, toppled dresser, and broken coffee table told a sinister story. Someone had been here. Were they still here? Their heart pounded in their chest, and they wanted to turn and run, but their feet were concrete blocks where they stood. They listened for shuffling, for footsteps, but the only sound was the hum of the refrigerator.

They must be gone, they thought. They hoped.

Ears straining for any sign of life, they took a measured first step. They pictured their phone in their pocket but didn't reach for it. The studio layout didn't require much searching. A quick pivot assured Ollie that no one was there. The violation sank in.

Who would do this?

The answer came in an instant. *Of course.*

Ollie pictured Carter's sneaky fingers finding the spare key above the door frame, laughing to himself as he vandalized their home. There was nothing of value to check on, all the art secondhand, and no jewelry to speak of. But then Ollie remembered.

Hobbes.

He was missing from the window where he usually spent his time, sunbathing and dreaming of catching lizards.

Ollie lifted overturned cushions, swatted through piles of clothing. Nothing.

Icy dread crept in. Hairs rose one by one on Ollie's neck.

"Hobbes!" Their voice cracked. "Hobbes, where are you?"

There was nothing. No sign of movement. No *meow.*

Ollie's pulse accelerated, thumped inside their ears. They searched the pantry, blanched by a snowfall of flour leaking from a torn bag.

"Hobbes!"

They crouched down on their hands and knees to peek under the couch, but only shards of glass from the shattered table and a stray sock were beneath.

Ollie's chest tightened. They imagined Carter kicking the orange tabby or dragging him out of the apartment in a burlap sack while he hissed and screamed. They lowered their body to the floor, nothing under the dresser, and flipped to their back. Glass poked through their shirt and their tears melted their view of the popcorn ceiling.

"Hobbes." A hoarse whisper.

And then a curt sound rose above Ollie's jagged breaths. *Mow.*

"Hobbes?" Ollie jolted upright. From the closet door, cracked a few inches, emerged orange fur, and Hobbes trotted over to Ollie and stood on their chest. Ollie released a voluminous breath. The glass beneath them dulled. Hobbes closed his eyes with pleasure as they stroked him, and laughter escaped Ollie's mouth as they wiped their tears into their spiky hair.

Hobbes pushed his butt into Ollie's face, forcing it sideways. They scratched the base of his tail, adrenaline dissipating with the sound of his purrs. Broken table, spilled flour, cracked picture frame. It could all be replaced. The tossed laundry and furniture could be straightened. The lock could be rekeyed. Hobbes was okay. They were okay. Sensing Ollie might move or some other atrocity, Hobbes leapt from their chest. Just in time for a thundering thought to jolt Ollie to a sitting position.

Breaking and entering, THAT is a crime.

CHAPTER SEVENTEEN

This was worth more than a phone call.

Without even a cursory glance in the mirror, Ollie dashed down the stairs and onto Main St. Williams would have to investigate now. He'd have to. What started as a jog, slowed to a brisk walk when Ollie noticed the suspicious eyes of passersby. The Rollins family paused beside their tan SUV. Brenda Rollins pulled her daughters, young twins, close. Ollie scratched at a tickle on their back where wind jimmied through holes in the fabric. Blood beneath their nails. The glass hadn't been so dull after all. The Rollins twins tugged at their mother's skirt, chattering about ice cream; and Ollie used the distraction to round the corner, out of sight.

Their steps landed hard on the brick, and the wind threw dry leaves in Ollie's face, forcing them to stop midway through a parking lot and bat debris from their eyes. The *Extended Stay* sign gleamed overhead, and, parked some twenty feet away, door hanging ajar, was Eva's car.

No fucking way.

They'd recognize the tan Lincoln town car anywhere after stalking it with Jenkins. The memory of Carter's hand around Eva's throat still intruded on Ollie's sleep, induced nightmares of Carter as a red-eyed devil. Eva lifted a slender leg through the open door. She hadn't seen Ollie yet, but now only fifteen feet away, they had no doubt that she soon would.

Eva had always carried herself with a proud grace. While cleaning, she held her body in regal poses, as if a photographer may jump from a broom closet to snap a shot. She looked down her nose at everything, the dirt she swept, the spiders she shooed, the muffins she baked. Her chin was permanently tipped up and her bust fixed aloft. But when she closed the door of her vehicle, her eyes lingered on the ground. Her shoulders hunched like a woman triple her age. Ollie forgot their mission for the moment, and they approached her as they would an old friend.

"Eva, it's—"

Eva jumped, clutching at the purse strap over her heart. "Jesus, Ollie, you scared me."

As Ollie drew closer, they noticed a juvenile bruise stretching from Eva's upper jaw to where her golden hair met her temple. The tender, pink edges deepened into a sickly purple, a puffy jewel tone that offset her emerald eyes.

"What happened?"

Eva covered the side of her face, smiled nervously. "It's nothing." She took two steps away, but Ollie followed.

"Did he do that to you?" Ollie jogged a pace to get in front of Eva. "Did Carter hurt you?"

Mascara clumped in her bottom lashes, ashy smudges at the corners of her eyes. "He's not a bad man," she said. And it struck Ollie how she said it. Like something she'd rehearsed. Repeated so often that it had become true.

Rage and disgust mingled in Ollie's shoulders. Flashes of their vandalized home, his fist poised to strike, the swollen bruise. "Why would you defend him?" Ollie's eyes searched Eva's. An answer seemed to lurk just beneath their surface, but her irises glazed over, as if she'd picked up on Ollie's intrusion and reinforced her defenses.

"I'm sure I don't know what you mean." She adjusted the strap on her shoulder, pulled the bag tight to her breast.

"Is it because he gave you a car?"

She took a step away, and Ollie jogged forward again.

"You don't owe him anything." Ollie felt, for the first time, pity for Eva. She was shrunken, diminished, and Ollie knew Carter was to blame. They just didn't know how or why.

Eva's jaw hung open. She shook her head. "A car?" she repeated back.

"I saw you together. I know."

Eva blanched. Her gaze sharpened.

Ollie had said too much.

She leaned forward, a breath from Ollie's lips. From prey to predator. "What is it you think you know?" she spat. The drawbridge had been pulled up. The turrets were manned.

"I know you're having an affair. You must love him, to defend him. Do you?"

Eva threw her hands over her face. Ollie thought she might be crying, the way her cheeks reddened, and her spine curled, but it was raucous laughter that escaped her lips.

"An affair." The words bounced over her chuckles through bared teeth. She stood straight and tall, collarbones pressing against her tanned skin. She dodged Ollie but let her shoulder bump them roughly on the way around. Gazelle-like legs carried Eva through the automatic doors, and the last golden tips of her hair disappeared into the lobby.

Ollie stood dumbstruck in the parking lot, Eva's strange reaction wriggling into their mind. They couldn't make sense of it. Turned toward the direction of home, they took a few steps before they remembered the break-in, Captain Williams. A shiver ran through their body, from the holes in their shirt or from Eva's strangeness. Only a few short blocks to the police station. Ollie continued on.

There's a version of this where everything makes sense. Bricks flew past under their feet. *I just have to find it.*

Inside the station, the air was stale. Ollie shoved the domestic violence pamphlet in their pocket just in case Eva decided to reach out. Jenkins avoided eye contact. His computer screen reflected blue light over his face, his eyes unmoving. Ollie gave him a wide berth as they made their way through the bull pen and into Williams's office, uninvited. They plopped into his tufted level chair, leaned their elbows on squared knees.

"This better be good, Alden."

"I'd like to report a break-in."

Williams looked up from his paperwork. Slid his glasses up the bridge of his nose. They had his attention. Ollie recounted the story, sparing no detail, no hand gesture, to make the relevant points. The exception, of course, was the stakeout they'd done with Brian Jenkins. They wouldn't threaten his job with this exposure, not when Williams would be forced to investigate the burglary. An investigation which, Ollie had no doubt, would lead straight to Alquist Ave.

CHAPTER EIGHTEEN

Mae awoke sweaty. Receding memories of disturbing dreams stabbed at the edges of her mind. Ollie's hands had been on her, warm caresses that sent blood coursing between her legs. But their tidy fingernails turned to long, scratching claws. Their hands swelled and sprouted coarse hair. Gripped by a beast she'd turned to see Carter, fangs in his mouth and blood in his eyes. She'd known he was going to kill her. Tear her flesh. Eat her piece by piece.

But the dream faded as her eyes adjusted to waking. She remembered that she loved him. The room was dark, and she wondered how long she'd slept.

"Babe!" she called out.

He said he'd check on me.

Mae's tea, half drunk, was cold on the nightstand. Silence had fallen over the house, explained by the white strip of paper Carter had left on his satin pillowcase.

You were sleeping so soundly, I didn't want to wake you. Had to take care of some things, back as soon as I can.

Love,

Carter

Mae rubbed at her eyes, hoping to wipe away the blur in her vision. Pressure from her fists shot purple light behind her eyelids. Her head throbbed. The skunky scent of a half-burned joint wafted into her nose, which she blocked with the back of her hand. Turning her head away from the culprit, she pushed it into her drawer and slammed it shut.

Think I'm good on that for a while. Even she couldn't deny that maybe the weed played a role in her unusual experiences and vivid nightmares.

Mae switched on the gas lamp beside her bed, and the wall exploded with light. The wallpaper's golds glittered more vibrantly than the day they were stamped, the reds deep and regal, and the patterns swirled into one another, morphed, shape-shifted, and swirled back into their positions. Mae's eyes dried. She forgot to blink. She spotted one swirl in particular which unfurled, the tip moving in a come-hither motion.

She'd never been high like this. She must still be dreaming.

As if guided by an unseen hand, she stood and followed it into the hallway. Mae ran her fingers over the railing, and as her palm passed over the wood, nicks and scratches disappeared, its cherry luster restored. She gasped, but still the curling wallpaper called her forward. As her feet moved across the strip of rug, it felt deeper, more plush. Stains vanished. Colors popped. Walls bent and warped around her, breathing in time with her own chest. She raised an open palm to feel the movement, but the fingers she saw were not her own. Too short. Too stubby. Wrinkles in all the wrong places. A pang of horror shot through her, and she studied her hands, flipping them back and forth.

These aren't mine. How did they get here?

Her concentration was broken by the hint of a whisper. It beckoned her forward. *Come,* the house seemed to say. It pulled her into the library. Inside, she heard a chorus of hushed voices, like she'd stepped into a fairy town, surrounded by thousands of tiny villagers all gossiping about her at once. The vitriol of a thousand pinprick mouths. It itched her eardrums and she stuck her finger inside to scratch it. The sliding ladder rolled toward her, or did she approach it? Impossible to tell. A familiar spot of rust between the rungs reminded her of her father's old warning.

"See that?"

She'd nodded, probably six years old.

"Never climb this, okay? You've got to promise. It's just for show. Not steady."

She clawed at the oxidized metal which flaked beneath her fingernail. Beneath it, trails of shining black iron, as if she removed a spot of ugly paint. She tore at the rusty shape with both hands now, until the whites of her fingernails turned orange, packed with rust. A puff of breath blew off the last of it, just dust now, and she observed the rolling ladder, brand new, as it must have been when it was installed. She climbed one rung and then two, and emboldened by her success, clung to the very top of the ladder and observed the library from her high perch.

The whispering was louder now, and she could tell it came from the books. The books full of words and their secrets. Their pretend worlds and wolves and happy endings. Stacks of lies, and now they tormented her, prying at her eardrums.

She released her grip on the ladder, balancing on the balls of her feet, plunging both index fingers deep into her ears.

"Stop!" she pleaded, but the voices whispered on. Stress leaked out through sweat on her feet, and her arches lost their grip. She slipped. Had to snatch at the top rung to keep from tumbling all the way down. This put her eye to eye with a purple bound book, its title gawking at her from gold lettering. *He Loves Her,* read the side binding. Her eyes hopped to the next, a burnt orange with black letters. *You Idiot.* And the next, teal with yellow script. *They're laughing at You. Stupid. Silly. Little. Girl.*

Rage erupted from Mae's throat in a scream. She grabbed the books and cast them down onto the floor one by one. Leaping from the ladder, she landed on top of them with a smack, and pain shot up through her ankles from the pressure. She stomped on the stack of books, which fought back, thrusting their dull edges into her bare feet.

"Fuck you!"

Her foot came down at a forty-five degree angle, snagging the nail of her big toe, which tore halfway down the nail bed. A sharp breath masked the pain for a moment, and then she felt the heat and watched the tear fill with crimson blood, blood that seemed to turn black the longer she looked at it. She tried to steady her jagged breaths as she hobbled toward the doorway, splattering the rug with each, uneasy movement. Warmth coated her foot, splashed up on her ankle.

When she reached the hallway, she grabbed the doorframe to steady herself, and the whispering stopped, all at once. Mae sensed eyes upon her and whipped her head in all directions to discover the watcher but found no one. Then she heard her, Lady Paola. The Lady sang the second movement of Tchaikovsky's *Violin Concerto.* As the notes rose and fell, so did the bounds of the hallway, the ceiling and floor, stretching and collapsing into almost nothing. She felt a presence at her back. The air cold against her flesh, and as if pushed by unseen hands, she took off running down the hallway, her steps percussion against Lady Paola's melody, and the sharp, stabbing pain flowed from her foot through her leg, and grabbed at her heart like a clenched fist. She reached her bedroom and flung the door shut behind her, locking it. Her injured foot now clung to the hardwood as her blood coated her heel and became tacky. She was ten years old again. Standing over her father's body. Knowing she needed help, needed to call someone. Footsteps thumped. A shadow passed under the door. She screamed and ran to her bedside table. Her fingers fumbled but were able to send a call to Carter, whose voice cracked on the other line.

"What? What's happening?"

Mae stuttered, eyes fixed beneath the door frame, where the shadow thickened and spilled under, a growing puddle of black. Mae tried to explain, tried to put words to the terror, but the sound from her lips was a long, high whine.

"Mae-by, calm down."

It expanded, a liquid void, until the size of a man, a swirling dark mass.

"Just calm down, I'll be home as soon as I can."

The phone dropped, screen cracking as it hit the unforgiving wood floor. Mae pressed her back against the nightstand. The knob dug into her shoulder blade. Her foot was a sticky mess, an offering of bloodied meat between her and the expansive shadow. She squeezed her lids shut, but it grew even behind her closed lids, standing upright into the shape of a man—no, a woman. The swirling void arched into feminine curves, grew snaking tendrils like flowing hair, and in its black hand something filled with color.

There was a glint at its edge and the blackness seceded into wood grain, a handle. The specter swung it in a circle with a flick of its phantom wrist, and whether Mae's eyes were opened or shut tight she saw the axe and felt the specter's eyeless gaze upon her. She clawed her way beneath the four-poster bed frame, shivered there like a terrified child, and watched beneath the comforter's reach for the encroaching shadow's steps.

Any moment now.

Her hands trembled, rattling against the floorboards. Her toe throbbed and streaked a bloody trail behind her. A grotesque, hobbled slug. Her jagged breaths punctuated whimpers she tried to smother with her palm. Lady Paola screamed now, wild crescendos of discordant staccato, and then heavy footfalls up the steps.

"Mae!" Carter yelled through her closed door. He twisted the handle and banged on the wood with his fist. The pressure reverberated, shaking the walls, and dust cascaded from high corners.

"I'm here!" Her words came through a shudder, and she knew she'd have to drag herself out into the open to unlock the door, stand before the vicious specter as it swung its terrible axe.

"Mae!" The pounding of his fists shook the foundation, and Mae feared that if she didn't move soon, it might bring down the house around her.

Unable to face the specter, she heaved herself forward with clamped eyes, feeling her way out from under the bed frame. Hands in front of her, she stumbled to her feet, feeling for the door and expecting at any moment for the monster's axe to tunnel through her skull. The knob was cold in her hand, and she felt the thing beside her, knew it raised its axe to strike, but she refused to look it in the face. The lock opened with a click and Carter crashed inside, grabbing Mae with both hands and pushing her several steps backward to keep from tumbling to the floor. He panted hot breath in her ear. Her body quaked in his embrace. Silence hung over the house, and Mae cracked open her eyes.

Ordinary. Just the room and not a thing out of place but the smears of blood painting her course around the room, staining the sheets.

"Mae, your foot." Carter crouched down, examining the gore.

Heat radiated within and Mae's eyes bounced over the scene, almost hoping to see it again, the feminine shadow, so Carter might understand. He eased her into a sitting position, and she felt her heart slow as he briefly disappeared into the bathroom and returned with the first aid kit.

"Did you see her?" Mae's voice was mousy, thin.

Carter didn't look up. He sprayed antiseptic over the bloodied toe and Mae winced at the cold.

"You saw her, didn't you?"

Wild hairs obscured Mae's vision, and she caught sight of herself in the vanity mirror. Her image reminded her of a book cover she'd seen, the title *Raised by Wolves*. Gray and pink smudges painted her cheeks, her eyes ghoulishly wide. She smoothed back a few errant strands, but it did little to salvage her image.

"We need to see Doctor Levine," Carter said finally. "In the morning."

Shame convulsed inside her, a venomous snake. Some old, town doctor would lecture her about 'side effects of marijuana', but Mae had been smoking for years and never experienced anything like this. Ultimately, she lacked the words for an argument. The trip was inevitable and fighting against it would only make the need seem more apparent, so she nodded.

"Why don't you get changed." He tossed a new set of pajamas onto the side of the bed. As he dipped through the door to offer some privacy, Mae caught a look on his face. Pity, maybe. And something else too. Something cold. She pulled her pjs over her head, the fabric sticking to her skin where it had soaked in sweat and blood, and it occurred to her the meaning of that look. It was just a presumption, really, but it felt like truth. As true as the screaming violin and the lady specter. *I love you less than I used to.*

Chapter Nineteen

Ollie stared at their dormant phone.

Stay out of it, he'd said, yet the urge to phone Mae gnawed at Ollie's insides. They were chaos within and chaos without. Strewn laundry, overturned furniture, and glass shards still littered their apartment. So, they started folding, shaking each piece to loose the glass, and making a neat stack of shirts on the righted couch. Surely some external order would settle their gut, the manual calm of placing things where they should be, of fixing. The coffee table couldn't be saved, so they dragged it to the door, wrestled it down the stairs and out to the curb for bulk pickup. Autumn had settled upon Landrum. Chilly breezes rattled dormant trees, spreading leaves of orange and brown and yellow through the quiet streets. They twirled in packs like tumbleweed. On the cusp of Halloween, the town had begun to decorate. Oversized webs and Shelob sized spiders inhabited the shop windows, illuminated by strands of lights, orange and purple. Ollie pushed a breath from the bottom of their lungs, examined the air for its cloud.

Too soon.

They turned to climb the stairs when a purring engine broke through the quiet. Turning on the adjacent road,

Ollie spotted it, a truck, muted green. A twitch of anxiety struck like lightning. Threat and promise warred within, but, bewitched by the possibility of discovering another clue, Ollie crossed Main St and poked their head around the corner of the tailor's shop. The truck parked in front of Dr. Levine's practice, and Carter escorted Mae from the vehicle, her steps slow and lifeless, into the waiting room.

Ollie remembered two years earlier, the graffiti at the school. They'd suspected Dr. Levine after spotting a red paint stain on his cuff and crept over this same route to listen beneath his window for a confession. They traced those steps, through the damp, water-stained alley and crouched beside those same dumpsters which smelled of rotting vegetables and a chemical sweetness. Sure, it hadn't been Dr. Levine, but Dr. Levine's son who'd spray painted obscenities on the gym's outer wall; and yes, they were no longer welcome at the medical practice after creating such a scene in the waiting room, but it would have been worth it if the experience led to uncovering something now, some vital missing cog in the machine of the infamous robbery and murder.

A warped metal bracket framed the window. It pressed cold on the crown of Ollie's skull. They heard rustling inside, a door creaking on its hinges. The sound came muffled through the brick wall, but when nurse Brenda asked Mae to take a seat, the words were as clear as if Ollie was in the room with them, hidden inside a cabinet.

"He'll be right with you," she said, closing the door.

Paper lining crumpled as, Ollie supposed, Mae sat on the examination chair.

"Just tell him what you saw." It was Carter's voice. "He can't help you otherwise."

"He's gonna think I'm..." Mae's voice was stifled, and Ollie pictured her face sunken in her palms.

The door squeaked open. "Mae Duvall," Ollie heard the flipping of pages.

"What brings you back in to see me? Everything alright with the medication?"

Ollie heard scratching, tiny nails on the brick, and looked down to see a rat darting into the dumpster. They muffled their gasp with a cupped palm and crouched further, hoping the sound didn't carry inside as well as it carried out.

"I don't ..." Mae trailed off.

"It's not working." There was a hard quality to Carter's words. "Tell him, Mae."

Blood pooled in Ollie's feet as they hovered. Acid poured into their stretched calf muscles, a deep burn. They bounced, tried to coax it to flow.

"Are the symptoms still present?" Doctor Levine asked.

Nails screeched against metal as the rat burrowed deeper inside the dumpster. Hairs raised on Ollie's neck. They imagined those claws digging into the soft skin at the base of their skull.

"Tell him what you saw," Carter urged, his stoic tone now spiked with frustration. "And about the weed."

Tissue rustled, and Ollie pictured Mae shifting uncomfortably on the paper sheet. Clicking of bone on bone joined the scratches as the rat chattered in frustration. The sounds moved up the side of the metal dumpster.

It's clawing its way out.

"It was playing again, the violin," Mae said finally, her words measured and cautious.

Ollie heard punctures in plastic, nearly at the top of the bin. Their body braced.

"And?" Carter pressed.

"And there was a shadow. I stubbed my toe and— everything was strange."

The rat squeaked, perched high above them, looking down from its plastic bag throne atop the waste bin.

"Well, as I'm sure you know. Marijuana can cause an increase in … this kind of thing. It's certainly not helping your situation." Doctor Levine sounded disappointed but not altogether surprised. "As for the medication, it's a bit of trial and error. I'd like to check your levels. Please fill the cup to this line. You can leave it on the table in the restroom when you've finished." Ollie heard the door close.

The rat's bulging eyes inspected Ollie.

Please don't jump down.

"I'm afraid for her, Doc. You should've seen her, twisted up, covered in blood, screaming. I'm not sure it's just the drugs. I think we should consider …"

"It's a possibility, Mr. Duvall. As we discussed, an inpatient unit can offer the time and structure needed to stabilize. Let's give it a week—"

Tiny claws gripped Ollie's scalp, a landing pad for the ambitious rat. They leapt from their crouched position, slamming their head on the metal window frame which clanged and sent black spots across Ollie's vision. Wild swings of their arms dislodged the creature from Ollie's head, and they sprinted down the alley without a thought to dampening the sound of their heavy footfalls.

Did they see me? They huffed as they ran. *Aw, fuck!*

They rounded the intersection and continued down Main St. The thin webbing between Ollie's thumb and index finger stung. Four points of blood leaked from holes the size of rat teeth.

FUCK. Probably have rabies now too.

They threw open the boutique door, taking the steps two at a time. Cool air dried Ollie's throat as they sucked in gulps, and they slammed their apartment door behind them and clicked the lock. They slumped down to the floor, catching their breath and appraising the damage. Their hand quaked as they held it aloft.

From recent research, Mae learned that no scientist would call the group of crows outside her window a *murder*. They would call it a flock. *Flock*, devoid of ominous connotation, sterile, might as well say *group* or *collection*. More interesting though, was the history behind why some chose the macabre title. Rooted in folklore and superstition, it was said that a gathering of crows may amass so they might collectively decide a member's capital fate. Avian judges and juries. Others believed a black mass of feathers to be an omen of death. Mae, not usually superstitious, couldn't help but lean toward the poetic resonance of *murder* as they tapped on her window, bleating and gawking at her through the glass before taking flight. Dark wings circled over the yard, visible through the night only when the moonlight refracted off their wings, casting a bluish hue.

How long had Carter been gone? Minutes? Hours?

The screaming birds and wailing strings emanating from above pecked at the edges of Mae's skull, inducing a throbbing ache that sent radiating white light through her line of vision. She sipped at tepid tea, pressed at her temples. And her own fingers, cold as death, sent shivers down the backs of her arms. Her glaring phone screen beat pain into the base of her eye sockets, and she was unable to read about the crows any longer.

A week. It was a short span of time to determine her sanity. She shuddered at the thought of itchy hospital gowns, feeling metal bars press at her back through a thin, plastic mattress. How much worse would the wailing be, she wondered, when it emanated from the mouths of fellow patients rather than from the ghost of Lady Paola, now nightly haunting the third floor?

She eyed the latest bottle of pills with suspicion.

Side effects may include: Dizziness, drowsiness, sleep disturbances, anxiety, vengeful spirits, lightheadedness, imprisonment ...

A journal entry detailed the visit. How Carter spoke on her behalf, how Dr. Levine regarded her much like an experiment. Like a beaker. A test tube. A spot of bacteria in a dish. She flipped forward in her entries to count the days since. *One, two,* it had been three, right? *Wait, the pages stuck together. Three, four, five?*

The latest entry was unfamiliar. She ran her finger over the date.

October 14

She'd penned no words beneath, but had sketched a drawing, a crude figure and an axe, disproportionately large, hovering above its head. Had she drawn that? She clamped the journal shut and returned it to its nest inside her drawer, took a seat in her chair overlooking the yard. The cushion imprinted her form, a steady perch.

The storm was silent at first. Silver sheets of rain gobbled up by starving grass. Mae pressed her ear against the cold windowpane, longing to hear the pattering drops, but all were devoured. All were swallowed up by the dry, cracking earth in a soundless gulp. Perhaps dodging the cold onslaught of raindrops, the crows landed en masse at the limit of her property, where the tall grass met the towering woods. *They formed a loose circle, perhaps deciding the fate of one of their flock*, Mae thought. Thunder rolled and strobing light illuminated heavy clouds. Then a blinding crack, a direct strike, seemingly at the murder's center. Mae drew a sharp breath, pressed her forehead on the chilled glass, and her exhale clouded her view in a plume of condensation.

Had it hit them? She waited for the surviving crows to take flight. A beat passed, and then another, and the rain poured down without mercy, and the sky blazed over the cemetery to the north. Had they all been killed? A headache twisted behind Mae's eyes. When had she slept? She shook the pain from her skull.

"Go."

The voice came through the wall of the neighboring room. Mae stiffened.

"It's your fault. Now, go!"

She jumped to her feet and her head whipped around in search of her raincoat.

"There's no time for that." It was flat, matter-of-fact.

Mae glanced down at her nightdress. The thin pastel fabric would be soaked through in seconds.

"Sssselfish," it hissed.

Her bare feet slapped against the hardwood, and as she reached the landing, lightning poured through the windows, casting long shadows on the walls. She squeezed her eyes shut but her feet continued, knowing the house, each step, inch by inch. Rain poured over her back in buckets, sopping earth sunk between her toes as she reached the backyard. The wind howled, echoed in her eardrums.

"GO!" it commanded, a low tone, the throaty voice of angry earth.

Her feet slid on slick mud which turned the bandage around her toe a dark shade of brown. Dying grasses whipped at her thighs as she cut through them. The cold sank its teeth into her chest, each breath like a thousand tiny needles stabbing at her lungs, and the raindrops landed like stones, beating her flesh. She pressed on, past the greenhouse which groaned under the storm's assault and reached the clearing where the earth became rocky, jagged edges ripping at her tender feet. She slowed to a hesitant walk. Three crows, no four, spied her approach. They called to another two. They were raised up, perched on something. An uprooted tree? No, Mae moved closer. A mound of rags?

Mae squinted as water beaded over her eyelashes, crouched to make out the shape in the dark. She wiped the puddles from her eyes, now close enough to reach out and touch it. The perched crows took to the air, revealing a mangled visage.

Mae's scream split the night in two. The storm moved away, as if knowing to step aside, to allow this main act to take center stage. She'd seen him before, at the Fall Festival, and tucked inside a hidden memory, somewhere else too, much earlier.

It was the good half of his face she recognized, the other little more than haggard meat, bits of exposed bone. His jaw hung open, immortalized horror, as did his remaining eye. Mae trembled, took a stilted breath in, and let it go in another scream, weaker than the first. She fell to her knees, sobbing. Her tears blended with the falling rain.

Soggy footsteps approached from behind, boots sucked at by the muck, set her nerves aflame.

"Mae?" It was Carter's voice, and she leapt to her feet, tried to speak, but the sounds she made were intelligible. She pointed at the ravaged carcass in the woody overgrowth.

"What is it?" His brows stitched together.

Mae pointed harder. "Look!"

Carter shook his head in confusion. "What am I looking at, Mae?"

"He's right there!" Her voice was high, erratic.

He curled her arm around her shoulders. "You're soaked through, let's get you inside."

Horror curled inside Mae. "We can't just leave him here, we have to call someone, do something."

"Who?" He pressed her into taking reluctant footsteps away from the body, back toward the Victorian.

"The Captain, Captain Williams, didn't you see him? You have to look!" Rage mixed with fear and shock. *Why won't he do something? Why is he acting this way?*

"Shhhh," he rubbed Mae's shoulder with his palm, but the attempt to calm her only incited her further.

"Carter, what the fuck?" She ripped her body from his grasp. Her tone was shrill. "His body is right—" She tried to turn and point back to the ravaged corpse, but Carter caught her and pressed her further toward the house.

"You have to calm down, Mae. You're having another episode."

"Like hell I am." The grit in her tone shocked even Mae herself, and Carter responded by strengthening his stranglehold on her arm.

Mae twisted, a reflex, and when she felt his grip loosen, she ran. Throbbing pain in her toe intensified as her feet hit the dirt, but she pushed herself forward, feeling a predator threat at her back. Blackhaw bushes tore strips from her thigh. Chokeberry branches snapped under her weight and dug into her exposed flesh. His footfalls were heavy on the sopping earth and splattered mud onto the backs of Mae's calves, just a single step ahead of him.

"Mae!" He yelled through huffing breaths. "Fuck!" Carter yelped, but Mae resisted the urge to turn and see how he was injured.

More time. More distance.

North was the only clear path forward. Towering woods of Eastern Hemlock blocked every other route, so she dipped beneath the wire fence that separated the cemetery from her land, confronted now by the weather-beaten headstones illuminated with moonlight through sheets of freezing rain.

"Help!" she cried, but she knew the nearest property, the Dalroy's, was too far to hear. She weaved through untidy rows of graves, her foot catching on the odd, rotten stem, abandoned at the base of an epitaph, left to wither. Whatever injury Carter had sustained, it slowed him long enough for Mae to glance around for a hiding spot. The clearing spanned the length of a football field, and with the searing pain from her foot, Mae doubted she could reach the woods at the other side. A mausoleum stood some fifty feet away, nestled between overgrown hedges. It would have to do. She dragged herself through the merciless rain, the whistling wind pushing against her, to the vault's opening.

"Mae!" His voice carried on the roaring wind.

She ducked inside, and her breath came out in hurried huffs, which hung in the damp air as a cloud. The storm beat against the stone roof and Mae strained her hearing against it for the sound of Carter's footsteps. Thunder ricocheted through the night, and a flash of lightning flooded the vault with strobing light. Mae thought she could make out the letters on the tomb. She thought they might spell her own name. She ran her fingers over the etching, crouched in the corner like a trapped rat. She tried to make herself small. Her heart punched at her chest. Wind roared against the walls, and she squeezed her eyes shut.

Thump.

No.

Thump. Thump. thump.

She refused to look. If she wouldn't look, perhaps she would disappear.

A mighty hand wrapped around her head. It dug into her ear, pushed her lips into her teeth. She felt her skull tip back and launch forward. And then nothing at all.

TWENTY

The hallway, the lobby, the waiting room, the ward. All had been stripped of color, the patients undeserving of yellow's warm nuzzle, of purple's velvety feel. And red? Out of the question. Angry, violent red could never be allowed inside. Not to influence these ravaged, wild minds. Give them ideas. No, the walls, the tiles, the sparse furnishings, all were a grimy white illuminated by an overabundance of fluorescent lighting. The cold plastic bench was built into the floor, lest Ollie decide to chuck it at a passing nurse, and the scent of disinfectant tried too hard. It rested atop secrets, the ugly truth of the place which the staff was employed to hide. The only noise was the movement of doors. The buzzing of electronic locks, a whoosh of air, and the metallic clank of them shutting. Five doors Ollie had passed through. Each opening only for the touch of a key card.

Locked alone between two heavy sets, Ollie did their best to ignore the camera pointing at them from a high corner and flipped on their phone in an effort to pass the time. *Terrarium*, a pattern-finding game with a turtle theme, refused to load, the circle spinning and spinning with no sign of progress.

Of course, there's no service.

Ollie shifted as the hard seat numbed their left butt cheek, and they opened their camera roll. They flipped through myriad photos: Hobbes asleep, belly up, beneath the window. Hobbes snuggled beneath the pink and green crocheted blanket. Hobbes on top of the refrigerator. A selfie of Ollie with a beaming smile, holding Hobbes close to their face while Hobbes grimaced. They flipped and flipped until they landed on one they'd nearly forgotten. Mae held Ollie close with an arm hooked over their shoulder. Her dimpled smile shone through her hazel eyes and Ollie remembered how she'd smelled of lavender that day, just slightly, around the tips of her dirty blonde hair. Ollie's mouth hung crooked, and a pang of embarrassment reminded them of the exhilaration they'd felt with Mae so close. It was always the unavailable ones they obsessed over. Typical.

"You're here to see Duvall?"

The jarring voice ripped Ollie from their memory, and they jolted up from their seat to see a scowling nurse. She held a clipboard close to her lilac scrubs, her deep red curls defying gravity.

"Mae," Ollie answered. "Yes, Mae Duvall."

"Mhmm," the nurse responded, eyes back down to her clipboard. "You're gonna need to store that."

Ollie glanced at their phone, then around at the bare walls, eyebrows slightly raised.

"Through here." The nurse held the door so Ollie could pass through behind her, and the neighboring hallway held a wall of lockers.

"In here?" Ollie opened one.

The nurse grunted.

Phone stowed, the nurse led Ollie through another set of doors and into a small room with wide windows housing thick glass. "Just a moment." The lilac nurse dipped out of the room and allowed the door to lock behind her.

Distant moaning and raised voices down the hall emerged through the heavy metal door. The chemical smell was tinged with ammonia, and the metal table was bolted to the floor, as were the metal chairs. The lilac nurse led a woman by the arm, her back hunched and feet sliding across the floor in thick socks. Teal ties of her hospital gown slacked at her back creating a gap in the fabric, but the exposure didn't seem to bother the hunched woman, who took shuffled steps forward, face buried beneath a nest of hair, eyes on the grimy white tiles. When the concave woman reached for the door handle, and the lilac scrubbed nurse unlocked it, Ollie said, "That's the wrong—"

But as the woman slumped down into the metal chair, she gazed up at Ollie with Mae's hazel eyes, familiar apart from the deep recesses of her purple eye sockets.

Ollie held in the gasp.

Mae's cheek bones bulged around her sunken face, her complexion blanched, her gaze listless. Black sutures yanked at the skin around her hairline, and stray hairs tangled with the jagged ties, crusted with black, dried blood. Her eyes wandered over Ollie with no sign of recognition, stuck between some state of dreaming and wakefulness.

"Twenty minutes," the nurse said firmly, and disappeared behind the heavy door.

"What are you doing here?" Mae's voice was low and hoarse.

What was Ollie doing here? It felt presumptuous, seeing her now, to insert themself.

"There's an empty bed down the hall. The one in my room is taken, but we could be neighbors if you move in."

"I came to visit you." The sentence came out with an uneven pitch.

"You know I kissed you in a dream." Mae's eyes twitched and wandered like a feral animal caught in a trap.

Ollie's heart tore, and they swallowed to keep from crying.

Mae leaned across the table. "Do you want to kiss me, Ollie? Is that why you do what you do?" It was a whisper, accusatory. And she was right. They did want to kiss her. But not like this.

Mae sat back, folded her arms. "Have you heard from Carter?" Her eyes were wide, bloodshot at their tips. "Did he send you to check on me?"

Ollie picked at the skin around their fingernails. "No, I— I just came. On my own."

Mae bounced her head and her eyes fixed on a spot outside the window.

"Come to spread more rumors then?" Her voice was sharp. "More lies?"

Ollie felt an uncomfortable twinge. "What?"

Mae exhaled a ragged breath, shook her head rapidly and sunk it between her hands. Her fingers dug into her tattered hair. "I just don't know," she whispered into her palms. "Just don't know anymore."

"Know what?" Ollie leaned down, hoping to entice Mae to meet their eye-line.

Mae released a staggered giggle and pulled her hands from her face. Her lips twisted into a smile. "You must think … "

"I think, I mean I heard, in town, that you were here. And I just, I wanted you to know that I'm still trying." Ollie felt the wave of pity building from low in their gut. Seeing Mae here, gaunt, frazzled, confused. It was almost too much.

"Oh yes, your little game of Clue." Mae spat. "How's that going by the way?" She strummed her uncut fingernails across the metal table. "Lemme give you a hint," she whispered. "It was my husband, with the rock, in the mausoleum." A double flick of her eyebrows and Mae descended into a giggle fit.

Ollie stroked their pants. It was a bad idea to come. They didn't know—they weren't qualified to—the words came up like vomit. "I came to tell you you were right, Mae. There is something up with Eva. The car she's driving, it's registered to Babineaux. Remember? The same guy who wrote that letter? The one to your dad?"

Mae's brows knitted together.

"You remember, don't you?"

Ollie watched Mae's irises follow a half circle on the ceiling. "Of course, I remember." She stood up. "If you take me home, I can show you. I wrote it down in my journal. It's just inside my nightstand. Just take me home and I'll show you." She moved toward the door, seemingly waiting for Ollie to rise and walk her out of Springbrook.

"I can't take you home, Mae." Ollie's heart sank as Mae gripped the doorknob. "I'm sorry."

Mae deflated but returned to her seat without argument.

"There's more too. I tried to tell you, but Carter, he found me in the yard. He chased me, threatened me. I thought he was gonna kill me."

Mae scoffed, "Who, Carter?" She shook her head dismissively. "He wouldn't—"

"He broke into my house. Threw all my shit around." Ollie heard their voice rising higher, tension building in their chest from Mae's incredulous expression. "He hid a signal jammer in the barn. Did you know about that? He's been cutting you off from the world. And you just said—"

"No." Mae's voice was an exhale, a denial pointed at no one in particular. "I get confused sometimes. And the weed, it … that's all."

Ollie dug their fingernails into their palms. "And now Captain Williams is missing. They're writing it off at the station, saying he must've taken an *overdue holiday*, but that's horseshit. The man hasn't missed a day of work since—he brags about it. Lost his marriage over it. There's just no way."

Mae's head stilled. For the first time on this visit, her eyes met Ollie's. "Captain Williams is missing?"

"Not officially, but yeah, he didn't show up for work. Didn't call in."

Mae's lips wrapped around her teeth. She took a long, deep breath in and huffed it out, all at once.

"Do you know something, Mae?"

Mae bounced her knee beneath the table, she dipped her head back into her hands.

"What is it?" Ollie leaned closer.

"Everything's just … it's all mixed up. I feel like I can't even tell anymore."

Ollie wrapped their hands around Mae's, guided them gently away from her face. "What can't you tell?" Their voice was soft.

Tears welled in Mae's eyes, overflowed her lids, streamed down her sunken cheeks. "What's real. What's not real. What's a fever. What's a dream."

Ollie wanted to leap across the table, encircle Mae in a smothering embrace. Smooth her hair. Kiss her face.

"Can you help me?" A flicker of hope appeared, and, for a moment, Mae resembled herself more closely.

"How?"

"I can tell you something, and you can tell me whether it's real or not real."

A dull scream snaked down the hall, dampened by layers upon layers of doors.

"There was a scream just now." Mae spoke quickly. "Real or not real?"

"Real." Ollie felt it too now, the rising hope.

"Eva and Carter, there's something between them. Real or not real?"

"Real," Ollie confirmed though they felt guilty shattering the illusion that it may not be. "I saw them kissing, remember?"

Mae nodded. "And there's something wrong with the house? Something inside?"

Ollie swallowed hard. "Just the water damage on the third floor."

"And Carter …" Mae's eyes filled with tears again, as if her last thread of hope rested on the coming words. "He's hurting me somehow, isn't he?" Her upper lip twisted and tears dripped onto the metal table. "And he doesn't love me, does he? Real or not—" Her voice cracked. The streams down Mae's face trickled onto her arms.

"Mae." Ollie waited as she wiped her arms on her pant legs. "Do you know something about Captain Williams?"

"It was just a dream." Mae nodded, her eyes vacant. "Just a bad dream."

Ollie held space for the silence. "You can't go back to the house. You can stay with me if you'd like, or I can help you get a motel room in town, but you can't go back home. It's not safe."

Mae shook her head. She wiped at her face and when her hands dropped to her sides, she cracked a defiant smile. "It's my house, Ollie. Don't be crazy."

Ollie noted the irony but didn't comment on it. "Carter is dangerous. You should've seen the way he—Mae he put you in here. I don't know exactly what he wants, but whatever it is … Look at you!" Ollie regretted their harsh tone and Mae sunk back into her chair.

"It's *my* house." Mae folded her arms.

The lilac nurse knocked on the window with the back of her fist. "Time's up," she said through the glass.

CHAPTER TWENTY-ONE

Mae shivered beneath the thin, polyester sheet, the fluorescent bulbs blaring overhead even in the dark, early morning hours. Jolene mumbled in her sleep from the twin bed opposite hers. Mae could face the bulb or the corner. She avoided the corner, choosing instead to allow the cruel light to pulse at her sockets, leaving blue trails in its wake. Even through her closed lids, the white beams penetrated, stealing sleep, denying rest. She faced it until she couldn't anymore, when the pounding in her head made her turn to the dark corner. Willing her lids to remain shut, she told herself, *it isn't real. Just a trick of your imagination.*

But inevitably, curiosity would drive her to crack open her right eye. She'd inspect the corner, hoping each time that her logical mind would be ratified. That she would see only white walls and white ceiling staring back at her. But this time, as every time, it started with a dark swirl where the wall met the ceiling in a neat line. Bottomless, it seemed, the blackest black. A tiny shadow at first, barely noticeable, but it stretched out, as it always did, swallowing light and growing further as it gained power. The black would encompass the corner, the hole growing deeper. And Mae could do nothing but watch as it ate another ceiling tile, swirling outward. Mae thought if she threw herself into it, her whole body into the spinning void, she might land somewhere unknown, somewhere unlike this hospital, somewhere, perhaps, far worse. This fear kept her prisoner in her metal bed, like some small vermin stuck in a trap, until the sun broke through the barred window and nurse Angela appeared to collect her for breakfast.

All the food was soft. A fluffy biscuit, a scoop of grits, a banana. Mae scooped grainy mush and let it drip in chunks from her spoon. Muted voices leaked through the glass wall separating the lunchroom from the hallway, where a line of patients collected their meds in disposable white cups. To Mae, they looked like condiment cups; and on the first day she half expected the black-haired nurse with the glass eye to fill it with a squirt of ketchup.

She didn't though.

She filled it with pills. Unmarked, unwanted pills.

The second cup was full of water. First cup. Second cup. *Open up.* There was a vulgarity to the ritual, opening her mouth wide to be inspected. Moving her tongue this way and that to assure the nursing staff she wasn't smuggling meds or skipping her dose.

After breakfast and pills came group, just in time for the haze to settle. Mae experienced the day, from that point forward, as though within a fishbowl. The feelings didn't feel quite so feeling. The smells and tastes didn't smell or taste quite so much. And though the void would appear in this corner or on that ceiling, she found it easier to ignore.

"Group time!" Nurse Angela's voice was an octave too high.

One by one, patients rose from the long cafeteria tables, discarded their cardboard trays in plastic trash receptacles, and filed into the group room. Mae avoided Patrick, the red head who mumbled to himself and shot daggered looks in her direction. She took a seat beside Jolene, whose bandaged wrists sported brown, linear stains. "Good morning, Jolene."

Jolene tucked her head down, a tiny acknowledgment, but said nothing. Beside Jolene sat a young boy, barely old enough to be in this place. His dark skin was sallow, eyes sunken like he too had forgotten the feeling of a good night's rest. "When's phone time?" he asked nurse Angela.

"Roderick, we've talked about this, haven't we?" Angela raised her brows and her lips curled into a kind smile.

"Yes ma'am," he nodded.

"Phone time's after lunch." She looked around the circle to make sure everyone heard. "You will all get your fifteen minutes of phone time after lunch. That's the schedule."

Four heads nodded in chairs.

"After lunch," the elderly woman in the plush pink bathrobe repeated. "Fifteen minutes, after lunch."

"That's right, Carol."

The mauve plastic chairs were the same ones Mae remembered from high school. Shiny metal legs and cold metal bolts that chilled through her clothes. Less so, now that she had her regular clothes back. She pulled her long sleeves over her hands.

"Today's group is life skills," Angela started.

"Life skills!" Carol chirped. "Every day's life skills." She gave Angela a wide toothy smile.

"That's right, Carol. And in today's life skills group, we're going to discuss our living spaces. How do we make them a calm, clean place? A place we want to be."

"I clean every Sunday and Thursday," Carol offered. "Sunday is for vacuuming and Thursday is for Wiggins's cage."

"Wonderful, Carol. Thanks for starting us off. And who's Wiggins?"

Carol toyed with the collar of her robe, rolling the fabric between her fingers. "Oh, he's my best man. African gray parrot. The smartest bird in the world, you know."

"How do you know?" Roderick asked, his eyes narrow.

Carol tugged at the hem of her robe. "Well," she huffed, curling a wisp of ashy hair behind her ear, "it's science."

Roderick chuckled. "Bird science."

Angela halted the conversation with extended palms. "Thank you for sharing, Carol. Who else would like to share how they keep up a clean home environment?"

"My mom cleans," Roderick offered. "Can I call her soon?" His brows raised, hopeful.

"Just after lunch, Roderick. Is there anything you do to help?"

He sat back in his chair. "After my shower I hang up my towel on the rack. So it doesn't get germs."

"Very good, thank you." She turned her attention. "Jolene, what kinds of things do you do?"

Jolene stared at her stained, white tennis shoes. She angled her toes together, then angled them apart.

"Do you live alone?" Angela leaned closer, softened her tone.

Jolene stepped on the toe of her left shoe with her right.

Angela sat back. "Perhaps tomorrow you'll feel ready to share in group."

Mae's muscles tightened. She was next.

"And Mae, how about you?"

Images of Eva flashed through her mind, cleaning and cooking in her tank tops and leggings, her hair draping around her curvaceous frame. She grabbed at the sides of the chair, squeezed the hard plastic. "We've got Eva, she's our cleaning lady."

"Well, that sounds nice. I wouldn't mind having a cleaning person if we could afford it." Angela looked to the other group members who smiled and nodded their heads. "So how do you spend your time, Mae? Are you working? Are you in school?"

Mae felt her cheeks flush. "Not yet, but I'm going to go back."

Angela nodded affirmation. "I'm sure you will, dear. And tomorrow's group will be about finding employment, so maybe we can talk more about what you'd like to do then. Sound good?"

Mae forced a smile. Why hadn't she been working? Or going to school? Could she not even clean her own house or cook her own meals?

"I was a secretary for thirty-four years," Carol said, a smug grin curling her lips.

Jolene's icy stare made her slide back in her seat.

"My mom was a secretary. Gingam and Gingam Attorneys at Law, 1-877-645-5300." Roderick said. "Can I call her?"

Angela smiled. "Soon." Beside her was a stack of colored paper and a clear bin of crayons, which she handed to Carol. "Take one and pass it, please."

Carol flipped to the middle of the stack and selected a coral-colored page before passing the heavy stock to Jolene. Jolene pulled the blue paper from the top and handed the rest to Roderick who fanned them out onto the floor. His hand hovered over each color, and he mouthed words to himself, placing his fingers on the red sheet as if to grab it before changing his mind.

"Any color will do," Angela chimed in.

Roderick's eyes went beady, and he snatched up a yellow page, pushing the rest into a haphazard pile. Mae reached for the closest paper, a green one, but Roderick spied her hand and snatched it away before she could grab it, shoving it into his armpit. Angela placed the bin of crayons in the center of the circle and removed the lid. She handed Mae a purple paper as Jolene picked up a fistful of crayons and began drawing swirls.

"I'll give instructions in just a moment," Angela said, but Jolene's crayons continued in spirals.

The group room door was thrown open by Patrick who entered with a grimace that flashed his missing tooth.

"Welcome Patrick," Angela said, crossing her legs. "Grab a paper and some crayons, you're just in time."

He sulked across the tile with dramatic, heavy steps and collapsed in a lump just outside the circle.

"I want you each to draw yourself as a house. If you're feeling moody, maybe there are no windows or they are covered with shutters or heavy curtains. If you're carrying secrets, maybe there is a basement with a big lock on the door. Think about whether you're a big house with lots of room to move around, or if you're small and cramped and claustrophobic."

Mae looked around the group, her eyes falling on Jolene who pressed hard against the page, tearing a hole in the paper with the tip of her indigo crayon. She selected a few crayons without looking before Patrick snatched the bin and pulled it between his sprawled legs. He chose a black crayon with a dull tip and snapped it in half. Mae stared into her purple paper, heard him rummage through the bin, then snap another crayon.

The blank page stared at her.

If I was a house …

Mae thought about the tin can trailer, its porthole windows and thin walls.

Snap. Patrick's eyes bored holes.

Mae shut hers, pictured the shadowy Victorian, imposing, opulence in decay.

Snap.

Her lids flipped open, met by Patrick's cold blue stare. Her eyes darted to Angela. Immersed in helping Roderick form straight lines for his house, she didn't see the threatening gestures. Mae looked around the circle for help. Jolene folded her paper into a tiny triangle. Carol outlined her parrot. No one else saw when Patrick held two crayons up to his lips, made steady eye contact with Mae, placed them between his front teeth, and *SNAP.*

Rising anger, white hot, flamed up, poured from Mae's throat in a sharp, "Stop it!" The sound of crayons on paper stopped, all eyes drifting to Mae, who stood, but didn't remember standing. In her clenched fist was her paper, crumpled, its toothy edges digging into her palms. Patrick spit the broken bits of crayon onto the tile, his front tooth stained apricot.

Two male orderlies in mint scrubs rushed in from the hall, looking to Angela with furrowed brows.

"Mae?" Angela's tone was sweet.

Embarrassment pushed anger aside as Mae eyed the male orderlies. "I'm sorry," she said in a whisper. She wondered whether those padded rooms people joked about were real, and whether she'd find out for herself very soon.

"Why don't you go lie down."

The orderlies approached, one tall and heavy-set, his thick curls of body hair protruding from his scrubs, and the other short and lanky, his sparse hair combed over to conceal his bald spot. The too-much-hair orderly took Mae by the arm while the too-little-hair orderly held the door.

Mae matched their pace, hoping her obvious lack of resistance would show that she didn't need restraints. She was happy to cooperate. She sighed in relief when they steered her to her room. The nurse from the med line entered in her lilac scrubs; she held a small cup, two pills rattling around inside.

"These'll help you relax."

Mae took the cup, eyed the large white pills, and the nurse offered another small cup, this one full of water. One for pills. One for water. The pills grabbed at Mae's throat on the way down, and she had to swallow and swallow again to keep them from lodging in her throat. Left alone, Mae looked out the window at the naked woods. Gnarled and twisted trees stood bare, having dropped their leaves early. Exhaustion took hold, and Mae meant only to rest her eyes, but was awoken what felt like hours later when Jolene entered the room.

Mae sat up, wiped the sleep away. "Hello, Jolene." It was polite to greet her, even though she never responded.

Jolene faced Mae on her bunk. Her face scrunched up like she was thinking hard.

"What's up, Jolene?" Mae shifted her weight, crinkling the plastic mattress. Jolene had never paid her any attention before.

"You shouldn't have done that," she said. Her eyes were cold, distant. Mae saw the reflection of the naked trees in her dark irises, almost black in this light. Her heart drummed. Were Jolene and Patrick friends? She'd never seen them speaking. If Jolene launched herself at Mae now, would the orderlies come in before she could do any real damage?

"I—I didn't mean to yell at Patrick, he's just always staring at me and—"

"Not that." Jolene rolled her eyes.

The break in eye contact eased the tension and Mae felt her shoulders relax. "What then?"

Jolene glanced down at the picture from group clasped in her right hand, bold swirls in chaotic patterns from crayons pressed so hard the wax was smooth on the page. "Apologize. You should never apologize." She clawed at the drawing with her fingernail 'til wax collected like an ice cream scoop beneath it. "Trample them, like they would you. All men. Fuck 'em."

CHAPTER TWENTY-TWO

The Jenkins family lived in a stone craftsman, walking distance from Earle Elementary School. Ollie teetered on a curb amongst a swarm of children, uniformed and buzzing with end of school day energy. They felt a little silly waiting for the crossing guard, her orange vest over her stout form, shiny whistle at the ready between her teeth, but the cold look she shot Ollie when they hovered a foot onto the street before her signal meant Ollie had to cross with the kids. Sticky hands circled like sharks.

"Do it! Do it! You won't do it!" a ginger-haired boy goaded a demure girl in tiny pigtails.

She stuck out her tongue at him. Hard.

Sick burn.

He scowled and sucked his teeth.

The whistle rang out, cuing the flock of children to toddle through the crossing. Ollie stutter-stepped between their zigzagging paths, disoriented by their cacophony of high voices. *I'm never having kids. But I'd make a killer auntie.*

Disentangling themself from the herd, Ollie slipped behind the Jenkins's metal gate and closed it behind them with a clang. The stone path was bordered by evergreen ferns, defiantly vibrant against the sepia tones of autumn. From inside, Yorkie Jenkins was already yapping. Ollie knocked on the freshly painted purple door using the old school brass knocker.

Nice choice, Jenkins.

The Yorkie's barking crescendoed, and Ollie heard it carried away, probably locked in a guest room. Brian opened the door.

"Hey Willy Wonka. You gonna invite me inside your chocolate factory?" Ollie's eyes darted to the purple paint.

"You're a dick. You know that?" He gestured for Ollie to come inside, where baking cinnamon rolls wafted a sugary scent into the living room.

"Where's your brood?" Ollie asked, sinking into the deep couch cushions.

As if on cue, a child's wail echoed down the stairs.

"Jasper! Leave your brother alone!" Brian yelled back. He paused, listened for another yelp, and when one didn't come, curled his lips into a smug smile. "So, what brings you to casa de la Jenkins?"

Ollie leaned forward, resting their elbows on their knees. "I saw Mae."

Brian let out a heavy sigh. "And? How's she doing? I felt awful having to cuff her." He shook his head. "Shitty policy."

"Not great … Looks like she hasn't slept in days. Confused."

Brian nodded. "Yup, that's about how she looked when I brought her in."

"And that gash on her forehead. What's that about?"

Brian's fingers strummed his jeans. "I really shouldn't get into the details of it with you."

"Come on, Jenkins."

Brian pursed his lips. "Ugh, fine. Her husband said she was all riled up. He found her running through the cemetery in the rain, ran smack into the old mausoleum if you must know."

"She said—"

"She was a mess, Ollie." He drew his lips tight around his teeth. "Talking all kinds of crazy stuff when I got there."

Ollie leaned further forward. "Crazy like what?"

"You know, just nonsense. Saying he was gonna kill her, that she'd seen a body in the yard. We checked. Obviously. Nothing there, just a pile of brush."

"A body?" Ollie's brows knitted together.

"Yeah, and get a load of this, not just any body. She said it was Captain Williams. Dead. In her yard."

"Get the fuck out of here." Rising nervous energy made Ollie stand. They paced circles over the patterned area rug.

"It's all just paranoia, Ollie. She's sick. We touched base with Doctor Levine. He's gonna keep an eye on her while she's there, make sure she's stable before she comes home."

Ollie stopped. "What if it's not all paranoia, Brian? He didn't show for work, right?"

Brian shook his head, but Ollie went on. "I mean, you've known him how many years? Has he *ever* skipped out on a shift?"

Brian threw up defensive hands. "I mean, no, but he was burned out. Pressure coming down on him from all sides. He was long overdue for a vacation, been talking about heading to Mexico for ages now."

Ollie kneeled in front of Brian, forcing him to make eye contact.

"None of it's right Brian. The signal jammer, vandalizing my house *right after*. He threatened me! Plain as day. And then Captain Williams finally agrees to look into the case, and he's gone. Tell me you don't think that's normal. Come on!"

Brian's eyes wandered the room. "He's fine, Ollie. Give it a few days, you'll see." His eyes perked up. "But there is something else that will interest you. Steph!" he yelled. "Come down, Ollie's here."

Jarred by the invitation, Ollie took uneasy steps back to their spot on the couch. Stephanie jogged down the stairs, her pajama pants whooshing with her quick movements, her fingers interlaced in her hair. "They're monsters," she whispered to her husband, deadpan. "Monsters."

Brian chuckled. "I know, honey."

"Ollie, hey," she moved into the kitchen, and Ollie watched from the living room as she removed steaming cinnamon buns from the oven with a mitted hand. "Just another day in paradise," she said, rolling her eyes. After placing the hot pan on the stove to cool, she moved into the living room and collapsed into a loveseat. "Don't have kids, Ollie."

On her chest was smeared blue paint and her black hair fell around her shoulders in tangled clumps.

"I wasn't planning to." Ollie smiled.

"What was it you were telling me a few weeks back about the guy we saw over at Sigal, Carter Duvall?"

"Hah! Carter. Right." Steph's eyes bulged in mockery. "I recognized him. Detective asshole over here doesn't believe me," she said, glancing suspiciously at her husband, who smirked in return. "But I remember him. He had a B name. Bradly or something."

A shot of excitement jolted Ollie upright. "Brooks?" they asked, louder than they intended.

"Shit, yeah! Brooks. I ran into him one night at Louie's right before last call. He was even hotter back then, if you can believe it. Geesh, must've been a decade back."

Brian's face contorted in horror.

"Relax honey, it was before we met. You are also *unbelievably* hot." She winked in Ollie's direction.

Brian pursed his lips. "He must've been a real smoke show for you to remember him all these years later."

"No," she corrected. "I mean, he was," another wink, "but that's not why I remember. He bought me a drink, maybe thirty minutes before closing. And I thought it was a last ditch effort on his part, not wanting to go home alone and all, but I was willing to overlook it considering—"

"He was massively hot. Jesus, we get it." Brian rolled his eyes.

"Exactly. So anyway, I was sipping the drink, he was just starting to chat me up, you know, *what do you do* and the like, when some guy walked in and caught his eye. Next thing I know, he's left me at the bar and he's arguing with this dude. It was getting heated. First time I'd ever been blown off for some guy." She blew Brian a kiss. "First and last."

"Do you remember what they were arguing about?" Ollie sat at the edge of the sofa cushion, hanging on every detail.

"Nah, I was annoyed, and I didn't want to stick around for the brawl. I ducked out the back and went home. But I did look for him after that. Never saw him again, until recently."

"Well fuck." Ollie glared at Brian. "You didn't think to put this together? Some freaking detective."

"Okay, okay!" Brian raised his palms in defense. "I'm getting it from all sides here!"

"I mean, come on, dude. The letter, the car, and nothing? Nada?"

"Geez! I get it. Okay, so what? So you think Carter is actually this other guy? Brooks?"

"Brooks Babineaux. The same Brooks Babineaux who was writing to Mae's dad right before he died. No way that's a coincidence."

Brian sighed in concession. "Yeah, I suppose you're right."

Stephanie dug paint chips from beneath her nails.

"So, what now?" Ollie bounced their foot on the carpet. "I mean, I'd love to get all this info to Williams, but he's MIA." Their eyes wandered over to Brian. "I don't suppose you would be willing to look into Babineaux a bit more? Considering Williams agreed to reopen the case?"

Brian twiddled his thumbs.

"Come on, honey," Stephanie urged. "Don't be a—"

"Steph! I asked you not to call me that again."

She cracked a smile. "You're right sweetie. I'm sorry."

"Ugh, fine, Ollie." He shook his head. "I'll look into him. But I swear, if I catch shit for this from the Captain ..."

CHAPTER TWENTY-THREE

Days later, Ollie paced the sidewalk in front of Captain Williams' home, checking their phone at regular intervals.

"Jesus, Brian, come on," they muttered to themself.

Anxiety gnawed at their insides, and their eyes darted around at every barking dog, the whir of each car. The bungalow looked quiet, and a rolled newspaper sat on the porch, drenched by the night's rain. Ollie took a step to approach the door, but a stabbing dread made them hesitate, step back onto the sidewalk. Brian's Crown Victoria pulled onto the grassy swale beside Williams's property.

"About time," Ollie grumbled.

Brian hopped out of the car and jogged up to meet Ollie. "Sorry, sorry, I know I'm late, but it was worth it."

With Brian at their side, Ollie strode up to the light blue door with confidence.

"I guess we knock first, right?" Ollie held their balled fist upright. Brian shrugged. Three light knocks, libel to scare away a lizard but do little more.

"You're gonna have to do better than that."

Ollie turned their wrist and banged thrice more. "Williams!"

Brian peered through the window, cupping his hands around his eyes.

"Anything?"

Brian shook his head. "Come on."

Ollie followed Brian around the side yard. Unruly hedges reached into the narrow walking path, scraping the stucco and creaking on the window's glass. "So, what'd you find?"

They peeked into a bedroom window veiled by a sheer maroon curtain. Nothing.

"Well." They continued around to the back of the house. "Turns out Brooks Babineaux has a longstanding interest in old things." He knocked on the backdoor. "Captain?" he yelled.

Ollie slumped into a plastic patio chair. "He's not here."

"Let's just sit a while. Can't hurt."

Ollie nodded, eyes trained on the ground. "So, what'd you find?"

Brian pulled another chair beside them and sat down. "Well, turns out Brooks was raised up in the antique business. His father owned a small shop in Tennessee and, get this, made money on the side authenticating rare instruments."

"Get the fuck out."

"I will not. And there's more. Brooks inherited the shop when papa dukes died in 2003, but from his record, he was more interested in the money to be made than the love of antiquity."

"What kind of record?" Ollie slid to the edge of the chair. "Break-ins? Assault?"

Brian raised a palm. "Not quite. A little more small time. He got busted for forgery, tried to pass off a guitar as some super rare make. A Torres? Something like that. Got a slap on the wrist, but it must've been enough to ruin the shop's reputation because he sold it for next to nothing a year later."

Ollie sank back in the chair.

"Okay, so musical instrument, but forgery? Not really in the same league as murder."

"Would you let me finish?"

Ollie smirked.

"From 2004 to 2009 there wasn't much on him, but he must've still been at it because in 2009 he gets busted again for forgery, and this time he's got an additional charge for selling stolen property."

"The murder was 2008."

"Ollie, do you want to hear everything or not?"

"Yeah, yeah, okay, out with it."

"So get this. In 2009 he gets slammed with eighteen months on the forgery charge and eight years on the distribution of stolen property charge. And then in 2010, I find a marriage record."

"What?" Ollie sat up straight.

"That's right. Brooks Babineaux is a married man, goin' on a decade."

"No shit. And his wife?"

Brian's face relaxed into a smug grin. "Ivy Babineaux. And here's the thing." He pulled his phone out and tinkered with it, then faced the screen toward Ollie. "Quick social media search and I found her. She look familiar to you?"

Ollie's eyes sank immediately into her ample cleavage, her blonde locks spilling on either side of her chest. Shot from an upward angle, her emerald eyes glittered center-frame. "Eva." The words escaped their lips in a whisper.

"Turns out we pinned the wrong woman as the mistress."

Ollie clutched the phone, pulling it from Brian's hands to examine the photo more closely. It was unmistakable. Eva—No, Ivy stared back at them.

"Well this …" Ollie shook their head as the information sank in. "This changes things."

Brian took his phone back and tucked it away. "Sure does. Brooks has got a pair on him, eh? Bringing his wife and his fake wife to the same house." His expression suggested he might have been impressed. "Can you imagine?"

"Truly, I can't." Ollie shook their head. "What's this mean for our case?"

"For *my* case, it means that I need to have a talk with Ivy. If she married the guy in 2010, it's possible she knows something about the 2008 murder, *if*, and it's still an *if*, Brooks was involved."

Ollie scoffed. "If! Jenkins, he was an antique dealer. He got pinched trying to sell a fake rare instrument. How many rare instrument dealers do you know?"

Brian raised his lids, conceding Ollie's point.

"I wish Williams would get back from his little adventure already. He'd be a big help on this." Brian rose from the chair and pressed his face against the glass window in the back door. "Shit."

Ollie jumped up. "What is it?"

Brian waved them over. "Look at this."

Ollie pressed their face to the glass beside Brian's. Through the water stains and dust, they could make out the pine kitchen table. On it rested a ceramic napkin holder, salt and pepper shakers shaped like roosters, and a brown leather wallet.

Ollie's heart dropped into their shoes. They backed away from the door. "I fuckin told you, Jenkins. He's not on vacation. Something's happened to him. And if Mae's not as crazy as Doctor Levine thinks, he might be—" The word stuck in Ollie's throat. "Dead."

Brian dialed a number. "Ruthers, it's me. I'm at the Captain's residence and we've got a problem. We need to put out an APB on his vehicle …"

Ollie stumbled back into the chair.

Flashes of the ridealong streamed stop-motion through their mind. They were seventeen, bags not even unpacked in the new place. Williams was there. Bought them a coffee while he drank his after-shift beer.

"… file the missing person's report, get search teams ready, volunteers, the force, anyone who can help …"

They were eighteen. Rent was late. Only one job in town. Williams explained the ratios for mixing mortar.

"… Something's not right."

They were nineteen. Williams lugged his toolset up the stairs, helped Ollie carry out the busted water heater.

Brian ended the call, his jaw hanging slightly open. "Let's not jump to conclusions. You know how he was, running off and leaving things when he was caught up in the moment. He still might be—"

"On vacation? Without his wallet? Get real!"

"I know." He clenched and unclenched his fists. "I know."

"We should go in." Ollie made for the door, but Brian stopped them.

"We can't. In case … in case anything did happen, we need to follow procedure."

"We know what happened." Ollie's clenched jaw threatened to crack their molars. "Carter Duvall."

"We don't know that."

"Like hell we don't!"

"Evid—"

"Ivy's gotta know something. She's part of whatever's going on over there."

Brian nodded, head bouncing over the untamed rose bushes. "It's worth a shot."

Brian positioned the Crown Victoria so they could peer through its tinted windows. Eva's Lincoln rested in the same spot it had when Ollie saw the bruise. The bruise was a sign. Things were not well between them, and Jenkins agreed there was a chance. If they could get to her before Carter, she just might flip. She just might have had enough.

Beneath the *Extended Stay* sign, a figure approached.

"He beat us here."

Brian and Ollie watched him, arms overflowing with what must've been two dozen red roses, as he crossed the motel parking lot. He wore a blazer and fitted slacks, navy blue that made his jet-black hair shine darker.

"What do we do?"

Brian watched Carter step through the automatic glass doors.

"I guess we hope she doesn't accept his apology."

Ollie sank back into the seat and let a guttural sigh escape their lips. "Shit. Ten minutes earlier and we would've had her. I know it."

Brian turned the key in the ignition.

"Wait, that's it?"

His hand hovered over the gear shift. "You want to try to convince her to help us out with him standing right there?"

Ollie opened the passenger side door.

"What are you doing?"

They stepped out and ducked down to see Brian through the open window. "Just chill here a minute. I want to try to hear what they're saying. Maybe they'll give something away."

Brian killed the engine and reached for his door handle, but Ollie was already taking long strides toward the motel lobby.

"Goddammit, Ollie," Brian said, a harsh whisper through gritted teeth.

"Gimme ten minutes!"

Ollie's steps were quiet on the shallow, red carpet runner that lined the entryway. The bored attendant flipped through their phone from behind the desk and didn't bother to look up as the automatic doors swooshed shut behind them. Two long hallways stood empty on either side of Ollie, left and right. Hoping for a lucky guess, Ollie turned right and headed down the hall. A dying fluorescent light strobed from above, intermittently illuminating the mint green carpet, dingy from years of dirt squished between the fibers.

Gold and beige patterned wallpaper lined the walls in horizontal stripes. Ollie slowed as they neared the end of the hall. There was only one way to turn, left, but Ollie stopped before rounding the corner.

"Come on," said a muffled voice.

Ollie froze. It had to be him, just out of sight. They leaned against the wall.

Bang, bang, bang. His fist crashed against the door.

A creak sounded.

"These are for you."

Ollie imagined him holding out the bundle of flowers, red as her beaten face.

"I told you, I'm done." It was Eva, Ivy. No question.

"Come on, baby. It was a rough night, and I told you I'm sorry. But you know this is all for you. It's for us!"

Ollie couldn't help but sneak a lightning fast glance around the corner. Carter leaned against the wall, his body tilting inward toward the open door. They couldn't see Eva from their spot, but no doubt she stood in the doorway, just out of view.

"You're not even gonna take the flowers I got you?"

A small rustling told Ollie she did.

"Please just go." Her voice wavered.

"I can't go. I love you, you know that. It's always been us. Nobody's been there for me like you have."

Ollie rolled their eyes hard.

"It's getting too crazy, babe. This isn't what I signed up for."

Ollie startled at the sound of Carter's palm smacking against the wall.

"Signed up for?" Carter growled.

"You know what I mean."

Ollie wanted to jump from around the corner, to yell, *You gonna let him talk to you that way?* But they restrained themself.

"I really just don't understand you, Ivy. You say you want a home of our own, a place to settle down, some kids one day. And I try to make that happen for us, but it's not good enough for you. Because it's not *exactly* the way you want it." He let out an exasperated breath.

"It's not that." Her voice was soft.

"Not everything in life is gonna come on your timeline."

"All I do is wait for you!"

"Lower your voice."

"No, I waited while you were locked up, I waited for you to seduce another woman, I'm sick of waiting!" Her voice was high and cracked. Ollie was sure her eyes were filling with tears.

"You sound like a child," Carter said.

Plastic crinkled and a soft thud made Ollie sneak another peak. Roses littered the floor, petals spread out along the hall.

"It won't be much longer," he conceded.

"When?"

"Soon."

"No, when, Brooks? When are you gonna make her sign?"

"Tomorrow."

"Pfft. Why not today? I'm always waiting. I swear, you've got no problem at all making me wait, but for her everything's gotta be the perfect timing."

"Fine. Today!"

Today?

"You mean it?"

"For you, I'll do it today. We've got another ... two hours for visiting hours. I'll get it done. I know it's not what we hoped for, but we'll get the house on the market, and before you know it, we'll be settled into our own place, working on putting a bun in your oven."

Ollie imagined the smile. They'd seen this smile before on women's faces. The placated smile from a man telling his wife what she so desperately wants to hear. A man lying.

"Now, grab your shit, you're coming back to the house with me. Might as well enjoy our last bit of time there together."

"Ugh, do I have to? Just come in here. That place gives me the creeps."

Ollie heard the door shut and the electronic lock twist. They peered around the corner at the rose massacre and spun on their heels, taking long paces through the narrow hallway. The lobby attendant still stared into her phone and Ollie cleared the automatic doors and crossed the lot to find Brian waiting. "Well?" he asked, shifting his weight.

"They made up, doubt she'll talk to us now."

"Shit." Brian sprung the engine to life and put the car in reverse, spinning his head around to see behind him.

"There was something though."

As the car rolled backward, Brian shot a probing glance.

"They mentioned something about getting something signed and putting the house on the market. What do you think that's about?"

"They must want to sell the Victorian; guess they need Mae to sign off on it since she's the owner."

"He said he was gonna make her sign it today. You think we can beat him there?"

Brian eased the car into drive and let it roll up to the stop sign. A line of cars whooshed passed. "No sense trying to race him. Selling a house takes time. Whatever he wants her to sign, I'm sure it's just the first step of the process."

Ollie's eyes bounced over the passing cars. "You really think that's all it is?"

Brian shrugged. "What else could it be?"

Ollie twiddled a stray fiber on their cargo shorts. "I dunno, it doesn't sit right with me."

The car lunged forward, screeching into a small gap in traffic. "Anyway, I don't have time. Gotta get up with my unit, or did you forget about Williams? The search is a little more pressing at the moment."

Ollie's guts twinged. *The search.* "It started this morning, right?"

"Yeah. They started with his usual haunts, trying to figure out his last whereabouts before he went off the grid."

"And his phone?"
"Tried tracking it but it's off."
"You'll—"
"Yes, I'll keep you updated."

CHAPTER TWENTY-FOUR

Carter dressed too smartly for a psych ward. It set Mae's teeth on edge. Blurry shadows still lingered just outside of her vision, but she ignored them now, understanding the more she mentioned them, the longer she'd have to stay. It wasn't the same visiting room she'd sat in with Ollie, but it might as well have been. Four walls. Hard metal table. Metal threads woven through the glass window. He slid a briefcase, worn brown leather, onto the table between them. His nose crinkled. No doubt he smelled that signature scent, too clean. Clean with secrets. "How are you, babe?" His voice was stiff, the hint of a bad accent, like something he was putting on. Had it always been there?

Mae glanced left and right, let her shoulders rise and fall with a coy smile.

"You look …" He cleared his throat. "Dr. Levine said he spoke with you yesterday."

Mae wrapped a curly wisp of hair around her finger, twisted it beside her ear. "Yesterday, the day before that, and the day before that."

Carter folded one leg over the other. "He said you were more lucid."

Mae disappeared momentarily behind a long blink. *Lucid.* She opened her eyes and forced her teeth to show.

"Great. Did he say when I could come back home?"

"Well, he and I share some concerns." Carter ran his palm over the briefcase.

"Concerns?"

Outside the window Roderick whined, "She didn't answer, just one more time!"

Carter was distracted by the interaction, and Mae turned her head to see an orderly take him forcefully by the arm, leading him away from the landline phone at the nurses' station and toward his room, out of view.

"What concerns?" she pressed.

"Well, he mentioned the inherited account." Carter's mouth twisted into a passing sneer, but he kept talking as if he wanted to mask it. "And he and I are both worried that, with your current … *state*, you may struggle to manage things financially."

The muscles across Mae's abdomen tightened. A black void swirled in her periphery. She rubbed her eyes. "What are you saying?"

The snap closures of the briefcase clicked, and when she opened her eyes, the briefcase was open, revealing a manilla folder inside, thick with papers. Carter grabbed the stack and laid it on the table. He whipped open the folder, pushing a wave of chilled air onto Mae and thumbed through the top few pages.

"Just for now, Mae-by, I think, no I know, I will feel more comfortable if you let me handle the finances. You should be focusing on your health. We've got Eva to take care of the house, I'll make sure the bills are paid, and you can just take all the time you need to heal." Carter slid the paper across the table and spun it around so Mae could read.

South Carolina Durable Power of Attorney.

A sharp pain radiated through her chest.

"Why would you need this? We've been paying the bills just fine all this time."

Carter shook his head and blew a hard breath out. "Mae, *I've* been paying all the bills. And if you can't see why you're not the best person to manage money right now, well, I'm just not sure what to tell you. Maybe the meds haven't really kicked in yet." He reached across the table and started to pull the paperwork back toward himself, but Mae stopped him.

"I just—I don't understand."

Carter grasped her hand in his. "I'm sure this is hard to hear. It's hard for me to admit." His eyes sparkled even in the harsh light. "I thought I could keep us afloat with just my income, but it's been a struggle. I'm doing my best, but we're falling behind. I didn't want to add more stress on you by telling you, but if we're not careful with the money in that account … We're a team, right?"

A team.

"We don't need paperwork for this. I'll be careful with the money."

Mae thought she saw Carter's face tighten again. Had she seen it?

He sighed from deep in his chest. "I should've known better than to ask this way. It's clear you're unable to understand the depth of your illness." He pulled the papers back toward himself and shut them in his briefcase. "Dr. Levine warned me this might be the case."

Mae's veins flooded hot.

Carter rose from his chair.

"That what might be the case?" Mae rose too, standing in front of Carter as he moved to the door.

"You're not in any shape to be making decisions. I was hoping I wouldn't have to but …" His eyes drifted over the floor.

"But what?" Mae heard her voice becoming desperate.

"A Power of Attorney might not be the solution after all. Maybe it's guardianship we need."

"Guardianship?"

Carter pushed past her to the door and grabbed the handle, but then his pace slowed, and he turned slowly to face her. In a calm, even tone, he explained. "Well, Mae, a power of attorney only covers financial matters, but guardianship, on the other hand, would give me the ability to *truly* care for you. I could make sure you see the right doctors, take the right medication, and would be able to ensure that you always have an appropriate place to live." A smile moved across his face, sent chills through Mae's body.

Surely he can't …

"Dr. Levine said it might be the case. I didn't want to go there, but it's obvious to me that we've got no other choice."

Mae felt her knees sway, and she slumped back into her seat before they could buckle. Nurse Angela noticed Carter waiting at the window and led him away. The buzzing of electronic locks and the clinking of metal on metal as they opened and closed grew distant as the possibility whirled around in Mae's mind. *He can't do that. Right?* She rubbed at her temples. *There's no way he could prove …*

Mae remembered how Dr. Levine looked at her, like a scientific anomaly. And now Carter, with the same vacant stare, threatened to strip her of her freedom, her bodily autonomy, under the guise of caring. Her heart beat against her chest cavity.

"Time to go back to your room, sweetie."

Mae jumped at the sound but settled when she saw it was just nurse Angela. Her red, wiry curls threatened to escape her messy bun, and her mint scrubs were complimented by protruding long sleeves covered with cartoon animals.

She followed Angela down the hallway. "When do I see Dr. Levine again?" she asked as they approached her door.

"Gosh, I'm not sure." She furrowed her brow. "Can't remember if he's here this evening or if it's the ARNP. How about you lay down. I'll find out and I'll get back to you." She smiled and left before Mae could answer.

Jolene was in bed fiddling with her bandage.

"Hey Jolene," Mae said as she passed. But Jolene didn't answer. She hadn't spoken again since her big pronouncement.

The metal bed frame creaked as Mae sat, and she was struck with a sudden urge to call Auntie Bel. What would she think about all this? Laugh, most likely. *How the tables have turned, Mae! You abandoned me to get a taste of freedom, just to be deemed insane and have ALL your freedom taken away. Hah! Maybe you never had much potential after all.* Still, the sanitized room made Mae long for human connection. So, against her better judgment, she wandered into the nurses' station.

Roderick paced loops with the phone by his ear, mumbling into the receiver. A nurse Mae didn't recognize, with coral scrubs and warm, glowy skin sat behind the counter.

"Can I help you?" she asked.

Mae hadn't asked to make any phone calls since she'd been there. She wasn't sure of the process. "I was wondering if I could use the phone. After Roderick is done, of course."

The nurse's lips, painted a rich magenta, parted, exposing a wide smile. "Of course, sweetie. No need to wait." Her rolling chair slid away from the desk, and she hopped up and let Mae behind the counter. "You can use this one here."

A beige landline phone with a curly cord sat beside her. Mae spied her name tag, Brianne.

"Let me grab you a chair."

Brianne slid a mauve plastic chair, like those in the group room, over next to her, and Mae happily took a seat.

"Do you know the number?"

Mae nodded.

"Dial nine first."

Mae was grateful to have the phone number committed to memory. She realized it was the only one she'd memorized, except for Nat's. She took a deep breath in, imagining what Nat would say if she knew where she was now. Mae's finger sunk into the deep buttons, hearing the beep after each. Auntie Bel answered on the second ring.

"Who's this?"

Mae heard the podcast in the background and the annoyance in her voice.

"It's me, Auntie. Mae."

"You get a new phone?"

The background noise grew softer as if Auntie Bel was moving away from the source.

"Oh, no. This is—My phone died." Mae felt her cheeks flush. "How are you?"

Auntie Bel snorted. "Well! Roommate's a disaster. Damn idiot. But he bought me a little tablet thing for my podcasts so that's nice. How's married life?"

Mae watched Roderick move in tight circles, limited by the length of the phone cord. "It's, uh." His face contorted and he slammed the receiver down and stormed off down the hallway. "It's fine." Mae remembered how difficult it was to carry on a conversation with her aunt, her short temper and obscure interests. The podcast in the background grew louder. Mae heard the words *MKUltra*. "What's this episode about?"

"Oh!" Auntie Bel's voice went up in pitch. "It's a good one, this one. Government experimentation programs. Project Bluebird, Project Artichoke, MKUltra. I tell you what, our government is about as transparent as a brick. The shit those agencies are up to … makes my stomach turn."

"Oh yeah?" Relieved at even this warped kind of normalcy, Mae sought to keep the conversation going.

"You know, joke was on them though. If it wasn't for all their villainy, fuckin' around drugging American citizens with LSD, them hippies wouldn't have gotten their mits on those drugs. They started the whole counterculture hippy-dippy movement without knowing it!"

"They were drugging American citizens? Who?"

"The CIA of course! Thought they could figure out mind control, beat the Russians to it most importantly. Create some kind of sleeper cell super soldier. But all they got was some suicides and some seriously whacked out people. Thinkin' they were seein' shit, paranoid, goin' from lovey dove to foamin' at the mouth. Damn shame, living in a country where we can't trust our own government not to drug us and fuck us all up … "

Seeing things … As her aunt droned on, Mae thought about the body she'd seen, cut up and contorted in the brush. The wallpaper in the hall that swirled and summoned her.

She thought about the lady specter and the swirling void that followed her now.

"… some of them were never quite right again."

Mae heard a high-pitched beeping in the background.

"Well, I've gotta run. Food's ready. Thanks for callin', Mae. You take care now."

As Mae hung up the phone, Nurse Brianne rose and guided her back into the hallway.

"Hey, Miss Brianne?"

She paused. "Yes, sweetie?"

"How do you take LSD?"

Brianne's eyes grew wide, and she scrunched her mouth in disapproval. "Oh, girl, that's the last thing you need." She moved back around and slumped into her rolling chair, which slid a few inches back under her weight.

"No," Mae corrected, "it's not like that. I'm just curious."

Brianne leaned in close and whispered. "Well, it's just a liquid. Back in my mom's day, they used to drop it on pieces of paper and eat them, but I imagine you could put it on anything."

Mae nodded.

"But seriously, if you're in here, the last thing you need is a more distorted reality. You hear me?"

Mae's head bounced in agreement. "Of course. Thank you." As she wandered back to her room, she remembered Eva's muffins, her dinners, her pots of tea.

What if I'm not crazy at all?

CHAPTER TWENTY-FIVE

Ollie sat on the couch but kept both feet planted firmly on the floor in case they had to jump into action. Brian sat on a tufted chair, dingy, with a pink and yellow floral pattern, his eyes on Eva as she put a pot on the stove.

"It's really not necessary," Brian insisted.

"Oh, no," Eva called from the kitchen, not turning around. "It's nothing."

Ollie and Brian exchanged looks. They knew it was a long shot. Eva had stood by her husband through prison, abuse, and for all they knew, much worse. But Brian agreed they had to try. "Do you expect Mr. Duvall to be back soon?"

Teacups clinked on porcelain saucers from the kitchen. "I would think so, yes. He's just visiting his wife. The whole thing is just terrible." She wore a tight tank top, and from behind Ollie spied a small tattoo of a Chinese symbol on her shoulder.

"Interesting tattoo," Ollie remarked.

Brian shot them a chiding look. They'd agreed Ollie should let Brian do the talking, but Ollie couldn't resist.

"Thank you."

"What's it mean?"

Eva turned around and leaned against the cabinets. "It's my birth year. Year of the snake."

A cold smile twisted her lips.

"Of course," Ollie whispered.

"What's that?" Eva asked.

"Oh, nothing. My sister is year of the snake."

Eva nodded and turned back around to tend to the tea.

Ollie's phone buzzed.

Jenkins: SHUT THE FUCK UP

"Do you mind if I ask you a few questions?" Brian asked.

"Of course," she said, placing tea bags into the cups. "Though, I don't know how I can be of any help. I haven't seen the police captain."

Brian sucked his teeth. "This isn't regarding that, but ma'am, how do you know about that matter?"

Eva inhaled sharply. "I must've heard in town." She smiled. "But as I said, I haven't seen him."

"Would you mind coming in here please?" Brian phrased it as a question. It wasn't one.

Eva sauntered in from the kitchen and took a seat opposite Brian in the chair matching his. "What can I do for you?" She folded her hands in her lap.

"Well, we've done a little digging."

Ollie's eyes ping-ponged between them.

"On?" She smoothed a blonde hair behind her ear.

"On you, Eva. And on Mr. Duvall."

Eva sat up straighter. "Okay." Her face was somber, blank.

"Would you prefer I call you Ivy?"

A hitched breath rippled Eva's stomach. She forced her smile wider. "Why would I prefer that?"

Brian took a deep breath in and out. "Ma'am, I want you to really think about whether you want to do this with me."

Eva wetted her lips. Her eyes moved around the room.

"It's one thing to write letters to your husband in prison from the comfort of your own home. It's quite another, I'd imagine, to write them from your own cell. Don't you think?"

Ollie's nail dug into their thighs through their pants. The air was thick with tension, and they were reluctant to breathe it.

Eva swallowed hard. "What do you want?"

Brian leaned in, resting his elbows on his knees.

"We know your husband was involved in the murder of Richard Pruitt. And I think you know that as well as we do."

Eva pressed her back against the chair's regal frame. Foundation caked around her bruised orbital.

"We've got teams searching the town. They will find Captain Williams, and he'd better be alive when they do. So, here's what I know. You can help us out. Go back to having a jailbird husband, which sucks, don't get me wrong. Or you could keep playing dumb. Keep pretending to be some housekeeper named Eva, and when we find the Captain, because we *will* find the Captain, we will nail both of you to the wall."

The smile departed Eva's face. She twirled stray hairs behind her ear. "*If*, Mr. Duvall was involved in something, and I told you what I know, what would happen to me?"

Ollie's chest clenched.

"We're prepared to offer you a deal for your cooperation. Keep you out of prison. If you have information that leads to his conviction."

The teapot began to scream, and Ollie jumped what felt like a foot in the air. Eva rose gracefully from her seat and returned to the kitchen, where she removed it from the burner.

"So?" Brian pressed.

She poured the steaming liquid into the waiting cups, placed each cup and saucer on a serving tray. Ollie heard her whisper something.

"What's that?" Brian asked.

Eva emerged from the kitchen carrying the serving tray, steam pouring off each cup. She set the tray on the coffee table.

"How will you be able to keep up this little charade once Mae knows you're his wife?"

Eva's jaw trembled.

Ollie sat speechless.

"You won't be able to hang around here, sneaking kisses around corners. You'll be alone again. And they'll be together in this house, living the life you always wanted to have with him. Won't they?"

Eva's expression soured as if the picture left a foul taste on her tongue. She sat back in her chair. Ollie heard a buzz, and Eva reached into her pocket and answered a call. She turned her body away from them.

"She wouldn't?" Her voice was pressured as she spoke into the receiver. "Why not?" Eva's face twisted in contempt. "So, what now?" It was a forced whisper through gritted teeth. "Jesus, okay." She ended the call and sighed deeply.

Moments of silence stacked heavy in the air as Ollie watched Brian watch Eva. The trails of steam from the teacups thinned, now just a faint mist between cop and criminal. "Immunity," she said. Not a question, a statement.

"Impossible for me to guarantee. You could have something, or you could have nothing."

"I have something." Eva's emerald eyes glowed.

Brian worked to conceal his smile. "Something like what?"

"Texts, basically a confession." Eva stood and walked back into the kitchen. "But you'd better get going now. *Mr. Duvall* will be back any minute, and I have nothing else to say until I see my immunity agreement in writing."

Brian nodded. "Let's go," he said to Ollie.

Ollie, unsure how to appropriately bid Eva goodbye, did a half-curtsy before turning a violent shade of red and ducking out the front door. Brian followed close behind, shutting the door behind them and jogging down the porch steps to his car. "Better if we're not here when Babineaux gets back."

Ollie agreed and slid into the passenger seat. "So, what now?"

"Now I see the prosecutor about this immunity deal. If all goes well, I'll be heading to the State Attorney's Office, get us an arrest warrant for Brooks Babineaux."

Hearing *arrest warrant* and *Brooks Babineaux* in the same sentence flooded Ollie with warmth. It was happening, finally happening. Thanks in no small part to their push and the clues they'd discovered.

Surely Williams couldn't ignore this.

Williams. The thought of him sent a painful shock through Ollie's core.

"Any news on Williams?"

Brian grimaced. "Search parties are active, but nothing yet."

His office had no windows. Mae sat in a burgundy, leather chair, the queen version of Dr. Levine's throne which sat opposite her. His rectangular silver frames slid down his nose and he inspected her file. Mae created horror stories about what it might say.

Hopelessly, irrevocably mad.

Unable to care for herself in the simplest ways.

Lifelong dependence on others.

He cleared his throat. "How are you feeling, Mae?"

Mae pulled her sleeves over her hands, gripped the fabric in her fingers. "Much better."

"Hmm," he said without looking up at her. "Are you hearing any voices?" His narrow eyes met hers.

"No," Mae blurted.

"Haldol must be working then." He scribbled something down. "How about seeing things? Have you seen anything unusual? Lights, patterns, people? Moving shadows? Things other people can't see?"

"Nope." It was almost true. The shadow had diminished, and it was easy to ignore.

He checked a box, "Excellent," and flipped the file shut. "Any questions for me?"

Mae had been practicing how to ask. If she wasn't careful, she'd sound paranoid, unfit to be loosed upon the world. But she had to know. "One thing, yes. Just … out of curiosity."

Dr. Levine sat back in his chair, folded one leg over another.

"I was wondering, if I had accidentally ingested a drug, without realizing, could it have caused some of the things my husband mentioned?"

Dr. Levine's brows, the only hair yet to turn silvery-gray, stitched together. He threw the file open again and Mae's heart sank.She waited for him to pull out some big red stamp, to mark the file *FREEDOM DENIED*. He thumbed through pages and Mae steadied her breathing as no stamp emerged from his grandiose desk.

"Your UDS was positive but only for marijuana," he said finally.

"UDS?"

"Urine drug screen. We tested you upon admission. Any drugs in your system would've shown up there."

Mae felt her fingernails dig into her palm through her sleeve. "It tests for everything?"

Dr. Levine studied the page. "It's a standard, ten panel test, so no. Not *everything*. Is there something on your mind, Mae?"

This was it. No way around it but to ask directly and hope she didn't sound like Auntie Bel. "Does it test for LSD? I'm a little worried I may have come into contact with it. Would that explain my … symptoms?"

Dr. Levine strummed his fingers along the desk.

"Hypothetically, LSD can cause hallucinations, both visual and auditory, as well as rapid mood changes and paranoia, however, it's not a commonly found substance, and the odds that you would come across it *accidentally* in doses high enough to trigger your experiences is"—his mouth betrayed the smallest smile— "unlikely."

Mae's thoughts raced. *Rapid mood changes. Paranoia. Visual and auditory hallucinations.*

"It's important that you realize studies have shown that marijuana use may trigger and intensify underlying conditions like schizophrenia or schizoaffective disorder. It's in your best interest to stay away from it considering your diagnosis."

Diagnosis. Mae's stomach turned, but she pushed that thought away. "What if the weed I was smoking was laced with it and I didn't realize?"

He looked at her like a squirming fish on the end of a line. "Impossible," he said with a shake of his head. "Lysergic acid can't be ingested that way. It loses its effectiveness when burned."

"Snuck into my food?"

Dr. Levine's face stiffened. His casual eye contact turned analytical. "Snuck into your food?" he probed. "Who might want to do that?"

Shit. Mae forced a smile. "Oh, no one," she backtracked. "Just hypothetically."

He leaned forward, still examining. "Do you think someone is out to get you, Mae?"

She felt the catch-22. Of course, she suspected someone was out to get her, lacing her food with powerful drugs, but to say so would make her sound paranoid, in need of close observation. This man would not help her. This much she knew. So, she lied.

"Of course not." She shrugged and let her shoulders relax. "I think I've just been watching too many spy movies."

He nodded. "Well, your symptoms seem to be under control. I think we can look at discharging you today. I will have the case manager reach out to your husband so we can coordinate a time to get you home."

Home. The warm relief washed over her. She passed the test. Then the image of Carter returned. The cold, steady look on his face under bleating rain, his black hairs plastered to his temples. Her guttural horror at the policeman's ravaged body. His stoic disbelief.

"No need to bother him," she said.

Dr. Levine cocked his head.

"I can get myself home." She steeled herself, hoping there wasn't some rule against letting the recently crazy person out without an escort.

"Your paperwork has him listed as your emergency contact," though he didn't look back in the file. "It's standard procedure to reach out and let them know about discharge plans."

Mae tensed her shoulders and scowled before she regained control of her expression. "I'd like to change my emergency contact, now that you mention it."

"Is that so?" He eyed her suspiciously.

Mae nodded. Saying more might cast doubt on her impending release.

"You'd have to fill out some paperwor—"

"No problem." Mae smiled, putting on her best sweet-agreeable-woman face.

He sighed and pulled out one of his drawers, a myriad of hanging file folders inside. He rummaged through the papers and pulled out a blank form, sliding it across his desk to Mae.

Authorization to Release Information.

"You'll need to fill out all the fields with your new emergency contact's information. What's the name?"

Mae picked up a pen from his pencil-holder. She thought of Auntie Bel but cringed at the thought of her knowing where her niece had landed herself. "Ollie," she said finally. "Ollie Alden."

Dr. Levine gestured at the form, and Mae filled out her own name and address, all of Ollie's information she could remember, and checked the box for *discharge plan.*

"And my husband, I'd like to revoke that form please. I think I remember the intake person saying that was within my rights."

Dr. Levine huffed. "Of course, it is your right, but we won't be able to share anything with him if you do that. Not your medications, when you're leaving, your treatment plan."

His stare suggested he thought this might change Mae's mind.

"I understand."

"Okay," he relented.

Mae slid the completed form designating Ollie as her emergency contact back to Dr. Levine. He scrutinized it, no doubt looking for errors, but consigned himself.

"Very good. I will update this in the system right away."

Mae released her grip on her sleeves, and when Dr. Levine gestured for her to go, she happily showed herself out of the windowless room.

CHAPTER TWENTY-SIX

Ollie and Eva made an odd couple, sitting at the cafe opposite the police station, awaiting word on whether Eva's text messages were enough to grant her immunity. Even with Carter behind bars, the close proximity to him was unsettling. The cheese plate they ordered to appease the waitress sat untouched in the center of the small table as Eva sucked down her second glass of red wine. She looked jittery, unstable, as if a strong enough wind or the wrong inflection of a word might send her running. Her eyes were puffy, and where she'd wiped away her tears, she'd taken off her foundation, exposing the yellowish hue of the healing bruise on her cheek.

Ollie didn't expect to feel for her. She'd been part of it, after all, whatever conspiracy Carter had cooked up to profit off Mae's misfortune.

"I don't even know what to call you," Ollie blurted out. Their stomach clenched. Instant regret. Their harsh tone, luckily, wasn't enough to scare off the flighty bird. It just made her stiffen.

"Ivy," she said. "Or Eva. I don't really care, to tell you the truth." She shrugged and gulped down the last of her wine.

"I guess they're not too different." Ollie didn't know why they said it, why they felt the need to comment on it, except that the weighty silence was growing too much to bear. Each moment waiting for an update from Brian was torturous.

"What were the charges?" Eva asked.

Ollie shrugged. "I'm not a cop."

Eva snorted. "Could've fooled me." Her emerald eyes took a cool tone in the gray of the foggy afternoon. Main St was all but deserted. It was as if the town knew to stay away, just to make this waiting more insufferable.

Eva reached for a cracker, but didn't eat it, just moved it around the plate. "Do you know what will happen to him now?" Her tone softened a bit. Ollie recognized the sound and the distance in her eyes. Regret.

"I guess he'll be arraigned." Ollie stirred their straw around in circular motions. The ice clinked against the glass. "Can I ask … why did you—"

"Marry him?"

Ollie studied Eva's face, its perfect construction. Even with her hair pulled back in messy lumps, with her swollen eyes and in her pilled tracksuit, she was easily one of the most beautiful women they'd ever seen. But there was something that emanated from within. Like a stench. An ugliness, or perhaps, an emptiness. And despite her statuesque features, Ollie felt no attraction. Pity, but no attraction.

"I mean," Ollie stirred faster, the ice threatening to jump from the rim of the glass, "I get that he's good looking and all, charming even, but goddamn. He's an evil sonofabitch."

Eva rubbed her hand over her hair, scratched at her skull. "I went to Stanford. Did you know that?"

Ollie felt a twinge of disbelief, and their face betrayed it.

"Would've been top of my class too." Eva's mouth twisted into a melancholy smile. "I was studying History."

"History?"

That was definitely bullshit. The only historians Ollie had ever seen were old white men with salt and pepper hair sitting in front of stacked bookcases on TV.

"History, Philosophy and the Arts." The words flowed easily, lending them some credence.

"Okay?"

"I was home visiting my parents in Tennessee. And I went to his antique shop. I was looking for a—it doesn't matter. I didn't find it. Instead, I found him. Or he found me."

Ollie wondered then whether Eva had once been just like Mae. Young, inexperienced, something he desired.

"He'd say *Ivy, you're a vision. Ivy, you're a Greek goddess.* In the beginning anyway. My parents loved him. My friends loved him too, at first. He was, is, magnetic."

Ollie saw the joy of the memories dance across Eva's face, but they darkened into something else.

"Then it sort of turned. I'd tell him he was the most incredible man in the world, and he'd agree, and say nothing back. Subtle at first," she plucked a grape from the cheese plate and squeezed it, "and then less so." The grape skin tore beneath the pressure, its lumpy innards squirting around her thumb. "By the time they arrested him, I was hypnotized. He'd said, *you're lucky to be with me*, and I believed him. I felt lucky. When he offered to marry me, even from behind bars, it felt like an honor. It was a privilege to wait for him."

Eva wiped her fingers with the cloth napkin. "I'm not stupid," she said, her stare penetrating Ollie's chest, releasing a well of sadness that Ollie didn't know was there. "And I'm not sick. I know he is. I know that now. That's why I'm helping you."

A hitch in their chest made Ollie take a deep breath before they spoke. How foolish they would look, they thought, if they started to cry. "What will you do now?" The words seemed to reverberate around them, though there was no echo. Eva's eyes bounced around the cheese plate, as if it might offer some answers. Then finally, Ollie's phone rang.

Brian's voice was hoarse over the speaker, and Eva held her breath across the table, turned a shade paler.

"You're not gonna *fucking* believe this." He was winded, the words wedged between ragged breaths.

"What?" Ollie tried to put on an even tone, but from the way Eva leaned in, they knew the tension showed in their face.

"Come over here."

Ollie looked across the street to the station, where Brian jogged down the steps, phone pressed to his ear.

"Come on!"

Ollie tossed a few bills on the table.

"Where are you going?" Eva stood. "What's going on?"

Ollie held out their palm to silence her. "Jenkins—" The line was silent, and Ollie saw that across the street, Jenkins had opened the driver's side door of his Crown Victoria.

"I don't know," Ollie said, shoving their wallet back into their pocket, "but I've got to go." Eva threw her hands into the air, and Ollie turned away from her, feeling the creep of shame as they sprinted across the street to catch Brian before he pulled away. They didn't dare look back at her, the gnawing pit in their stomach wouldn't allow it.

The car was already in reverse when Ollie slid into the passenger seat. Brian's teeth were clenched, his head shaking back and forth as he mumbled to himself.

"What's going on?"

The car lurched backward, and Ollie had to catch themself so their head didn't slam into the dashboard. "Jesus, Jenkins!"

He threw the car in drive and Ollie clicked their seatbelt.

"Where are we going?"

"The Barlow house."

"Barlow?"

Ollie caught a glimpse of Eva standing beside the table, her head craning to watch them as they passed by, a stitch of guilt.

"Charles Barlow, the groundskeeper."

"What? Why?"

"Pfft!" Brian huffed.

Ollie hadn't seen him this angry since Ruthers beat him out for that promotion.

"They're letting him go." His eyes bulged, red capillaries angry and pronounced.

"The groundskeeper? Why? What did he do?"

The engine roared as Brian peeled away from the last stop sign on Main St. "He's dead. Barlow is dead and they're letting Babineaux go."

Brick shops gave way to wide open fields as they raced away from Main St. Mildewed wooden fences with busted boards contained fields of brown grass and the odd, decrepit barn. "What?" Ollie said through a gasp.

"Not enough to hold him after—" Brian slowed the car, pulled off the paved road onto a dirt one Ollie recognized from their bicycle trip here weeks back.

"After what?"

Brian shook his head and bit at his cheek.

"Eva gave us a written confession! I mean it might as well have been. Those texts were damning. No way a jury would've looked past them. What the fuck is going on?"

"But they weren't a confession, were they? Just innuendo." Brian spat. "And now we have a confession. A real one."

The car jumped over the dips in the country road. Outside, Lady lunged at her chain, snarling and foaming at the mouth. The groundskeeper's shack was dwarfed by the swarm of police activity. Streams of caution tape had already been erected, the entire department's cars encircled the property, lights blaring. "What are you talking about?"

"Charles Barlow was found dead," Brian said matter-of-factly. "Earlier today, suicide." He stopped short beside the rusted out corvette in the yard.

"What's that got to do with Babineaux?"

"He left a note. Said the guilt got the best of him, that he killed Richard Pruitt back in 2008, stole the violin, and kept working as the groundskeeper so he could search for that certificate of authenticity."

Ollie's jaw hung open.

"Said when Mae came back to town, the weight of what he'd done was too much, and when she went crazy, he blamed himself. Couldn't live with the pain he'd caused anymore." Brian killed the engine and dropped the keys into his lap. Took a deep breath in.

"There's no way," Ollie said. "After all the links to Babineaux. Just no way he wasn't involved."

Brian blew his breath out, long and steady. "You know that," his tone was calmer now, "and I know that. But with this," he gestured to the scene, "we're gonna need a hell of a lot more to prove it."

Ollie trailed Brian along the walk up to the house. They passed faces they recognized from the station, leaning against their cars, eyes down.

"Can I come in with you?" Ollie whispered.

Brian said nothing, taking long, purposeful steps to the door, so Ollie followed behind. There was a heavy feel inside, and Brian stopped in the entryway. Unable to see around him, Ollie eyed the collection of porcelain dolls on the right and shivers passed down their spine. Brian shook his head, and Ollie pressed their body against the door frame to slip past him. In the center of the small home, he lay. His head was mercifully obscured behind the sofa, but his torso and legs were visible from where Ollie stood, contorted into an unnatural position. Ollie's eyes wandered up to the ceiling, where blood and gray matter had sprayed, sending the occasional drip down to the couch. Beside his body was the handle of a shotgun, and Ollie stepped backward, not wanting to see any more.

They turned, ready to pass back behind Brian, get a gulp of fresh air outside, when they saw it resting on the couch. The Stradivarius was propped up on a pillow like a guest, its bow neatly placed beside it. It seemed to glow, demonic, from inside, and an ornate carving suggested its antique origin and incredible worth. On the coffee table before it was a torn sheet of paper. The suicide note, Ollie assumed. The confession. Their head reeled. They pushed past Brian, their vision doubled then righted itself, but black flecks moved in and out of their line of sight. How could it be? Even the porch and the wide open spaces all around felt claustrophobic. Ollie sucked hard at the air, trying to fill their lungs, but their breaths remained shallow. A gentle hand on their back made Ollie turn and they saw Brian beside them. He nodded, an affirmation.

"That's it," Ollie whispered. "That's Lady Paola." They slumped down into a sitting position and Brian followed suit. "I looked it up online. That carving, it's—"

"I know."

Shock gave way to anger gave way to despair. Ollie heard the codes called out over Brian's radio, watched the officers circle their cars, make calls.

"When are they letting him out?"

Brian stood up and extended a hand, which Ollie accepted. They followed him to his car.

"Today," he said on the way.

"But Eva …" Ollie imagined him finding her, wrapping his hands around her neck again, but not for a sultry kiss. "And Mae. We've got to warn them."

Mae stood in the gravel drive, the whir of the engine dissipating as the driver pulled off. *Empty*, she thought, as she took in the looming Victorian structure. It wasn't the absence of cars or the stillness at the windows, but a feeling of thinness about the walls which told her so. Sunlight pushed against the thick cloud cover but made headway only in spurts and odd streams which poured through the sparse branches overhead, dappling ashy light. Her phone buzzed in her pocket once again. Ollie. Calling over and over since Mae turned it on. Sporadic texts rolling in like waves.

Ollie: Hospital called and said you were getting out. Call me.

Ollie: Give me a call back ASAP

Ollie: We've got to talk about Carter. It's important, CALL ME BACK

Crows squawked in the distance, unseen through the fog. There were others, Mae recalled. Cardinals, bluejays, doves. There had been other birds. But now only the crows, for weeks and weeks, only crows cawing and screaming from the Eastern Hemlocks. A pinecone crunched underfoot as Mae moved up the porch steps. She remembered that night as a child when she'd been carried. The strong arms of an ambitious detective whisked her down this very path. The porch was whiter then. The house more rosy.

She'd thought, from the back of the social worker's car, *who will clean up the blood?*

She'd imagined, from the twin bed with purple Daisy sheets, it still stained the wraparound porch, streaked the hardwood. That rain would nightly chip it away in flakes as it turned brown against the stark white paint. And on the hardwood, she'd thought, it would rest permanently, without a father to clean it up, without a mother in sight, it would remain.

There were two of them now. First her father's, split in two by the heavy axe. And now the police captain's. The very same man, she thought, who might've carried her up these steps. The heads of two men, bashed, bloodied, bereft of life. Two brains spilled on the property at Alquist Ave. And she'd been witness to both. Had the latter been a dream? Had the former?

No. She felt quite sure that they were real. Carter's romance had felt real too, for a time. And the promise of their life together. But she was getting better at it now, with the time and her age and the distance from the house. Better at knowing real versus not real.

Her service was limited, just one bar, and she thought if she stepped inside it would falter to nothing. So she sat on the rotted rocking chair overlooking the yard, her eyes hesitating over the frazzled rope suspended from the oak bough. She dialed Ollie, her hand gripping the armrest, the wood soft and malleable under her fingernails. She scraped away the flimsy paint, unafraid of splinters.

"Mae! Thank God you called me back." Ollie's voice was stressed. Mae imagined stained armpits. "Where are you?"

Mae stripped another bit of paint from the rocker. "Home." Her voice sounded foreign, even to her.

"It's Carter—He's—There's so much I have to tell you."

A breeze carried a swirl of crumpled leaves across the porch. "Captain Williams is dead."

"Mae, you've got to meet me. Can you come to town? I can be at the coffee shop in five minutes. Can you meet me there?"

Mae could've sworn she heard the old Victorian groan, a deep exhale from the walls themselves. *It's my house*, she thought. *And if it is full of ghosts, they're my ghosts.*

"Mae?" Ollie's voice was climbing in pitch.

The Victorian's pull made Mae want to disappear inside the door, to climb the stairs, to find her way to her father's things on the third floor. She imagined them spread out around her, reading his papers, playing one of his records, splaying herself on the groaning floorboards of that top floor, the one she hadn't seen since she was a child.

"Are you there?" Ollie sounded desperate.

"I'm here."

"Carter will be back soon. Please, you've got to meet me. You could be in danger if you stay."

A quick shake of her head brought Mae back to the present.

The house can wait. "Okay, I'll meet you. *Brewed Awakening.* I'll start walking now."

CHAPTER TWENTY-SEVEN

Mae appeared changed when she took her seat across from Ollie. It wasn't the tiny purple sutures dissolving at her hairline or the extra layer of oil in her dirty blonde hair. Did she hold herself differently? Taller? Or something new behind her eyes? Something gone? Ollie wasn't sure, but her presence held gravitas. A stillness that didn't match their quaking innards.

Ollie inhaled to start pouring out the news, but as quickly as Mae had dropped her purse at the table, she excused herself to order a coffee from the barista.

Eva, Ollie remembered. They fired off warning texts, letting her know that Carter was getting out while avoiding the specific details. She didn't text back, and Ollie hoped it was because she was busy packing her belongings to run.

Mae finally settled, latte in hand, opposite Ollie.

"What's up?" Her tone was casual.

Ollie was afraid the breadth of what they had to tell her might shatter the bit of normalcy Mae had left, that she might collapse into a puddle on the sticky floor of the coffee shop. But the dread of Mae's reaction was pushed aside by the urgency of the news, the threat to her safety.

"Some shit went down while you were ..."

"In the psych ward?"

Ollie winced at her directness. "Right."

Mae stirred circles in her latte, eyes locked with Ollie's. "Well?"

"First of all, I'm really sorry to have to tell you all this. I know you must be—"

"Spit it out, Ollie. I'm not some fragile bird."

Ollie swallowed hard, watched Mae set down her stirrer and take a long sip. "Carter's a criminal, Mae." They stared into her face, waiting for a collapse.

"Hmm." Mae sounded unsurprised.

"He was arrested some years back for forgery and selling stolen property. Turns out he grew up working at an antique shop, and his dad specialized in authenticating rare instruments."

At *rare instruments,* Mae perked up.

"This is going to be a lot, but Carter isn't his real name. His real name is Brooks Babineaux. Remember? From that letter you found?"

Mae sat unblinking. "Go on."

"I've been working with Jenkins, he's an officer—"

"Oh yeah, Brian Jenkins, the one who hauled me off in cuffs."

Ollie shifted nervously. "Yes, that's him. Anyway, he and I interviewed Eva who was able to share some evidence. It was enough to arrest him but—"

"Eva?" Mae's body stiffened.

"That's the other thing. Again, I'm so sorry I have to—"

"Ollie!"

"Okay, okay. So, Carter's not the only one with a fake name. Eva's real name is Ivy. Ivy Babineaux. She's Carter's wife." Her eyelids twitched and Ollie thought the tears would break through at any moment, but to their surprise, Mae blinked them away.

"His wife?"

Ollie nodded. "She had these texts from him. They were completely damning, Mae, as good as a confession. It was enough that Jenkins arrested him. Would've convinced a jury too if you ask me."

Thin lines formed on Mae's forehead. "Carter is in jail?"

"Well, that's the thing. He was. But then something happened, and they had to release him. That's why I've been calling and calling you because it's not safe for you at home. Who knows what he's capable of." Ollie realized they were gripping the table and slowly released their hands.

"What?"

"You can't go home, Mae."

"No, what was it that happened?"

Ollie took a deep breath in. "There was this groundskeeper, employed by your father's estate. He actually worked there when you were—"

"Charles. I remember him."

"Well, he took his life and he left a note." Ollie reached across the table, took Mae's hand in theirs. Her hazel eyes bounced from Ollie's left to their right. "He confessed to your father's murder. He had the violin."

Mae shook her head. "No," she said, still shaking. "Maybe some other violin, but not Lady Paola."

Ollie applied soft pressure to Mae's hand. "I'm sorry Mae but it was. I saw it myself."

Mae ripped her hand away. "No! It wasn't her. I've seen her. She's at the house. I saw her in the library just a couple of weeks ago. It's not possible." Her jaw trembled. Her leg bounced.

Ollie leaned in close. "Please come home with me, Mae. Or let me get you set up in a hotel. It's not safe."

Mae turned her body away from Ollie, gnawed on her bottom lip. "It can't be right. Start over. Tell me everything you know, from the beginning."

Reluctantly, Ollie recounted all they knew: Carter's criminal past, his real name, his marriage to Eva. The arrest, the suicide, Carter's release. Each time they spat out a fact, it seemed to pass right through Mae, as if she hadn't quite heard it. Shock, maybe? They went on to the next piece of news, thinking each time that this would be the bit of information to sink in, that Mae's eyes would well with tears, or her face would turn scarlet and she'd explode in a scream, but it never came. Mae listened, her body positioned forty-five degrees away.

She avoided eye contact. Asked clarifying questions. And finally she said, "I have to go home."

"But Mae—"

She stood up. "I'm tired. I'd like to go home and rest now." She picked up her bag off the chair.

"It's not—"

"Thank you for meeting with me and letting me know everything that's happened."

Ollie walked behind her out of the cafe. A cold wind chilled their face as they stepped onto the sidewalk. "Please listen to me. He's threatened me. He conned you. He's a dangerous man. You CANNOT go back to that house."

Mae turned so fast her hair whipped Ollie's cheek. "It's *my* house, Ollie. This is not some game for you to win. He was *my* father, and this is *my* husband. It's not your problem to deal with. It's *mine*."

The force in Mae's voice made Ollie step backward. They nodded, and Mae spun around, taking purposeful steps back toward Alquist Ave. Her steps grew distant, and though there were other passersby on the street, Ollie felt the creeping sensation of deep loneliness. Their feet knew the way to the boutique, and, before they realized, they'd made it home, opened the apartment door and stepped inside. Mae's words echoed in Ollie's memory.

Mine, mine, mine. They'd only tried to help. Hadn't they?

Ollie slumped onto the couch, and Hobbes promptly hopped onto their lap. His orange coat had become glossy since moving indoors, and purrs reverberated from his now plump body. Ollie's fingers grasped at their phone.

Jenkins: He's out.

Icy shame leaked from somewhere deep inside. It flooded their chest, sinister fingers encircling their ribcage.

Was it all for Mae?

Ollie's fantasy of striding into the police station, high fives all around from the guys, being greeted by their smiling faces instead of masked sneers, blurred and melted away. The truth had always been there. It was just easier to believe their intentions were pure, noble. Did they want to be the hero? Of course. And hey, it didn't hurt that Mae was kind and warm and beautiful and made Ollie's stomach do backflips when they saw her.

But the truth remained. This was their shot. Solving the decade old murder was a surefire way to land a spot at the station, to stop being the Gen Z, genderqueer weirdo in town and start being actually seen, valued for what they could offer. Their dream job slipped away, one more con pulled off by Brooks Babineaux, though he'd never know it. And Captain Williams, more father figure than friend, the only one who would've known what to do, was missing. All their speculation, their investigating, their intentions (good, bad, or something in-between), had only made things worse. Perhaps it was best for Ollie to stay out of it for once. Head thrown back, Ollie stared at the popcorn ceiling, dragging shallow breaths into their heavy chest. And then Hobbes, whether ignorant and apathetic, decided it was a perfect seat, and laid his fattened body over Ollie's mouth and nose.

By the time Mae reached her property, the sun was low in the sky, casting a hazy orange glow through smears of cloud. The faded vibrancy reminded Mae of Ollie's hair, and an odd passing thought came that she would like, sometime, to reach out and touch the spiky shaved portion of Ollie's head.

Shadow lurked at her periphery, a phantom or just a bit of fog. Carter's muted green truck rested in front of the porch steps, making sporadic clicks and creaks as the engine cooled. It wasn't fear but interest that filled her as she approached. How might he be when he saw her? Surprised that she was released without his blessing? Fuming from his recent arrest? Would he assume she knew everything? More likely, nothing at all. It was this curiosity that drove her to turn the knob, which opened effortlessly at her beckoning.

There was rustling from his office, man-sized rustling, and as she shut the door behind her, Carter bolted into the living room. His wide eyes beheld her with a dash of begrudging respect.

"I'm home." She set her purse on the couch, wandered into the kitchen, and felt his eyes upon her. She imagined he was waiting for her to give herself away, to reveal what she knew and how he should proceed. Mae turned her wedding ring on her finger and perused the fridge for a snack, her stomach suddenly growling with hunger. There were light steps on the hardwood, and Mae turned to find Carter staring at her from the living room, observing her like a scientist.

"Do we have any bread?"

His shoulders fell. "Not sure," his words were slower than normal, "did you check the breadbasket?"

Mae shut the fridge and glanced on the counter, finding a wicker basket with a half-eaten loaf. "Of course." She shot him a smile, which he greedily returned.

She picked out two slices and popped them into the toaster when his hands wrapped around her waist. They pulled her closer until her back pressed against his body, her head resting between his pecs. She closed her eyes, languishing in the strange sensation: the delight of being held so affectionately by someone likely incapable of feeling any such thing. There was comfort in his warm embrace. A temptation to believe this physical proximity might be the result of love.

The scent of burning bread wafted into her nostrils, and she forced her eyes open, pulled away from him enough to pop the slices from the toaster. He stepped back, and when she turned to meet his eyes, she found a satisfied look.

Chilled butter pads dug divots into her toast as Mae tried to spread it. Giving up, she stacked the warm slices on top of one another to melt the stubborn butter and joined Carter in the living room.

"Why didn't you call me when you got out? I would've picked you up."

Of course, he's not going to tell me. And why should he assume I know? Me, his mad wife. No—not even that.

"I didn't want to trouble you." She rubbed one slice of bread over the other as a makeshift knife. "And I thought some time alone might do me some good."

"To think?" A darkness crept at the edges of his demeanor.

"About what you said," Mae added quickly. "Whether I'm up for managing the finances."

Carter rubbed his lips against his teeth.

Mae was reminded of a predator, wary of walking into a trap. "And?"

Mae took a bite of her toast, chewed while she thought of the most advantageous response. She wiped a bit of grease from her chin. "I understand where you're coming from. Dr. Levine said the new meds are working well, so I'd like to see how the next couple of weeks go, but I think it's not out of the question." She took another bite and watched his expression for clues.

His mouth flattened and he nodded, as if considering this was not a total loss.

"Where's Eva?" A pang of anxiety shot through Mae as she asked, but the temptation was too great. She had to know how Carter would attempt to explain this. "Will she be by to make dinner tonight?"

His posture straightened. "I gave her some time off while you were … well, you know. Didn't expect you home tonight, so no, I don't expect her to be here." His lies were a fluent, second language. His eyes were vacant. "We could go out, if you'd like." His canine crept free from his upper lip as it curled into a grin. "Unless you'd rather stay in?"

Mae recognized the challenge. "I'd love to go out."

The smile spread to his eyes. "Maybe somewhere nice? It's been too long since we had a fancy dinner." Upping the stakes.

Setting down the plate of toast, Mae leaned forward. "I'll go pick out a dress." She crossed the room and had begun climbing the stairs when he added:

"Try the green one. You look like you've lost weight, bet it will fit you now."

The jab pricked like a tiny arrow in the back, but Mae continued climbing, not looking back.

As long as he thinks he's winning, I'm safe.

She reached the top landing and glanced back at him. He sat, knees parted, back straight, like a king.

I need all the time I can get to search.

He beamed up at her and she returned his genial look, raising him a kiss blown into the air.

They'll bring back the noose for you if I have anything to do with it.

CHAPTER TWENTY-EIGHT

The stilted but otherwise uneventful dinner the night before had eased Carter enough to leave Mae alone in the house. She crept into his office, which had been her father's study and was still soaked in the grandeur of a superior man. The rich maple desk held his off-brand laptop and crowded behind the plush chair were stacks of books he'd never read. For all of Carter's intelligence, he seemed to have no use for fiction, especially the classics. Illustrious hardcover editions of *The Iliad, Grapes of Wrath, As I Lay Dying, Of Mice and Men, The Picture of Dorian Gray* lined the oak shelf, coated in a layer of dust. A Tiffany lamp cast muted light over a pewter sewing machine, a brass jewelry box, and a swivel mirror with decadent leafy details around the oblong face. Mae eased herself into his tufted leather chair, her father's chair. She pulled her reflection close, letting her vision settle upon her image.

My hair used to shine.

She ran her hand over it, half expecting her fingertips to collect dust as they might if she ran them across the forgotten bookshelf behind her. Brittle strands poked out at odd, wiry angles. At her crown the sutures were disappearing, clutching her skin together at a gathered fold. A black scab sat at the center, a half-moon of dried blood.

She remembered the rain that night, the rain and the fear. Officer Williams's mangled visage was a stark vision implanted in her mind. It kept her company, especially at night when she searched for peace enough to sleep.

He chased me, of that much she was sure. But had she slipped? Had the wind picked up with enough force, the stone floor of the mausoleum slick enough with rain that she lost her balance? Smacked her skull against the marble? A wind inside her stomach swayed and tipped, the feeling of being grasped, pulled back, launched forward. It might have been his hand that gripped her skull. He might have beat her with a rock. But what did it matter now, she supposed. The brass handle was cold in her palm and the drawer slid open with a creak. Her eyes passed over the contents: a few manilla folders, yellow highlighter, smattering of capless pens. She eased it shut again and a strangling feeling grasped at the top of her lungs, shallowing her breath. Clicking her phone to life, she dialed Ollie, left the phone on speaker atop the desk while she slid open the second drawer.

"Hey." Their voice was thin.

"Ollie, hey, listen, Carter is out but he'll be back soon. I'm in his office and—what should I be looking for? This is where he goes but it's all just," she brushed around the items in the second drawer, a stapler, paperclips, a spare phone charger, "it looks normal."

Mae stared at the phone awaiting an answer. The beam of light from its face illuminated a trail in the hazy room. Lint wandered in and out of its glow.

"I really don't know."

Mae snatched up the phone. "What do you mean? We need evidence, right? Something to show he was part of it."

A hopeless breath passed over the receiver. "Mae, I'm sorry I just really don't know. I'm not a detective." Their voice grew sharp edges.

"Well, do you think we could meet? Try to get a game plan? I'm here now, I can help." Mae's eyes passed into the office's shadowy corners. "There's gotta be proof in this house."

Silence hung on the line.

"Ollie?"

"Yeah." It flew out on an exasperated breath.

Mae waited, scraping a bit of corrosion from the jewelry box with her fingernail, but when Ollie finally spoke, they said, "Look, everything I've done has made things worse. You need real help, from the real police." A few moments of silence and then, "I really gotta let you go. I volunteered for a search party, and I should really start getting dressed."

The cracked skull of Captain Williams flashed in Mae's mind. *The axe.* Mae kept the thought to herself, wished Ollie luck with the search, and promised to let them know if she found anything. Ollie, half-heartedly, thanked her before hanging up.

Could it still be in the barn? Mae checked the time, 3pm, and knew Carter would be back within half an hour. She did a once-over of her outfit, billowy shorts, a T-Shirt, and not an undergarment in sight. Taking the stairs two at a time, she dashed into her room and tossed on a pair of pants and a sweater. She pulled on her boots and clamored back down the staircase, slipping outside through the stained-glass door.

Wind whistled through the backyard's long grasses. Brown and dry, they chafed at her clothing, snagging with tiny blades along the leaves. She passed the greenhouse, and through the water-stained panes were bursts of green, unruly vines and untended bushes overflowing their pots, an oasis amongst the fall decay outside the glass. It hit when she reached the barn. The longing. She stood in the open space, straw crunching under her boots, remembering the photo she'd taken with Ollie, before the madness, before the betrayal, when she thought everything was coming up ros—

The whirr of an engine and the crunching of gravel under tires made her freeze. Her eyes bounced over the tree stump where an axe was lodged, but not the one from her memory. This one was smaller, the blade a metallic black. The gap between the rusted lawn mower and the wall was too slim for her to hide between. A car door slammed. On her right was the old tack room. Its flimsy plywood door hung on by a single hinge. The thought of the insect life inside made her shudder. She listened. Boots on gravel then pine.

He's headed to the front door.

One.

Two.

Three.

Mae sprinted out of the barn, knowing she only had a brief window when Carter would be occupied putting his key in the lock and might miss her running from the barn to the rear door. She couldn't bear to look, so she wasn't sure if she was seen. She reached the house in a blur, huffing, and shut the door behind her.

Her heart punched her rib cage. Three sharp knocks rang out from the door. One gentle step at a time, Mae crept across the house. She peeked through the glass and saw a most unwelcome face on her doorstep.

"Officer Jenkins," she chirped, wearing a sarcastic smile.

"Mrs. Duvall." He stared at his shoes.

"What can I do for you?" Mae leaned against the door frame, an exaggerated gesture of relaxation.

He held up a clear plastic bag marked *Evidence* in red print. "Your husband left this down at the station." Inside was a wallet.

Mae stiffened. "You can leave that in our mailbox, please."

Brian looked at the bag, raised his brows.

"In the mailbox. Please," Mae repeated.

Brian sucked his teeth and turned away.

"It's just—" Mae called after him, "I don't think my husband would appreciate you so carelessly throwing around information about him. What if he hadn't told me he'd been to the station? Could cause some kind of fight or misunderstanding. You see?"

He nodded, relaxed his face into a smile. Before he could turn to go, Mae added, "And hey, I heard about the old groundskeeper. Just awful."

Brian perked up. "Mind if I come in? I'd be interested to know what you remember about him."

Mae glanced at the time, 3:12, and shook her head. "No, that's not possible I'm afraid."

Once again, Brian turned to go, but Mae stopped him. "I heard about the Stradivarius," she blurted. "When will it be returned to me?"

Annoyance or pity or suspicion crossed his face. "We've contacted the trustee of the estate. It will be returned to its rightful owner as soon as it's processed for evidence."

"Which will be when?"

Brian didn't linger on the porch this time, instead taking leisurely steps to his Crown Victoria and calling over his shoulder, "Couple weeks. But I wouldn't expect it. Call the estate lawyer, that's all I can say."

The estate lawyer?

Memory of the business card came rushing back. With, she checked, fourteen minutes before Carter was expected home, she rifled through her wallet, spreading loyalty cards, IDs, and business cards out like a blackjack dealer across the kitchen counter. *Robert Feinstein,* she snatched it up, ran her thumb over the gold embossed lettering. He answered on the second ring.

"Ms. Pruitt, I've been expecting your call."

The sound of her old name was like a warm hug. "Mr. Feinstein, yes. I was told to call you for information regarding my father's Stradivarius violin. You heard it was found?"

"Yes, of course. I was contacted by the police who assured me they would take the utmost care of it while it was in their custody."

"When can I have it back? They said they need to process it for evidence. How long does that take?"

"Unfortunately, I can't speak to that, however, I have checked into the ownership of the Stradivarius violin," Mae heard papers flipping in the background, "named and referred to as Lady Paola in your father's Will and Testament. It will be returned to the beneficiary set forth in your father's documentation. I'm sure you recall from our prior meeting, you were named the beneficiary of the estate and nearly the entirety of your father's possessions therein, however, this was one of the few items bequeathed to someone else."

Mae's memory of that day was a flurry, and this detail was nowhere within her recollection. "Someone else?"

"Correct," he restated. "Elizabeth Tompkins."

The shock was numbing, and while the vague memory of this name poked at the periphery of her memory, the idea that her dad would've given Lady Paola to someone else was a cold betrayal. "Who is Elizabeth Tompkins?" she asked, her tone more serpentine than she intended.

"I'm afraid it would be unethical for me to disclose anything more. Apologies, however, I'm sure you understand. Just as you wouldn't appreciate my giving out your information to others, I can't very well hand out information about Ms. Tompkins. Is there anything else I can do for you, Mae?"

The familiar sound of crunching gravel outside caused Mae's diaphragm to contract. "No, that's all," she spoke quickly. "Thank you."

Mae tucked her phone into her pocket, gathered up the contents of her wallet and shoved it back into the slots at odd angles. It was barely back in her purse when she heard Carter's key in the lock.

Elizabeth Tompkins. The name had invaded Mae's dreams, echoed in her mind as she woke, and was scrawled across the pages of her journal. Gray morning light poured in through the window, touched the skin of her knees as she sat on the bed, but provided no warmth. The comforter remained tucked in on Carter's side. When midnight had come and he hadn't returned home, there was no stitching anxiety, no hairline wrinkles on the forehead of a worried wife. Relief had come instead.

Dancing around him in the daylight was exhausting enough. She didn't have the energy for method acting, putting on airs during the night as well. Her satin robe offered gentle tenderness as she slid it onto her skin. She floated downstairs, checked the driveway for his truck.

Gone. Good.

If the lawyer wouldn't tell her who Elizabeth was, maybe Auntie Bel would offer a clue.

Nine a.m. was early for her aunt. She pictured her curled up on the couch, shoes still on, or splayed across her mattress, jaw hanging while snores abound. But Mae dialed anyway, no longer willing to tiptoe around.

To her surprise, her aunt answered. "Yeah?" Her gruff tone was unsurprising.

Mae offered a brief pleasantry, then got down to it. "Elizabeth Tompkins." Not a question, but a statement.

"Who?"

"Elizabeth Tomkins," she insisted. "You recognize that name?"

"Tompkins …" there was a shuffling in the background. Auntie Bel unleashed a flurry of coughs, and just as Mae's gut sank, she heard, "Ah, Lizzie. Whatta 'bout her?"

Mae jumped up, began to pace. "You know her? Who is she?"

Auntie Bel harrumphed. "Ain't nobody worth knowin'."

"Auntie, this is important."

Plastic crinkled on the other end of the line. Mae knew the sound well and could picture her aunt's hand in the frozen waffle bag.

"This ain't the right way for you to hear 'bout this, honey."

Clammy dread strangled Mae's lungs. "It's important."

Auntie Bel's fingers strummed over a hard surface.

"Auntie," Mae pressed.

"She's yer mama, alright? But she ain't worth a damn. No woman leavin' her baby's worth her weight in whiskey."

The words pushed the remaining air from Mae's lungs.

Of course. Who else would her father leave a priceless heirloom to? Mae's response rode out on a whisper. "Was she sick, Auntie?"

"Sick?" She snorted. "I dunno 'bout sick. Drunk as Cooter Brown. That's for sure. Richie, yer daddy, he deserved better than her. Same as you. Y'all were better off when she left. Can't make a silk purse outta a sow's ear. That's what I always told him, that's what I'm tellin' you now."

"Where's she now?" Mae heard the southern drawl returning to her speech.

"God knows. Could be any bar east of the Mississippi."

"Thanks." She didn't think to say goodbye, just disconnected the call, and found herself wandering, the accusations about her mother flying around her head. *Insane. Drunk.*

Mae wandered the grounds. Autumn cold crept under the satin fabric of her robe. Dry grass tickled her feet. The back door hung open in her wake, and she reached out her hands on both sides, letting the longest weeds brush her palms.

The sun's weak rays barely penetrated the greenhouse, and inside was grayer, dimmer. Shards of broken ceramic pots crunched underfoot, and at her waist were rows of tables crowded with untended vines and ferns, some shriveled, some dead, some flourishing in their state of neglect. Grainy dirt on her fingertips, she lifted a boisterous fern, smoothed its leaves. Crows squawked in the distance, sending a shudder through her core. She remembered blood, his contorted limbs.

She checked her phone, surprised to have service in the glass enclosure.

One missed call: Robert Feinstein. One voice message.

His voice was softer on the recording, his message softer too. "Ms. Pruitt, this is Bob Feinstein. While it would be unethical for me to provide contact information for Elizabeth Tompkins or to disclose any identifying information about her, I have considered your situation and decided it is within my scope to forward a message to her regarding your inquiry. Please return my call at your earliest convenience. I will hold off on contacting her until I have your go-ahead to share your contact information. Thanks."

It was something. Mae returned the call, making short work of providing her approval of his plan while she twisted a decaying vine. It was a long shot that she'd hear from her. Clearly her mother hadn't wanted any part in her life. She'd had two decades to reach out. Why should now be any different? And anyway, she would probably assume the call was financially motivated, that Mae wanted the violin for herself, and reached out only to plead with or guilt her.

Mae yanked the mushy vine, but instead of snapping from the stalk, it toppled to the floor, smashing the pot. She knelt down, instinctively began collecting pieces despite the disarray surrounding her, and through the metal table legs, she spotted an out of place object in the corner. Most of the greenhouse appeared forgotten by time, coated in a thin mildewy layer, speckles of dirt, fallen leaves, but this was untouched by the decay and wedged into a corner, invisible to anyone standing. She crawled, blackening her knees and staining her robe, through the table's legs. Her arm stretched though, fingers fully extended, and grasped the wooden handle. It was heavy, and as she pulled it toward her produced the squeal of metal on concrete. She knew it at once. Yes. How could she ever forget? She cradled it in her arms, thinking of her father, of Captain Williams, of Ollie fleeing the property. The axe.

Her heart beat rhythms against her ribs. Brown smudges were visible on the blade and the handle.

Of course.

It was the one thing that could tie him to it. They could test the DNA, brush for his fingerprints. And Carter, in his infinite hubris had hidden it here, surely thinking the last thing Mae would do would be to start gardening. Potential hiding places rolled through her mind like movie credits, but before she could decide on one, that familiar crunch of tires on gravel alerted her that she was out of time. She pushed the axe back into its hiding place, did her best to wipe the dirt from her knees, and took brisk paces back toward the house.

She reached the back door before he could reach the front, and one race was won. But how could she explain the dirt and grass stains on her robe? The remnants of muck on her skin? She flew up the stairs, taking the steps two at a time, dashed into the bathroom, and locked the door just as she heard Carter's footsteps on the hardwood. Stripping off the robe, she turned the shower as hot as it would go, watching the steam collect on the mirror, obscure her form. She bundled the robe into a ball and shoved it in the middle of the laundry basket.

"Mae!" she heard him call over the pattering of water.

"In the shower!"

Slipping inside, the droplets scorched her back, but she didn't resist nor make any attempt to change the temperature. The scathing heat was a welcome distraction from the news which threatened to rock her like a ship caught at sea in a storm. Her mother. The murder. The evidence. The abandonment.

Carter's steps grew closer. The knob turned but stopped short of opening.

"You locked the door?"

Mae cleared her throat. "Must've slipped the lock when I closed it."

"I'm gonna cook."

The lady specter loomed large in Mae's mind, threatening to return should Mae eat whatever he offered.

"Thank you, but I've been snacking all day."

He grunted, displeased, tried the knob one more time.

"I've gotta tell you something."

She froze. Water ran into her eyes.

"Oh?" It sounded strange, but hopefully not strange enough to raise suspicion.

"Eva quit."

Eyes closed, Mae let the water stream down her face. She felt her skin turn red.

"So you'd better get used to my cooking," he added, then slunk off, steps fading away as he did.

CHAPTER TWENTY-NINE

The police station was quieter than Mae expected, and Officer Jenkins looked less imposing in stature sitting behind his desk than he had the night he'd restrained her. That incident and the several hours preceding were still hazy, coming in vibrant flashes that made her stomach lurch like a bad dream. But she remembered his face: the mix of hesitation, pity, and fear as he put on his authoritarian posture like an ill-fitting suit jacket, led her into his handless backseat. He'd avoided her gaze as she stared through the metal mesh at his rearview mirror, daring him to face what he was doing. She'd hated him then, but if she was going to trap Carter, she would need his help.

Her feet clicked on the broad off-white tiles as she swung her legs back and forth. She'd decided to stop picking at her hangnails, her nail beds raw and inflamed, and foot swinging was the next best thing. An older cop with a sour face made fleeting glances. She wondered as she waited, what the rumors were about her around town. The crazy woman in the old house.

"Mrs. Duvall," he finally called without looking up from his desk.

Mae crossed the bullpen, stares on her back. She didn't turn to see who was looking, avoiding any movement that might be interpreted as paranoia. Maps sprawled across Jenkins's desk. Red pen outlined search areas, some slashed through. She settled in the uncushioned metal chair. "Any progress finding him?"

With quick but careful folds, Jenkins reduced the map to a small triangle and stowed it away in his desk drawer. "What can I help you with, Mrs. Duvall?"

"It's about Captain Williams," she said, thinking this would get his full attention. She was right.

His eyes perked, his posture straightened. "Do you know something about his location?"

Mae exhaled, long and slow.

"I'm sure you remember that night, when—well, anyway, I think I may have found some evidence related to his disappearance."

"Is that so?" He eyed her as if he thought she'd say Williams had been beamed up by aliens.

"I found an axe in my greenhouse." She kept her voice low, unsure whether she'd be heard or if she'd already been pegged as the hopelessly unstable housewife.

"Most of the farmhouses have axes, Mrs. Duvall."

"Please, call me Mae."

"Mae."

"I understand that, sir." She thought she might appeal to his sense of authority, "but I assume most axes aren't bloodstained. With all due respect."

"Bloodstained?" He tilted forward, subtle, as if trying to subdue his interest.

"It was tucked away in a corner, like it wasn't meant to be found."

Jenkins rolled a pen back and forth across his formica desk. "I can think of few better hiding places than a greenhouse. Why there?"

Mae folded her hands in her lap, squeezed her fists, resisting the urge to pick. "My husband thinks I'm useless, on top of being insane. He'd see no reason for me to go into the greenhouse. It's defunct anyway. And I've never had a green thumb. I suppose he stashed it there in a hurry, then never found a better spot. He's reckless, my husband."

The pen's little arm clicked as it made contact with the desk, back and forth he rolled it. "So, I assume you're also supposing that your husband, who recently had you committed, murdered Captain Williams with this axe? The same body you claimed to see the night of your ... institutionalization?"

Mae sighed, placed both palms flat on the desk, slid them toward him as she leaned in close. "What I *suppose* is that you have no leads. Your captain has been missing for days now, and you'd very much like to find him." Her eyes narrowed, her voice a hissing whisper. "I'm sure you'd prefer thinking he's alive, perhaps just stuck somewhere with no way to get in touch. I'm sure you'd prefer thinking that I *am* insane and utterly useless. But I also *suppose* that I've given you your only lead, and that it would irresponsible, no, unconscionable not to follow up merely based on your assumptions about the state of my mental health."

Jenkins ground his lips around his teeth. "It's our duty to follow up on every lead, and of course, we will. However, DNA testing takes time."

Mae nodded, relaxed back into her chair. "I know you were investigating him for my father's murder, arrested him even. Is it such a stretch to think he killed again?"

"My deepest condolences on the death of your father, Mae. But that case has been recently closed. I'm sure you were contacted by one of our staff. Charles Barlow confessed to the crime before taking his life. Your father's possessions were found in his home. We were wrong about your husband." His face suggested the words tasted bitter leaving his lips. "He was cleared of all charges."

"You know as well as I do how convenient that was. You must know Carter was involved. I'm giving you a chance to prove it."

Jenkins's face tilted.

"I'll find a way to prove what Carter's done. I have no job, I'm not in school, I barely care for the house as my husband points out at every turn. I have nothing but time. Time and access to all Carter's things, all my father's things. I found that old letter, and I'll find more. Mark my words: I will put Carter away, for the captain's murder, and for my father's. And I need to know that when I find what you need to lock him in a cage, that you'll come and escort him out in cuffs, as I already know you are well capable of doing."

A smile cracked Jenkins's face, a begrudging respect. He nodded, and an alliance was formed.

"We'll send some officers to the house. We have your permission to search your grounds including the greenhouse, correct?"

Mae nodded.

"Excellent. Keep me informed."

Despite his buttoned-up countenance, Mae detected stubborn hope in his tone. Not enough to match her own, but now at least, she had an ally in uniform. No more telephone games through Ollie. No more tiptoeing around Carter. The game was on.

Ollie's tires needed air. They slumped over hills and depressions in the earth, but Ollie pressed forward, charting a path through the blanket of leaves. The towering Eastern Hemlocks held tight to their evergreen needles, but surrounding oaks tossed buckets of brown leaves into the forest with each gust of bone chilling wind. Ollie had sworn they wouldn't return. Not after fleeing for their life into these woods. But they'd ignored the gnawing pull to find Captain Williams for too long, and if Mae was right, they knew where to look.

Lady kept pace easily, eager for the exercise after being penned up in Ollie's apartment. Charles hadn't lied. Her bark was worse than her bite, and to Ollie's surprise, Lady didn't snarl at Hobbes, didn't raise a single hair on her back. After their first night at the apartment together, Ollie awoke to find them cuddled together in a crescent shape, soaking in the warmth of dawn beneath the window. Ollie harbored a deep love for strays. They were a stray too, after all.

They laid down their bike a hundred feet before the break in the trees. Mae's property looked quiet. From here, Ollie couldn't see the driveway, wasn't sure if the muted green truck was there. Lady at their side, they felt emboldened. Brooks Babineaux may think twice before he tangled with a snarling German Shepard. Sniffing the ground, she pulled her leash taut. Her pointed ears hung limply around her head. She closed her eyes to take in the scents.

"You don't happen to have any police training, do ya girl?"

Lady glanced up, showing a sliver of white in her eyes.

"It's okay, didn't think so."

Ollie's steps sunk into piles of leaves that rose up mid-calf. Lady stepped easily through the underbrush while

Ollie's feet fumbled around unseen rocks. Crouching behind a thick tree trunk, Ollie observed the property.

He has to be here.

As Ollie scanned the ground for signs of Williams's body, they both wanted to find him and shamefully hoped that Mae *was* unstable, that what she'd seen *was* a hallucination. Ollie wanted to locate his remains, to have him laid to rest. But more so wanted him to return in a taxi, to tease the police force for worrying, to make Ollie feel foolish for hypothesizing, one more time.

Lady caught a scent, jerked on her line, tugging Ollie along with her. She lurched onto the Alquist Ave property, away from the shelter of the trees, and Ollie stumbled to keep up, their head swiveling around, anxiety clawing at their throat. Whimpering as she pulled, tail wagging with excitement, Lady led Ollie to the property's northern perimeter. Gazing up with adoration in her eyes, she sat on a pile of overturned earth. Ollie tossed a treat which she caught in the air. They crouched down, moved some rocks aside. A rancid smell wafted up from disturbed earth. Ollie's fingers caught a bit of cloth mixed in with the dirt, Lady emitted a throaty bark, and Ollie stumbled back, landed on their ass.

Their head whipped around in the direction of Lady's fixed stare. She held her head low, a trail of hair raised along her spine. Her lip quivered, showing flashes of her long canines. In the vacant field between the barn and the greenhouse, Ivy stood. Her long black skirt billowed in a passing breeze, stretching in the same direction as her curled blonde hair. Green eyes reflected the forest all around and stared, unmoving. Her hand dropped to her side, clutched in her palm, a phone. She mouthed something, and though it was impossible to read her lips with certainty from this distance, Ollie thought they spelled *I'm sorry.*

Surprise became fear.

"Ivy," Ollie called, the lowest volume they could muster to clear the distance between them.

Lady snapped at the air.

Ivy took a step backward, then another. She looked over her shoulder.

Adrenaline screamed at Ollie to run, and they scrambled to their feet. The way back to their bike took them closer to the house. Lady fixated on something in the distance.

"Let's go," Ollie whispered.

While they made for the break in the tree line, Lady pulled in Ivy's direction, slowing Ollie's pace. A jog pulled into sidesteps by Lady's lunging was the best Ollie could muster, still one hundred feet away from the cover of the trees. A shot rang out, whizzing past Ollie's head.

"STOP."

Ollie froze, expecting at any moment to feel the searing entry of a bullet. Lady cowered, startled by the gunfire. She whimpered, looked to Ollie for guidance.

"Tie up the dog." His voice was cold, unwavering.

Ollie knew without having to look. They heard the snapping twigs and crisp leaves beneath his footfalls. As he approached, Lady's hairs raised once again. She growled, low and menacing. Showed her impressive canines. Her bottom jaw trembled. Foam collected on her lips, dripped in white chunks.

"Tie it up," he commanded.

She snapped at the air.

"Or I'll shoot it."

Carter moved his gun's sights from Ollie to Lady. Ten feet away, he was within point blank range. There was nothing in his eyes. Cold nothing. And Ollie knew somewhere deep he would do it. Hands shaking, they tied the leash around a nearby branch, hoping it was too thin to hold, that if Carter got too close, she'd lunge, snap the line. That he'd meet the same fate as Jezebel.

"Hands behind your head and walk to me."

"It's okay," Ollie whispered to Lady, but her eyes remained locked on the threat. Palms folded on the back of their head, Ollie forced their legs to move in Carter's direction.

"I warned you about coming back here, didn't I?" His voice was smug, and Ollie's stomach turned at the feeling of his hands on their body, patting them down. Lady snarled and lunged at her line, the sound of the branch cracking but not giving way. Carter's fingers wandered into the pocket of their cargo pants, scooping out their Swiss Army knife. The gun's muzzle, still warm from the fired shot, pressed into the back of Ollie's neck. "Walk."

He took them into the barn, forced open the plywood door which concealed the tiny room Ollie had hidden in before, where they found the signal jammer. He threw Ollie in, folding them into dust and hanging cobwebs, and pushed the door shut behind them. They heard wood squeal against wood, and knew he was barricading them inside. The thin strip of light beneath the door disappeared. Ollie was alone, a prisoner in utter black.

CHAPTER THIRTY

Mae heard the explosion outside. *Fireworks?* And a dog barking in the distance. Carter had slipped out only moments before, and a guilty thought crept into Mae's mind.

I hope he was shot.

There was an urge to investigate the source of the noise, but she'd already wasted so much time chasing auditory ghosts, and there was so little time left. In the back of her mind, like a stuck, haunting melody, was the pull of the third floor.

Mae's mind drifted from question to question as she climbed the stairs, reached the second-floor landing, and kept climbing. Why had he boarded it up? Were the boards truly rotted through? Would Ollie have lied, or could they have been mistaken?

The railing was still broken off where he'd claimed she pushed him. She stood between the splintered edges where the missing length of rail provided a clear shot of the fall to the ground. Vertigo threatened to take hold. The space around her warped and twisted, and Mae reached back to steady herself on the remaining rail. She couldn't have pushed him. Right? The thirty-foot fall would've done more harm than a few scratches. Would've at least broken an arm.

Against her will, Mae envisioned her own neck snapping, a trail of blood from her mouth as she lay beneath, soaking into the oriental rug. Shaking herself back to the present moment, Mae studied the plywood boards that sealed the third-floor entrance. Her fingers found purchase on the edges, and to her delight, she saw that Ollie had used shallow brad nails to secure the boards. She pulled, bracing herself on her back leg, knowing if the board gave way too suddenly, it would send her stumbling back through the gap, tumbling down three stories to the oriental carpet.

Two nails in the corner popped free, and a stir of elation rose up inside her. She stopped pulling, surveyed her progress. Pinpricks of blood emerged where the splinters went in. She'd need a tool to rip the rest of the board from the doorframe.

A buzz in her pocket.

Her heart skipped.

Another buzz, a call.

Unknown number.

Heart fluttering, Mae reached the safety of the second-floor landing before taking the call.

"Hello?" Her voice hesitant.

"Hello, this Mae Pruitt?" It was a woman with a syrupy Southern drawl.

"Speaking." Mae's pulse thumped in her temples.

"This is Liz Tompkins. I understand you been tryin' to reach me."

Mae sat on the top step, felt the fibers in the carpet runner. Time seemed to pause around her at the sound of her mother's voice, speaking to her for the very first time. She hadn't thought she'd have an accent. She hadn't known what to expect. "Mrs. Tompkins—"

"Miss," she corrected.

Mae cleared her throat.

"Miss Tompkins." Mae did her best to formalize her tone, like she was speaking to a bank teller, a customer, someone who'd never held her heart in their hands, then left it beating unprotected on a sidewalk. "I was calling about my father's estate. I understand you were a beneficiary and I—"

"You wanted to know why, no doubt."

"That's right." Mae was grateful Liz couldn't see her trembling lip.

"I s'pose Richard always was nostalgic. Lady Paola was a fond memory we shared. I never asked for her, of course, would've been improper, but they sent me the paperwork when he passed nonetheless, informed me of the theft as well."

Mae's brow perked. "Paperwork?"

"Yes, such an old, fine piece accompanies paperwork. To prove its authenticity, should it ever go to auction, and to inflate the ego of the owner, too, I should think. I've felt quite silly holding onto it all these years without Lady Paola herself to pair it with, but I guess I'm not immune to nostalgia myself."

Pieces materialized and shifted into place in Mae's mind. *Of course, that's why they were never able to find it. Not the police, not Carter, not Charles (if he was involved after all).*

"But none of that answers your question properly. I've thought many years on how I might explain myself to you, Mae, and in all that time, I'm embarrassed to admit that I've never come up with an adequate explanation, suffice to say I thought we'd both be better off."

She took a deep breath in, wind rattled over the line. "I hope we can leave it there."

The ultimate betrayal stood between them, the distance between an abandoned daughter and a mother who did the leaving.

"Thank you for calling," was all Mae could think to say. The call ended without fanfare. No tearful goodbye, no heartfelt apology, no grasping at explanations, no plea for forgiveness. Having expected nothing consciously, to Mae's surprise she still felt let down, one more time by her mother.

But she hadn't sounded mad. No, her Southern diction was lyrical, her syntax was that of an educated woman whose thoughts were organized, complex, stitched together with intention. Perhaps, Mae thought, her legacy was one of evasion more than madness, of neglect, or irresponsibility, of want for freedom no matter the cost, not one of tragic mental instability.

Instability. The memory came in an instant. The pry bar. She'd seen it in the library while they were moving, watched him use it to loosen old nails. Her feet carried her there without thought to the lady specter who haunted it in her last visit. She didn't check the corners for black molten shadows. Didn't read book spines for taunting messages. It lay unassuming on a corner table. And next she knew, she was prying the remaining brad nails from the plywood boards, stacking them on the stairs, and stepping into the cool dusty light that streamed in through the third-floor window, the thick scent of memory and mothballs filling her nose.

Mae felt as if she'd crossed a portal to another time, surrounded by her father's things, some cloaked in white sheets, some strewn about. The fear that Carter would appear at any moment vanished, as if this place was reserved for her and her father, an impenetrable pocket of family and loss, in which he had no place. Boxes overflowed with books, others marked *Clothes*, a tarnished candelabra webbed with spider's silk was perched upon a rolling desk. A faded green trunk, the lock cut, sat open in the center of the creaking floor, its contents littered over the surrounding area. She blinked floating specks of dust from her eyes, sat crossed-legged amidst the tornado of memory.

Sale, a bin read. It was clear plastic, a departure from the antique chests and cardboard moving boxes. Inside she found silver cutlery, a small landscape painting, jeweled cufflinks, her father's gold watch. Beside the window was a metal framed bed, its plastic-coated mattress layered in soot the shape of shoe prints, a grimy sheet crumpled in the corner. She eyed the window frame, conspicuously free from dirt and debris, and pushed up on the glass which slid open without complaint. *Unlocked*, she thought. Grasping it, she leaned her head outside. Below an old trellis wound down the siding, its wooden structure wide enough for feet, spaced apart enough like ladder rungs. The ivy that grew there had withered in the autumn cold but was also stripped away in a vertical line from the ground to the window. She pictured Carter shimmying up while she slept, his heavy footfalls above her as she tried to sleep in her room below, driving her anxious dread.

"So, you've been up here," she said aloud. Leaning back inside, she noticed her father's old record player, also free from dust and cobwebs. She placed the needle on the disc, let it play as her father had shown her. Strings bellowed from its speaker, her father's rendition of Tchaikovsky's *Violin Concerto*. She hadn't known he had recordings. Had rarely seen him play Lady Paola. Yet, here it was, the answer to her question of madness.

Carter had discovered his recordings, used them to taunt and torture her. As Lady Paola sang high notes, Mae's rage bubbled like molten steel. He'd planned it all out, this intricate, maddening design. And she had fallen for it, hook, line, and antique sinker. What delight he must've felt when he caught her during the seance. What sick pleasure must have swirled in his belly to know that his plan was working, that she suspected supernatural intervention before his betrayal.

Steps rang out on the staircase, growing louder, but it wasn't fear that filled Mae, it was wicked, feminine rage. She tossed open a nearby cabinet, hoping to find a knife or some other weapon to wield, but instead found a collection of papers. The steps grew louder, closer.

"Mae!" The voice carried up the stairs through the open door.

She inspected the papers, odd writing, repeated lines, and a name scrawled over and over again.

Charles Barlow.

Charles Barlow.

Charles Barlow.

The script was unlike Carter's, yet it must've come from his hand. He was practicing. It had to be. The only solution that made sense. He came up here to practice forging the groundkeeper's handwriting, paying special mind to his signature to forge the suicide note, the letter where Charles confessed. Carter was a forger, after all, convicted, served time. How hadn't she seen it before? And now the proof was before her, clear as day.

"Mae." The voice quieter now, quieter and closer.

Mae's eyes rose from the papers clutched in her fist, passed over the bohemian black skirt, the lacy white top which barely held in her overflowing chest, the curls of blonde hair descending her shoulders. Ivy's emerald eyes were fixed, her expression unreadable.

"Ivy." Mae mirrored her stoicism, unwilling to give Ivy the pleasure of knowing the pain she'd caused.

"You shouldn't be up here." Her tone was fragile. If Mae hadn't known better, caring. More footfalls on the landing made Ivy step aside, create a clearing in the open doorway. She sucked in her lips, as if restraining her response.

Carter's muscular figure appeared in the space between Ivy and the door, his hair pushed to odd angles, held in disarray by sweat. Jaw clenched, he observed his wives in the third-floor room, sucked his teeth as if they'd invaded his privacy.

"Mae," he cleared his throat, "it's not safe up here. You need to go back downstairs."

He passed Ivy without looking, as if she was transparent, like a ghost. "I wouldn't want you falling through the floor."

The boards groaned under his weight, and Mae stiffened as he took deliberate steps toward her. "You are far too precious to me," he said, straightening the sleeve which had fallen below her shoulder.

Ivy balled her hands into fists.

Vicious barking echoed over the grounds beneath.

Mae looked for malice inside his honey-colored eyes, but either it was absent or so well-hidden that she found none. He wrapped his arm around her rigid frame. His fingers felt at once alien and cunning, strong and reassuring. Her guts twisted. Papers in her hand crunched as she crushed them, her hands clenching with battling emotions. His arm around her like a vice, he stepped toward the open doorway, still regarding Ivy as a specter, a ghost, a thing unseen. The air thickened, weighed down Mae's lungs as she tried to breathe. Each step felt like slow motion. She glanced back, her eyes locking on Ivy's vibrant green irises, spread wide with five alarm fire. Mae faced the stairs.

She heard the crash, heavy metal on bone, and felt Carter's weight drag her down as he fell. Mae slipped from beneath his arm before he could bring her with him to the floor. Ivy held a bronze statue in her quaking hand, an owl, her father's favorite. It had once sat in the foyer.

Carter's eyes rolled. Blood leaked from a chasm in his head, slicked his black hair. His lashes fluttered, lids closed. Ivy hovered, and Mae feared she'd be next, bleed out beside her forgery of a husband. But Ivy dropped the statue, the weight of it shaking the floor.

"Go," she said. "To the barn."

Mae fled down the stairs, skipping steps and crashing onto the second-floor landing. She glanced behind her, saw Carter's body slide away, then disappear into the third-floor room. Mae should've kept running. She knew that, and a moment later Ivy appeared, her lacy white shirt now stained crimson, in the open doorway.

"Wait," she commanded. "Stop."

Mae froze. She knew she should run, but her feet held her in place.

"What's that in your hand?"

Ivy floated down the steps, all the grace of Victorian spirit. "Give me that."

Knuckles white, Mae unfurled her fist revealing the scrawling letters, Carter's practice runs for the suicide note. Ivy snatched the papers away, and Mae's feet finally became unstuck. Sound fell away, and she saw only the blur of carpet patterns beneath her feet, felt the whir of air on her cheeks as she sprinted toward the back door. Ivy followed, and Mae thought she'd catch her, drag her down to the hardwood, finally take her revenge on Mae for stealing away her husband, until Mae reached the bottom of the staircase. Mae turned left. Ivy turned right and moved into the foyer. Mae dipped through the back door, but curiosity made her hesitate. She watched with bent knees, ready to run, as Ivy tossed the letters into the roaring fire.

CHAPTER THIRTY-ONE

Eyes blurred with panic and confusion, Mae took off toward the barn.

What did Ivy want?

To kill Carter? Or to save him?

When she reached the barn door, she threw it open and dashed into the dark interior. Panting, she realized she didn't know why she'd come. Did Ivy have a trap waiting for her here?

"Hello?"

Mae's chest contracted. "Hello?" The word caught in her throat.

"Mae?"

Recognizing the sound at once, Mae pushed the trunk that blocked the flimsy plywood door. She ripped it open, and revealed Ollie, their skin grey from a coating on fine dust. They threw their arms around Mae with a force that pushed her backward several steps.

"Thank God," they said. "Thank God."

Mae felt warm tears drop onto her shoulder. She wrapped her arms around Ollie, returning their embrace.

"I think I found him," Ollie panted through ragged breaths. "On the north side of the property, there's some freshly dug soil, the smell and—I felt the cloth—" Ollie buried their face into Mae's sopping shoulder. "You were right, Mae. Carter killed him. You were right all along."

As Mae held Ollie's trembling body, she caught sight of the tree stump, Ollie's axe buried in the center.

"You left it here …" Mae drifted away from Ollie's embrace, enchanted by the beam of light which laid upon the blade.

Ollie wiped snot from their nose. "Yeah I—"

They rambled on with some explanation, but Mae couldn't hear them. In her mind a bow sawed across strings. An arpeggio punctuated her steps toward it. Bits of dust wafted through the sun's rays, dappled light over the smooth, wooden handle. She gripped it, and a few of Ollie's words broke through.

"What are you—"

Mae braced with her foot on the stump, yanked the axe from its resting place. It was heavy in her hand. No, the perfect weight. A deep breath in, and Mae swung it round with a flick of her wrist. She'd breathed in the darkness of the old Victorian, day in, day out. She'd inhaled it all. There was no darkness left in the house. No fear. It had taken residence inside her lungs, settling at the base like black mold.

"Be careful …"

Ollie's voice faded away as she swung it once more, faster this time, and a wide grin illuminated her face. The darkness spread from her lungs, crept through her veins to every vital organ. Black as char they were. Midnight blood ran through arteries beneath pale skin. She was the shadow now. The lady specter, axe wielding creature to be feared.

"Do you have your phone?"

Ollie came into focus, wiping their nose on their shirt sleeve. "No, I must've dropped it."

They clutched Mae's free hand in theirs. "Come on, follow me."

Leading her through the barn door, Ollie jogged along the path. Lady barked and yanked at her tether, eager to be freed. Mae slowed her pace at the sight of the dog's frothing muzzle, stopped short as the branch cracked, holding the beast back by little more than a sapling.

"It's okay, girl," Ollie assured, hands out in a stop motion.

Ollie took steady steps toward the dog, within striking distance, but Mae stood back. "Ollie ..." The dog spit saliva with a guttural bark. Stepping away, Mae heard a crunch, felt something smooth beneath her heel. Glancing down, the reflection of the fading light sparkled off the cracked phone screen.

Ollie untied the dog from the broken sapling as Mae lifted the phone and brushed away dirt from its surface.

"It's busted."

Holding the leash, Ollie deflated. "Shit."

Mae tossed Ollie the phone to see. After mashing a few buttons, Ollie wrapped the leash around their palm. "I'll get help. My bike is in the woods just over there. Run to a neighbor. Seriously, Mae. He's got a gun. Get yourself as far away as possible."

Mae nodded, walked with Ollie to the tree line, giving the snapping dog a wide berth.

Leg swung over the side, Ollie mounted their bike. "The force will bring down hell on his ass. Don't worry. He's not gonna weasel out of this one." Pedaling through the brush, Ollie's figure grew distant.

No, he won't weasel out of this one, Mae thought. Standing tall, she glanced at the Dalroy's house, barely visible through the trees, then turned her back on it. She moved through the property on Alquist Ave, determination in her steps, axe in her hand, revenge in her heart.

CHAPTER THIRTY-TWO

Ivy rocked on the off-white porch, leaves swirling at her feet with the passing wind. Her swollen under-eyes were tinged with a purplish hue. Back and forth she rocked, as if soothing an invisible child in her arms. Mae sat in the matching chair, pushed her feet to rock in time. The axe blade dragged against the wood, carved shallow crevasses.

The chairs creaked, and the distant squawking of crows and shifting of dry leaves harmonized the wheezing wooden tones. "Tell me," Mae said.

Ivy planted both feet, abruptly stopped her rocking.

"What do you want in all this?"

Her head turned smooth and slow like an owl, her expression thoughtless, and Mae thought for a moment, there was a distinct possibility it may slide all the way around. Ivy chuckled. Shook her head. "If he goes down, I go down right with him. He saw to that."

"I found the axe." Mae glanced down at the one in her grasp. "The one in the greenhouse. The one he used to—" What started as an offer of consolation died in an onslaught of rising rage. Eva had known about Williams's murder. "I already told the police about it."

"And whose DNA do you think they'll find on the handle, right alongside his?" Ivy snorted with hissing ire.

And who might deserve the cell beside him? Mae shot her a look that said as much.

"I didn't kill him, if that's what you're thinking. He made me stash it like his errand girl." Her gaze drifted to the dangling rope from the oak bough. "That's what I've always been." Her fingers gripped the arm rests, nail digging into the wood. "I think he loved me … once."

Mae's memory wandered back to early days, stolen meetings at the trailer park pool, lingering glances, his fingers through her hair, the glitter in his eye when she smiled.

Sometimes, he loved me too.

"How could we have known?" Her words were feather soft; a balm meant to soothe them both. They rocked in time. A distant groan clawed through layers of drywall and flooring, climbed down from high above. Mae's skin goosed.

She didn't want to ask, but she had to. "What did you do to him?" The words came out thin, danced across the air between them like a ballerina.

"He's waiting for you," she said, eyes still locked on the rope as it twisted in a gust. "Upstairs."

The rocking chair bucked backward as Mae stood. "You should get out of here." A sinking feeling of pity settled over her, as if she was looking at her own narrowly avoided future. "The police will be here. You should run."

Ivy stood, bending in the breeze like a waif. Aimlessly, she batted at her purse, strung backward over her arm.

"Wait," Mae said.

Ivy turned, met her with bulging eyes.

"Do you have your phone?"

Ivy's slender hand drew the phone from her purse, handed it over with a glazed expression, then plodded down the steps, an empty husk.

"Where will you go?" Mae called over the town car's roof. Concern for Ivy came as a surprise but laid thick upon Mae's heart like a weighted blanket.

Ivy shrugged, flashed a hopeless smile.

Mae clicked on the phone, called after her, "What's the passcode?"

Fingers over the door handle, Ivy smirked. "All zeros." Her lips parted into a toothy smile. "What else would it be?" She slid into the driver's seat. The engine roared.

Mae punched in Jenkins's number, was ready to dial when Ivy called out from her rolled down window. "Mae!"

Her heart lurched. Maybe she had second thoughts, wanted to save Carter after all. "Sorry about the letters. My fingerprints were all over them."

Mae shrugged, twisted her mouth into a forgiving smile.

"And the strings."

"What?"

"It was all I could find."

Before Mae could ask, Ivy rolled up her window, accelerated down the gravel drive with a force that kicked gravel stones out behind her. They rained onto the porch steps, mercifully missing Mae's legs by inches.

Jenkins answered, quick and questioning. "Hello?"

"This is Mae. It's time."

Ascending the stairs, Mae hoped the vague and ominous nature of her words would spur Jenkins to come, but perhaps delay him a few minutes while he decided whether or not to heed the call. She had unfinished business, after all, and needed time to conduct it. Each step felt like a walk to the gallows, shrouded in shadow.

Whispers nipped at the corners of her mind as she drew closer to the second-floor landing, bit at her ears as she climbed to the third.

Swirls of darkness obscured her periphery. Overtaken by the heavy sense of the lady specter, her movement toward the door strained, as if she carried on her back a thousand secrets and misdeeds. She envisioned the terror she'd witnessed that night, the axe-wielding woman, faceless, made of mystery and fear. And she was not afraid. The woman was no threat, in fact, not a woman even separate from herself.

The lady specter surrounded, then became her. Another groan wafted out from the third-floor room, wrapped her in fortitude. Indeed, she walked to the gallows. But not as prisoner, as executioner.

In the faded daylight, the third-floor room was more mausoleum than house. Stepping over the dusty boxes and chests and bins of her father's items destined for sale, she ignored Carter's cries, placed the needle on the record to drown them out with her father's music. Lady Paola's melody lifted her spirit. How could these very same notes have filled her with dread mere weeks before? Her disgraced husband and captor lay fixed to the metal bed frame beneath the window, writhing like a fish on a hook. Steel violin strings wrapped around his wrists and ankles, bit into his flesh raising hairline slices of blood where he struggled.

Mae crawled into the bed beside him, axe nestled to her left. She felt his wide eyes on her skin. Slithering her body like a snake across the musty sheets, she tried to curl up, to rest her head in the crook of his neck, but his bound arm got in the way.

"Ugh." She wriggled out in frustration and stood over him. Static raised her hair to a lion's mane, she felt it stand on end like a dirty halo. "Tell me your name."

"I know you love me, Mae." His voice was demure, pleading. "And you know I have always loved you, since the moment I saw you. You know that."

His body stretched, arms yanking his shoulders nearly out of their sockets, legs pulled taut and fastened to opposite bedposts, the wire string twisted around each post, unforgiving as barbed wire.

Mae stood over him, watched his pupils dart back and forth between hers.

"Tell me your name, *husband.*"

"Give me one last chance." He licked his lips. "I know I screwed everything up before, but that's all done. You've gotta see that. Eva's gone—"

"Ivy," Mae stopped him. "Her name is Ivy."

"What does it matter?" he shrieked. "She's gone and it's just you and me now. Like it always should've been. We can put all this shit away, be a real husband and wife. We can get a whole pack of goats if you want them! Have *kids.* Remember?"

Mae turned her back. "Herd."

"What?"

"Not a pack of goats, a herd."

Carter shifted his weight, groaned as another line of blood formed around his ankle. "Of course, a herd."

"Did you forget your real name?"

He coughed out a laugh. "Brooks, okay? It's Brooks. But I've always been *Carter* with you. I wanted to start over. That's not a crime, is it?"

Mae turned away, dragging the axe behind her. Finger stripping a line of dust from an antique armoire, the words echoed, *not a crime, not a crime.* Her finger crusted gray with dust, she looked to him.

"In the dresser." He motioned with his eyes. "There's a knife. Get it. You can cut the strings."

Mae raised the axe above her head. "I should cut the strings."

The whites of his eyes flashed. He strained against the wire. Blood leaked from deep cuts and rolled to his elbows.

Mae giggled, dropped her arms and the axe crashed onto the strained floorboards. "That would be *crazy.*"

"Mae, please. In the drawer, just get the knife and cut me free. It'll be like we always wanted it."

Seeing him splayed turned her stomach, but she was unsure if it was pity or disgust. "First, tell me what you did. Tell the truth for once in your life."

Sweat seeped into the fabric around his armpits. "It doesn't matter. You're always focused on the wrong things, Mae. That's your problem. I told you I'm sorry, what more do you want?"

Mae turned toward the window, the entry he'd used so many times to riffle around, to try and make his fortune off her lost childhood, her father's agonizing murder.

"I want you to tell me the whole truth. Then I'll cut you free." Mae stood taller than she ever had in his presence, dwarfed his bound figure beneath her. "Better hurry. I've already called the police. I imagine they're on their way."

"Are you serious?" His muscles clenched, but the unwavering metal strings that bound him held tight, coated now in his dark red blood. "Okay, okay." He spoke fast, no stopping for breath. "I was appraising the Stradivarius, years ago, when Charles came to me. He wanted to steal it but didn't know how to sell it. He didn't have the connections." The betrayal of her father's trust bit into her as if it was her own. His groundskeeper plotting his demise, conspiring against him while he signed his paychecks.

"I agreed to unload it for a 50/50 cut. No one was supposed to get hurt, but it went wrong. Richard, your father, wasn't supposed to be home. Charles told me he grabbed the closest thing, the—you know—the axe and ..."

A gathering of crows swirled above the greenhouse, landed one by one on the lawn.

"The idiot didn't know I needed the certificate of authenticity to get even close to what the Stradivarius was worth. I tried to pass off a forgery, but the buyer spotted the fake. So, Charles stuck around, tended the grounds, and searched the property until the moron broke a window and scared himself out of looking anymore. When I got locked up, we lost touch; but when I got out, I needed the cash. How else was I supposed to make a new start? I'd lost my business, everything. Mae, you've got to understand. I would've been on the streets."

No, it wasn't pity. Mae was sure now.

"So, I found you, figured I'd find the thing myself. I didn't count on falling in love with you."

The last sentence changed inflection, lit a fire inside Mae that threatened to leak out her eyes, or her fists. "And Captain Williams?"

A deep guttural sigh, "I had no choice. He showed up here, fishing around. I thought he was an intruder. I did what I had to do."

Mae nodded, her vision blurred.

"Hurry, Mae. Please. Grab the knife." His eyes were all whites.

"I'll get it," she said without facing him. She floated to the dresser, opened the top drawer. The knife inside was long, silver with an embellished handle. The cold metal made her hand remember its strength. She gripped it. Her knuckles turned white. Taking methodical steps toward Carter, she held the blade out toward him. Light bounced off the shiny surface, reflected in his hazel eyes. Carter's jaw hung open a crack, wide enough for an insect to fly in.

"I don't see a knife," she said. "You must've put it elsewhere."

"Mae?"

She twisted it so the window's light reflected onto the walls. "Maybe you just imagined you put it there."

"Mae, please." The words came slow, measured.

She pressed the blade against the thin skin of his throat. She remembered the glare of fluorescent lights in the hospital. The captain's decimated visage. "I think you need some sleep, Carter. You don't sound well."

Beads of sweat formed on his brow. He swallowed, and his Adam's apple pressed against the blade.

"But wait," Mae withdrew, "I'm the one who's unwell. Right, baby? It's me who had to go to the hospital. Your sweet wife. Mae-by. Mae-by I'm crazy!" She let out a high-pitched squeal and tossed the knife across the room with a clang. "I'm always seeing things and hearing things and acting *queer*. Isn't that right, baby?"

"Mae—"

Mae smacked her forehead. "Oh gosh, that was the knife, wasn't it? I got confused again and lost it. I'd better look for it. Don't you think? It's your only chance to get out of here before the cops show up." Mae toppled a set of books atop a dusty cardboard box. "If I don't find it and cut you free, you'll be angry with me again." Mae chucked a fallen book over her shoulder. "And we can't have that. 'Cause if you're angry with me, you'll have me

locked up again. Won't let me wriggle out of there a second time. Not before I sign away my estate, my freedom."

Carter stared, incredulous.

"I'd better find it." Mae flipped an end table sending a plume of dust into the air. "Is it here?"

She feigned a look. "No, not here." A stack of papers cascaded to the ground as she cleared them from a shelf. "Here?" She stared back at Carter. "Ivy would've known where to look."

"Ivy never mattered, babe. She was a means to an end, that's all."

"Well, she's gone now. Strung you up and left you."

As Mae pulled open a low dresser drawer, Carter said, "Not that one," his words quick.

Inside glittered an ornate barrel key. "Oh, look." Mae held it up for him to see. "I've finally found it, baby. The key you knew I'd lose. And here it is." She shoved it deep into her pocket. "But a key won't cut those wires." She paced wild patterns, weak floorboards curled around her stomping. "Do you see how I'm trying to help you? But how can I help you? My head is so full of ghosts. How can I possibly help you escape?"

"You're not crazy!" His voice sounded fragile, a panicked laugh. "You know you're not!"

"That's the catch-22, isn't it? Crazy people don't know they're crazy, right? That's what the book says. But I do. In fact, I'm quite sure of it, thanks to you. You've reminded me so, so many times. So tragic, that I've gone the way of my mother."

He twisted against his binds, whimpered as his skin tore around them. "I made it up, okay? I don't know anything about your mother. I'm sorry. Just help me. I love you. We can be together. Please!" His watery eyes had a quality Mae had not seen in them before, utter desperation.

She approached, one pounding step after another. Through gritted teeth she said, "Maybe if I weren't crazy, chasing spirits and music around the house, tearing myself apart for your amusement, I could've helped you. Maybe I could've even forgiven you. But your plan worked, Carter! You've dismantled me piece by piece. There's no empathy left inside. No way for me to save you."

Deep in her pocket, the phone rubbed against her thigh. She withdrew it, held it up to his face so he could read the screen.

Recording.

"Mae, no." His skin faded to pale white. Three floors below, a jostling at the door.

"I think we have a visitor," Mae said, her expression blank. The timer on the recorder ticked on.

"Mrs. Duvall!" The authoritative voice whooshed up flights of stairs.

"Up here!" Mae chirped back.

Carter's head bobbled back and forth, his jaw trembling.

Careful, quiet steps led Mae to the landing where she was met by Jenkins, horror stricken at the sight of her bound prisoner. Stopping the recording, she handed him the phone.

"You won't have to release him this time."

Clamoring for the handcuffs on his belt, Jenkins moved across the creaking floorboards.

"Who the fuck are you?" Hissed the flailing child strapped to the mildewed bed.

"You don't remember me?" Jenkins eyed him with a raised brow. "Maybe I'm just a figment of your wife's imagination then." He fixed the cuff to Carter's wrist, began to unwind the violin string that held it in place. "What do you prefer, Mr. Babineaux? That I call you Carter or Brooks?" Jenkins moved toward the window side, pulled Carter's cuffed hand to meet his other, securing him as he unwound remaining wires.

A sudden change came over Carter's expression and tone as he realized to whom he spoke. "Officer, look what she's done to me. My wife is sick, I don't blame her, but you must see what she's done, tied me up like an animal. I don't want to press charges but—"

"Save it." Jenkins lurched Carter into a sitting position, trained his service revolver on him. Following from behind, Jenkins pressed Carter to move down the stairs, and Mae followed, leaving a full flight of space between them.

Straining his neck to catch glimpses of her, Carter called behind to Mae. "I don't expect you to understand." There was a wild sadness about his face, like his whole life had been played in a minor key. "She was always wedged between us, Lady Paola, gleaming like she was on fire within." In his hazel irises danced an image of her ornate carving, her delicate neck, and Mae saw him as a man hopelessly entangled in her thin metal strings.

EPILOGUE

Late December

Lady Paola arrived the day after Christmas, transported in an armored truck, escorted to the door by an armed guard. She made the journey inside a pine box, nailed shut like a coffin around her case. Affixed with string was a handwritten note, one line only.

She belongs in Landrum.

The hammer strung through the belt loop in Ollie's pants pulled the denim low around their hips as they climbed the ladder. They braced for balance against the stone hearth, crinkled their nose as the burnt aroma from the blazing fire the night before wafted upward.

"Need help with that?" Mae asked as the ladder shifted under Ollie's weight.

She rushed over, bracing the uneven footing. Warm sugar had seeped into Ollie's T-Shirt from the cookies they'd baked together. Gift wrap in greens, reds, and golds lay shredded around the foyers, bows scattered from persistent attacks by Hobbes.

The drill whined as Ollie pushed the bit through hardened spackle; they hammered anchors in where anchors had been before. Violin display cases follow a general look: wooden borders around plate glass, a colored background to offset the wood tones, and this one matched to an uncanny likeness, the one Richard Pruitt had hung before. The same burgundy background, the same maple wood frame, hooks on the back in the same position.

You sure you want it there? Ollie had asked. Mae had nodded, *It's the heart of the home.*

Lady watched, rawhide in her canines, as Ollie inserted screws at just the right depth to catch. They jimmied the hooks until the case had a secure hold on the wall behind. Mae stepped back as Ollie descended the ladder, but not so far that their body didn't brush against hers. Side by side, their toes dug into the area rug as they looked up at it.

"It's perfect," Mae said.

Ollie couldn't help but blush. Mae removed Lady Paola from her velvet lined case, cradled her as if she were a newborn. It was Ollie's turn to hold the ladder still as Mae climbed, to brace the uneven legs as Mae placed Paola's delicate neck into the slot. Glass sealed around her, and fingerprints rubbed from the sheen, they beheld her.

"She really is something." Ollie reached for Mae's hand, fingers grazing her palm.

Birdsong drew Mae's attention to the bay window where a female cardinal chirped from the porch rail, muddy red, cheeks painted orange. "Look," Mae urged.

Ollie turned to face the window, following the line of Mae's extended finger.

"They usually travel in pairs. I'm sure the male is around here somewhere."

The cardinal cocked her head, observing them sideways.

"Where's your mate?" Ollie cooed.

The bird hopped along the railing, scuttled upward in a flurry of wingbeats.

"I think she's alone," Mae said, pulling Ollie close at the hips.

Ollie cracked a smile. "I don't blame her."

Glancing at the grandfather clock in the corner, Mae squeezed Ollie's hand. "Isn't it time you got to work?"

Smoothing the wrinkles from their blue button down, Ollie tucked in their shirt tail, tightened their black leather belt. Mae ran her finger along the sewn patch, *Landrum Police Dept.*

"You're right. If I'm late, Jenkins will have my ass." After a kiss on the cheek, Ollie asked, "What's for dinner tonight?"

Mae flashed a mischievous smile. "You're spoiled. Better enjoy the easy meals while you can. Won't be around to cook for you every night once classes start in the spring."

ABOUT THE AUTHOR

Rae Knowles (she/her) is a queer woman who has always leaned toward the dark and strange. Her characters tend to be queer and defy gender norms, and her writing circles around themes of obsession, narcissism, and unstable reality. She holds a BA in English Language and Literature with a minor in Creative Writing.

Rae has multiple works forthcoming from Brigids Gate Press, including her sapphic horror novella, Merciless Waters, due out winter '23, and her collaboration with April Yates, Lies That Bind, in early '24. She's sold a number of short stories to prestigious publications such as Dark Matter Ink, Nightmare, Seize the Press, Nosetouch Press, Cosmic Horror Monthly, and Taco Bell Quarterly. Recent updates on her work can be found at RaeKnowles.com and you can follow her on twitter and TikTok @_Rae_Knowles

ACKNOWLEDGEMENTS

First and foremost I would like to thank my wife for supporting my dream of holding my book in my hands, even when it felt impossible. You made space for me to write, both literally and figuratively, read my roughest, earliest work, and never stopped believing that I could become a published author. It would take volumes to describe how much I love you.

To my parents and son, thank you for listening to me drone on and on: about writing, about books, about stories. For celebrating my wins and for encouraging me during the tough moments.

This book would not be in existence if not for the unwavering support of the Coven, a group of writing friends who read early drafts, commiserated with me, promoted my work, and otherwise cheered me on. Each a talented author in their own right, please check out the work of Tanya "That Bitch" Pell, Amanda Casile, Thea Lyons, Jessica Mitacek, Taylor Grothe, and Teagan Olivia Sturmer.

I would be remiss if I didn't thank my critique partner and coauthor on our upcoming novel *Lies that Bind*, April Yates.

Our shared google docs and instant feedback are endlessly motivating, and even though you didn't acknowledge me in Ashthorne, I suppose I am a better person than you.

Finally, a huge thank you to my editor, MJ Pankey, and sensitivity reader, KBW. Your feedback was invaluable. And, of course, I am massively grateful to my publishers, Heather & Steve, who took a chance on my work and continue to champion me, as well as exist as all-around stellar human beings.

CONTENT WARNINGS

depictions of transphobia, homophobia, gore, violence, anxiety, drug use, psychosis, emotional & physical domestic abuse

MORE FROM BRIGIDS GATE PRESS

According to Dante, a sin is the misdirection of love—the human will, or essentially, the direction of our beings. Love the Sinner is an examination of just how those sins can kaleidoscope into horrific consequences creating a distorted and deadly landscape. These stories stand stark before you in full glaring misstep and macabre to show the human psyche in all its twisted reality.

From grief and its rage to medical meddling to ensure a new world order to bloody revenge within a quantum leap, these stories seek to solidify one absolute truth: man is the scariest monster.

Prepare for adventure as Juliana, a nineteen-year-old Brazilian, finds herself forced to run from an occult overlord, leaving her sister in peril. Temporarily safe, Juliana works to save money for Vilma's rescue—and along the way, meets Patrick, a rich-boy mountain climber with friends in high places.

Angus Addison wants to see his corporate flag on the summit of Mount Everest—carried there by the first woman in history—but the Himalayas are no joke. Failure could cost both sisters their lives.

Juliana weighs the risks and rewards—for even if she raises the cash, she still must figure a way to free Vilma from the same man she ran from—a man known to his disciples as The Farmer.

Who are we if not for the monsters that we keep?

They Hide: Short Stories to Tell in the Dark collects thirteen chilling tales that weave through the shadows, exploring the nature of fear, powerlessness, and control.

- A series of murders in a New England colony
- An untamed beast in pre-revolutionary France
- A mysterious stranger who invades 18th-century Ireland
- A traveling circus that takes more than the price of admission
- A gathering of the Dark, telling tales on the longest night of the year, and more.

Come play with vampires, werewolves, ghosts, zombies, ghouls and the devil himself. Make sure you check under the bed and don't turn out the lights.

In an Old West overrun by monsters, a stoic gunslinger must embark on a dangerous quest to save her friends and stop a supernatural war.

Sharpshooter Melinda West, 29, has encountered more than her share of supernatural creatures after a monster infection killed her mother. Now, Melinda and her charismatic partner, Lance, offer their exterminating services to desperate towns, fighting everything from giant flying scorpions to psychic bugs. But when they accidentally release a demon, they must track a dangerous outlaw across treacherous lands and battle a menagerie of creatures—all before an army of soul-devouring monsters descend on Earth.

The Witcher meets Bonnie and Clyde in a re-imagined Old West full of diverse characters, desolate landscapes, and fast-paced adventure.

Visit our website at: www.brigidsgatepress.com